Here are twenty-four brilliant stories, by five-star mystery-minded chefs, designed for the connoisseur of crime.

An uncharacteristic meal ordered in a restaurant serves to break an alibi – when Hercule Poirot is on the case;

The death of a terrapin, and the loss of a baby-spoon, are catalysts for murder in two stories by Patricia Highsmith;

Bootleg liquor is used to bring a con-man to justice – the special kind of rough justice meted out by The Saint;

Poison is concealed in the icing of a birthday cake or an old woman's bedtime milk;

A cup of cocoa, a whisky bottle and a flask of water are small clues which each solve a case;

But there is another, ghastly way in which murder and eating are combined – as Roald Dahl shows in a horrifying little story.

The Gourmet Crook Book is a feast of tales by world-famous writers for whom murder and suspense are meat and drink . . .

THE EDITOR

Tony Wilmot, aged 41, was born in Peterborough. After leaving King's Grammar School he served in the R.A.F., then worked as a reporter on several provincial newspapers. His first Fleet Street reporting job was in the Ludgate Circus building which bears a memorial plaque to Edgar Wallace. When he began to write short stories he often looked at that plaque and wondered whether he would follow in Wallace's footsteps. In 1974 he won the Edgar Wallace Award for a story.

He has written more than 120 short stories and a novel; and has also won the Crime Writers' Association Short Story Competition. He now works on the magazine *Weekend* and is married to the writer Shelagh Shone. They live in Wimbledon.

The Gourmet Crook Book

Edited by

TONY WILMOT

EVEREST BOOKS LIMITED
4 Valentine Place, London SE1

Published in Great Britain by Everest Books Ltd, 1976

A paperback original

ISBN 0905018 028

Introduction and linking text
Copyright © Anthony Wilmot 1976

Printed in Great Britain by
Richard Clay (The Chaucer Press), Ltd.,
Bungay, Suffolk

MENU

INTRODUCTION

Over the years the detective story has been defined as a story in which the detective, professional or amateur, detects by sifting the evidence, looking for clues, interrogating suspects and eventually brings the thief/murderer/blackmailer/con man to justice. The crook story, on the other hand, is one in which the crook (the 'hero') is the protagonist and by skill, daring or luck outwits the forces of law and order, usually for some kind of profit motive.

Most of the stories in this anthology fall into one or other of these two categories. But some, like Ray Bradbury's *The Veld*, Roald Dahl's *In the Ruins*, Stanley Ellin's *Speciality of the House* and Daphne du Maurier's *The Old Man* do not fall strictly within the terms of reference, but are crime stories with a specially macabre flavour. Edgar Lustgarten adds a dash of stark reality – a true life murder case. And Christianna Brand has created a Brand-new recipe for *The Gourmet Crook Book* called *The Whispering*.

In selecting the chefs for the collection I have endeavoured to excite the reader's palate and stimulate his imagination by including stories with a food or drink content – a content invariably lethal. The chefs are from all genres of fiction: Sci-Fi, Historical novel, Black Magic, Racing, Psychological creepy and, of course, the Detective story. I'm sure that every connoisseur and aficionado of criminology will find ingredients to suit his particular taste . . . from political assassination and the perfect murder to arsenic poisoning in the classic tradition.

Buon appetito!

TONY WILMOT

Sbirro's was a gourmet's delight. His guests were truly appreciative of his gastronomic delicacies – and lived in hope that the maestro would invite them into the inner sanctum . . .

SPECIALITY OF THE HOUSE

Stanley Ellin

'And this,' said Laffler, 'is Sbirro's.' Costain saw a square brown stone façade identical with the others that extended from either side into the clammy darkness of the deserted street. From the barred windows of the basement at his feet, a glimmer of light showed behind heavy curtains.

'Lord,' he observed, 'it's a dismal hole, isn't it?'

'I beg you to understand,' said Laffler stiffly, 'that Sbirro's is the restaurant without pretensions. Besieged by these ghastly, neurotic times, it has refused to compromise. It is perhaps the last important establishment in this city lit by gas jets. Here you will find the same honest furnishings, the same magnificent Sheffield service, and possibly, in a far corner, the very same spider webs that were remarked by the patrons of a half-century ago!'

'A doubtful recommendation,' said Costain, 'and hardly sanitary.'

'When you enter,' Laffler continued, 'you leave the insanity of this year, this day, and this hour, and you find yourself for a brief span restored in spirit, not by opulence, but by dignity, which is the lost quality of our time.'

Costain laughed uncomfortably. 'You make it sound more like a cathedral than a restaurant,' he said.

In the pale reflection of the street lamp overhead, Laffler peered at his companion's face. 'I wonder,' he said abruptly, 'whether I have not made a mistake in extending this invitation to you.'

Costain was hurt. Despite an impressive title and large salary, he was no more than clerk to the pompous little man, but he was impelled to make some display of his feelings. 'If you wish,' he said coldly, 'I can make other plans for my evenings with no trouble.'

With his large, cowlike eyes turned up to Costain, the mist drifting into the ruddy, full moon of his face, Laffler seemed strangely ill at ease. Then, 'No, no,' he said at last, 'absolutely not. It's important that you dine at Sbirro's with me.' He grasped Costain's arm firmly and led the way to the wrought-iron gate of the basement. 'You see, you're the sole person in my office who seems to know anything at all about good food. And on my part, knowing about Sbirro's but not having some appreciative friend to share it is like having a unique piece of art locked in a room where no one else can enjoy it.'

Costain was considerably mollified by this. 'I understand there are a great many people who relish that situation.'

'I'm not one of that kind!' Laffler said sharply. 'And having the secret of Sbirro's locked in myself for years has finally become unendurable.' He fumbled at the side of the gate and from within could be heard the small, discordant jangle of an ancient pull-bell. An interior door opened with a groan, and Costain found himself peering into a dark face whose only discernible feature was a row of gleaming teeth.

'Sair?' said the face.

'Mr Laffler and a guest.'

'Sair,' the face said again, this time in what was clearly an invitation. It moved aside, and Costain stumbled down a single step behind his host. The door and gate creaked behind him, and he stood blinking in a small foyer. It took him a moment to realize that the figure he now stared at was his own reflection in a gigantic pier glass that extended from floor to ceiling. 'Atmosphere,' he said under his breath and chuckled as he followed his guide to a seat.

He faced Laffler across a small table for two and peered curiously around the dining-room. It was no size at all, but the half-dozen guttering gas jets which provided the only illumination threw such a deceptive light that the walls flickered and faded into uncertain distance.

There were no more than eight or ten tables about, arranged to insure the maximum privacy. All were occupied, and the few waiters serving them moved with quiet efficiency. In the air was a soft clash and scrape of cutlery and a soothing murmur of talk. Costain nodded appreciatively.

Laffler breathed an audible sigh of gratification. 'I knew you would share my enthusiasm,' he said. 'Have you noticed, by the way, that there are no women present?'

Costain raised inquiring eyebrows.

'Sbirro,' said Laffler, 'does not encourage members of the fair sex to enter the premises. And, I can tell you, this method is decidedly effective. I had the experience of seeing a woman get a taste of it not long ago. She sat at a table for not less than an hour, waiting for service which was never forthcoming.'

'Didn't she make a scene?'

'She did.' Laffler smiled at the recollection. 'She succeeded in annoying the customers, embarrassing her partner, and nothing more.'

'And what about Mr Sbirro?'

'He did not make an appearance. Whether he directed affairs from behind the scenes, or was not even present during the episode, I don't know. Whichever it was, he won a complete victory. The woman never reappeared nor, for that matter, did the witless gentleman who by bringing her was really the cause of the entire contretemps.'

'A fair warning to all present,' laughed Costain.

A waiter now appeared at the table. The chocolate-dark skin, the thin, beautifully moulded nose and lips, the large liquid eyes, heavily lashed, and the silver-white hair so heavy and silken that it lay on the skull like a cap, all marked him definitely as an East Indian of some sort, Costain decided. The man arranged the stiff table linen, filled two tumblers from a huge cut-glass pitcher, and set them in their proper places.

'Tell me,' Laffler said eagerly, 'is the special being served this evening?'

The waiter smiled regretfully and showed teeth as spectacular as those of the major-domo. 'I am so sorry, sair. There is no special this evening.'

Laffler's face fell into lines of heavy disappointment. 'After waiting so long. It's been a month already, and I hoped to show my friend here ...'

'You understand the difficulties, sair.'

'Of course, of course.' Laffler looked at Costain sadly and shrugged. 'You see, I had in mind to introduce you to the

11

greatest treat that Sbirro's offers, but unfortunately it isn't on the menu this evening.'

The waiter said, 'Do you wish to be served now, sair?' and Laffler nodded. To Costain's surprise the waiter made his way off without waiting for any instructions.

'Have you ordered in advance?' he asked.

'Ah,' said Laffler, 'I really should have explained Sbirro's offers no choice whatsoever. You will eat the same meal as everyone else in this room. Tomorrow evening you would eat an entirely different meal, but again without designating a single preference.'

'Very unusual,' said Costain, 'and certainly unsatisfactory at times. What if one doesn't have a taste for the particular dish set before him?'

'On that score,' said Laffler solemnly, 'you need have no fears. I give you my word that no matter how exacting your tastes, you will relish every mouthful you eat at Sbirro's.'

Costain looked doubtful, and Laffler smiled. 'And consider the subtle advantages of the system,' he said. 'When you pick up the menu of a popular restaurant you will find yourself confronted with innumerable choices. You are forced to weigh, to evaluate, to make uneasy decisions which you may instantly regret. The effect of all this is a tension which, however slight, must make for discomfort.

'And consider the mechanics of the process. Instead of a hurly-burly of sweating cooks rushing about a kitchen in a frenzy to prepare a hundred varying items, we have a chef who stands serenely alone, bringing all his talents to bear on one task, with all assurance of a complete triumph!'

'Then you have seen the kitchen?'

'Unfortunately, no,' said Laffler sadly. 'The picture I offer is hypothetical, made of conversational fragments I have pieced together over the years. I must admit, though, that my desire to see the functioning of the kitchen here comes very close to being my sole obsession nowadays.'

'But have you mentioned this to Sbirro?'

'A dozen times. He shrugs the suggestion away.'

'Isn't that a rather curious foible on his part?'

'No, no,' Laffler said hastily, 'a master artist is never under the compulsion of petty courtesies. Still' – he sighed – 'I have

12

never given up hope.'

The waiter now reappeared, bearing two soup bowls which he set in place with mathematical exactitude, and a small tureen from which he slowly ladled a measure of clear, thin broth. Costain dipped his spoon into the broth and tasted it with some curiosity. It was delicately flavoured, bland to the verge of tastelessness. Costain frowned, tentatively reached for the salt and pepper cellars, and discovered there was none on the table. He looked up, saw Laffler's eyes on him, and although unwilling to compromise with his own tastes, he hesitated to act as a damper on Laffler's enthusiasm. Therefore he smiled and indicated the broth.

'Excellent,' he said.

Laffler returned his smile. 'You do not find it excellent at all,' he said coolly. 'You find it flat and badly in need of condiments. I know this,' he continued as Costain's eyebrows shot upward, 'because it was my own reaction many years ago, and because, like yourself, I found myself reaching for salt and pepper after the first mouthful. I also learned with surprise that condiments are not available in Sbirro's.'

Costain was shocked. 'Not even salt!' he exclaimed.

'Not even salt. The very fact that you require it for your soup stands as evidence that your taste is unduly jaded. I am confident that you will now make the same discovery that I did: by the time you have nearly finished your soup, your desire for salt will be non-existent.'

Laffler was right; before Costain had reached the bottom of his plate, he was relishing the nuances of the broth with steadily increasing delight. Laffler thrust aside his own empty bowl and rested his elbows on the table. 'Do you agree with me now?'

'To my surprise,' said Costain, 'I do.'

As the waiter busied himself clearing the table, Laffler lowered his voice significantly. 'You will find,' he said, 'that the absence of condiments is but one of several noteworthy characteristics which mark Sbirro's. I may as well prepare you for these. For example, no alcoholic beverages of any sort are served here, nor, for that matter, any beverage except clear, cold water, the first and only drink necessary for a human being.'

13

'Outside of mother's milk,' suggested Costain drily.

'I can answer that in like vein by pointing out that the average patron of Sbirro's has passed that primal stage of his development.'

Costain laughed. 'Granted,' he said.

'Very well. There is also a ban on the use of tobacco in any form.'

'But good heavens,' said Costain, 'doesn't that make Sbirro's more a teetotaller's retreat than a gourmet's sanctuary?'

'I fear,' said Laffler solemnly, 'that you confuse the words *gourmet* and *gourmand*. The gourmand, through glutting himself, requires a wider and wider latitude of experience to stir his surfeited sense, but the very nature of the gourmet is simplicity. The ancient Greek in his coarse chiton, savouring the ripe olive; the Japanese in his bare room, contemplating the curve of a single flower stem – these are the true gourmets.'

'But an occasional drop of brandy or pipeful of tobacco,' said Costain dubiously, 'are hardly over-indulgences.'

'By alternating stimulant and narcotic,' said Laffler, 'you seesaw the delicate balance of your taste so violently that it loses its most precious quality: the appreciation of fine food. During my years as a patron of Sbirro's I have proved this to my satisfaction.'

'May I ask,' said Costain, 'why you regard the ban on these things as having such deep aesthetic motives? What about such mundane reasons as the high cost of a liquor licence, or the possibility that patrons would object to the smell of tobacco in such confined quarters?'

Laffler shook his head violently. 'If and when you meet Sbirro,' he said, 'you will understand at once that he is not the man to make decisions on a mundane basis. As a matter of fact, it was Sbirro himself who first made me cognizant of what you call "aesthetic" motives.'

'An amazing man,' said Costain as the waiter prepared to serve the entrée.

Laffler's next words were not spoken until he had savoured and swallowed a large portion of meat. 'I hesitate to use superlatives,' he said, 'but to my way of thinking, Sbirro represents man at the apex of his civilization!'

Costain cocked an eyebrow and applied himself to his roast,

which rested in a pool of stiff gravy ungarnished by green or vegetable. The thin steam rising from it carried to his nostrils a subtle, tantalizing odour which made his mouth water. He chewed a piece as slowly and thoughtfully as if he were analysing the intricacies of a Mozart symphony. The range of taste he discovered was really extraordinary, from the pungent nip of the crisp outer edge to the peculiarly flat yet soul-satis-fying ooze of blood which the pressure of his jaws forced from the half-raw interior.

Upon swallowing, he found himself ferociously hungry for another piece, and then another, and it was only with an effort that he prevented himself from wolfing down all his share of the meat and gravy without waiting to get the full voluptuous satisfaction from each mouthful. When he had scraped his platter clean, he realized that both he and Laffler had com-pleted the entire course without exchanging a single word. He commented on this, and Laffler said, 'Can you see any need for words in the presence of such food?'

Costain looked around at the shabby, dimly lit room, the quiet diners, with a new perception. 'No,' he said humbly, 'I cannot. For any doubts I had I apologize unreservedly. In all your praise of Sbirro's there was not a single word of exag-geration.'

'Ah,' said Laffler delightedly. 'And that is only part of the story. You heard me mention the special, which unfortunately was not on the menu tonight. What you have just eaten is as nothing when compared to the absolute delights of that special!'

'Good Lord!' cried Costain. 'What is it? Nightingales' tongues? Filet of unicorn?'

'Neither,' said Laffler. 'It is lamb.'

'Lamb?'

Laffler remained lost in thought for a minute. 'If,' he said at last, 'I were to give you in my own unstinted words my opinion of this dish, you would judge me completely insane. That is how deeply the mere thought of it affects me. It is neither the fatty chop, nor the too solid leg; it is, instead, a select portion of the rarest sheep in existence and is named after the species – lamb Amirstan.'

Costain knit his brows. 'Amirstan?'

'A fragment of desolation almost lost on the border which separates Afghanistan and Russia. From chance remarks, dropped by Sbirro, I gather it is no more than a plateau which grazes the pitiful remnants of a flock of superb sheep. Sbirro, through some means or other, obtained rights to the traffic in this flock and is, therefore, the sole restaurateur ever to have lamb Amirstan on his bill of fare. I can tell you that the appearance of this dish is a rare occurrence indeed, and luck is the only guide in determining for the clientele the exact date when it will be served.'

'But surely,' said Costain, 'Sbirro could provide some advance knowledge of this event.'

'The objection to that is simply stated,' said Laffler. 'There exists in this city a huge number of professional gluttons. Should advance information slip out, it is quite likely that they would, out of curiosity, become familiar with the dish and thenceforth supplant the regular patrons at these tables.'

'But you don't mean to say,' objected Costain, 'that these few people present are the only ones in the entire city, or for that matter, in the whole wide world, who know of the existence of Sbirro's!'

'Very nearly. There may be one or two regular patrons who, for some reason, are not present at the moment.'

'That's incredible.'

'It is done,' said Laffler, the slightest shade of menace in his voice, 'by every patron making it his solemn obligation to keep the secret. By accepting my invitation this evening, you automatically assume that obligation. I hope you can be trusted with it.'

Costain flushed. 'My position in your employ should vouch for me. I only question the wisdom of a policy which keeps such magnificent food away from so many who would enjoy it.'

'Do you know the inevitable result of the policy *you* favour?' asked Laffler bitterly. 'An influx of idiots who would nightly complain that they are never served roast duck with chocolate sauce. Is that picture tolerable to you?'

'No,' admitted Costain, 'I am forced to agree with you.'

Laffler leaned back in his chair wearily and passed his hand over his eyes in an uncertain gesture. 'I am a solitary man,' he

16

said quietly, 'and not by choice alone. It may sound strange to you, it may border on eccentricity, but I feel to my depths that this restaurant, this warm haven in a coldly insane world, is both family and friend to me.'

And Costain, who to this moment had never viewed his companion as other than tyrannical employer or officious host, now felt an overwhelming pity twist inside his comfortably expanded stomach.

By the end of two weeks the invitation to join Laffler at Sbirro's had become something of a ritual. Every day, at a few minutes after five, Costain would step out into the office corridor and lock his cubicle behind him; he would drape his overcoat neatly over his left arm and peer into the glass of the door to make sure his homburg was set at the proper angle. At one time he would have followed this by lighting a cigarette, but under Laffler's prodding he had decided to give abstinence a fair trial. Then he would start down the corridor, and Laffler would fall in step at his elbow, clearing his throat. 'Ah, Costain. No plans for this evening, I hope.'

'No,' Costain would say, 'I'm footloose and fancy free,' or, 'At your service,' or something equally inane. He wondered at times whether it would not be more tactful to vary the ritual with an occasional refusal, but the glow with which Laffler received his answer, and the rough friendliness of Laffler's grip on his arm, forestalled him.

Among the treacherous crags of the business world, reflected Costain, what better way to secure your footing than friendship with one's employer? Already a secretary close to the workings of the inner office had commented publicly on Laffler's highly favourable opinion of Costain. That was all to the good.

And the food! The incomparable food at Sbirro's! For the first time in his life Costain, ordinarily a lean and bony man, noted with gratification that he was certainly gaining weight; within two weeks his bones had disappeared under a layer of sleek, firm flesh, and here and there were even signs of incipient plumpness. It struck Costain one night, while surveying himself in his bath, that the rotund Laffler himself might have been a spare and bony man before discovering Sbirro's.

So there was obviously everything to be gained and nothing

17

to be lost by accepting Laffler's invitations. Perhaps after testing the heralded wonders of lamb Amirstan and meeting Sbirro, who thus far had not made an appearance, a refusal or two might be in order. But certainly not until then.

That evening, two weeks to a day after his first visit to Sbirro's, Costain had both desires fulfilled: he dined on lamb Amirstan, and he met Sbirro. Both exceeded all his expectations.

When the waiter leaned over their table immediately after seating them and gravely announced, 'Tonight is special, sair,' Costain was shocked to find his heart pounding with expectation. On the table before him he saw Laffler's hands trembling violently. But it isn't natural, he thought suddenly. Two full-grown men, presumably intelligent and in the full possession of their senses, as jumpy as a pair of cats waiting to have their meat flung to them!

'This is it!' Laffler's voice startled him so that he almost leaped from his seat. 'The culinary triumph of all times! And faced by it you are embarrassed by the very emotions it distills.'

'How did you know that?' Costain asked faintly.

'How? Because a decade ago I underwent your embarrassment. Add to that your air of revulsion and it's easy to see how affronted you are by the knowledge that man has not yet forgotten how to slaver over his meat.'

'And these others,' whispered Costain, 'do they all feel the same thing?'

'Judge for yourself.'

Costain looked furtively around at the nearby tables. 'You are right,' he finally said. 'At any rate, there's comfort in numbers.'

Laffler inclined his head slightly to the side. 'One of the numbers,' he remarked, 'appears to be in for a disappointment.'

Costain followed the gesture. At the table indicated, a grey-haired man sat conspicuously alone, and Costain frowned at the empty chair opposite him.

'Why, yes,' he recalled, 'that very stout, bald man, isn't it? I believe it's the first dinner he's missed here in two weeks.'

'The entire decade more likely,' said Laffler sympathetically. 'Rain or shine, crisis or calamity, I don't think he's missed an evening at Sbirro's since the first time I dined here. Imagine his expression when he's told that, on his very first defection, lamb Amirstan was the *plat du jour*.'

Costain looked at the empty chair again with a dim discomfort. 'His very first?' he murmured.

'Mr Laffler! And friend! I am so pleased. So very, very pleased. No, do not stand; I will have a place made.' Miraculously a seat appeared under the figure standing there at the table. 'The lamb Amirstan will be an unqualified success, hurr? I myself have been stewing in the miserable kitchen all the day, prodding the foolish chef to do everything just so. The just so is the important part, hurr? But I see your friend does not know me. An introduction, perhaps?'

The words ran in a smooth, fluid eddy. They rippled, they purred, they hypnotized Costain so that he could do no more than stare. The mouth that uncoiled this sinuous monologue was alarmingly wide, with thin mobile lips that curled and twisted with every syllable. There was a flat nose with a straggling line of hair under it; wide-set eyes, almost Oriental in appearance, that glittered in the unsteady flare of gaslight; and long, sleek hair that swept back from high on the unwrinkled forehead – hair so pale that it might have been bleached of all colour. An amazing face, surely, and the sight of it tortured Costain with the conviction that it was somehow familiar. His brain twitched and prodded but could not stir up any solid recollection.

Laffler's voice jerked Costain out of his study. "Mr Sbirro. Mr Costain, a good friend and associate.' Costain rose and shook the proffered hand. It was warm and dry, flint-hard against his palm.

'I am so very pleased, Mr Costain. So very, very pleased,' purred the voice. 'You like my little establishment, hurr? You have a great treat in store, I assure you.'

Laffler chuckled. 'Oh, Costain's been dining here regularly for two weeks,' he said. 'He's by way of becoming a great admirer of yours, Sbirro.'

The eyes were turned on Costain. 'A very great compliment. You compliment me with your presence, and I return same with my food, hurr? But the lamb Amirstan is far superior to

19

anything of your past experience, I assure you. All the trouble of obtaining it, all the difficulty of preparation, is truly merited.'

Costain strove to put aside the exasperating problem of that face. 'I have wondered,' he said, 'why, with all these difficulties you mention, you even bother to present lamb Amirstan to the public. Surely your other dishes are excellent enough to uphold your reputation.'

Sbirro smiled so broadly that his face became perfectly round. 'Perhaps it is a matter of the psychology, hurr? Someone discovers a wonder and must share it with others. He must fill his cup to the brim, perhaps, by observing the so evident pleasure of those who explore it with him. Or' – he shrugged – 'perhaps it is a matter of good business.'

'Then in the light of all this,' Costain persisted, 'and considering all the conventions you have imposed on your customers, why do you open the restaurant to the public instead of operating it as a private club?'

The eyes abruptly glinted into Costain's, then turned away. 'So perspicacious, hurr? Then I will tell you. Because there is more privacy in a public eating place than in the most exclusive club in existence! Here no one inquires of your affairs; no one desires to know the intimacies of your life. Here the business is eating. We are not curious about names and addresses or the reasons for the coming and going of our guests. We welcome you when you are here; we have no regrets when you are here no longer. That is the answer, hurr?'

Costain was startled by this vehemence. 'I – I had no intention of prying,' he stammered.

Sbirro ran the tip of his tongue over his thin lips. 'No, no,' he reassured, 'you are not prying. Do not let me give you that impression. On the contrary, I invite your questions.'

'Oh, come, Costain,' said Laffler. 'Don't let Sbirro intimidate you. I've known him for years and I guarantee that his bark is worse than his bite. Before you know it he'll be showing you all the privileges of the house – outside of inviting you to visit his precious kitchen, of course.'

'Ah' – Sbirro smiled – 'for that Mr Costain may have to wait a little while. For everything else I am at his beck and call.'

Laffler slapped his hand jovially on the table. 'What did I tell you!' he said. 'Now let's have the truth, Sbirro. Has anyone, outside of your staff, ever stepped into the sanctum sanctorum?'

Sbirro looked up. 'You see on the wall above you,' he said earnestly, 'the portrait of one to whom I did the honour. A very dear friend and a patron of most long standing, he is evidence that my kitchen is not inviolate.'

Costain studied the picture and started with recognition. 'Why,' he said excitedly, 'that's the famous writer – you know the one, Laffler – he used to do such wonderful short stories and cynical bits and then suddenly took himself off and disappeared in Mexico!'

'Of course!' cried Laffler. 'And to think I've been sitting under his portrait for years without even realizing it!' He turned to Sbirro. 'A dear friend, you say? His disappearance must have been a blow to you.'

Sbirro's face lengthened. 'It was, it was, I assure you. But think of it this way, gentlemen: he was probably greater in his death than in his life, hurr? A most tragic man, he often told me that his only happy hours were spent here at this very table. Pathetic, is it not? And to think the only favour I could ever show him was to let him witness the mysteries of my kitchen, which is, when all is said and done, no more than a plain, ordinary kitchen.'

'You seem very certain of his death,' commented Costain. 'After all, no evidence has ever turned up to substantiate it.'

Sbirro contemplated the picture. 'None at all,' he said softly. 'Remarkable, hurr?'

With the arrival of the entrée Sbirro leaped to his feet and set about serving them himself. With his eyes alight he lifted the casserole from the tray and sniffed at the fragrance from within with sensual relish. Then, taking great care not to lose a single drop of gravy, he filled two platters with chunks of dripping meat. As if exhausted by this task, he sat back in his chair, breathing heavily. 'Gentlemen,' he said, 'to your good appetite.'

Costain chewed his first mouthful with great deliberation and swallowed it. Then he looked at the empty tines of his fork with glazed eyes.

'Good God!' he breathed.

'It is good, hurr? Better than you imagined?'

Costain shook his head dazedly. 'It is as impossible,' he said slowly, 'for the uninitiated to conceive the delights of lamb Amirstan as for mortal man to look into his own soul.'

'Perhaps,' Sbirro thrust his head so close that Costain could feel the warm, foetid breath tickle his nostrils, 'perhaps you have just had a glimpse into your soul, hurr?'

Costain tried to draw back slightly without giving offence. 'Perhaps' – he laughed – 'and a gratifying picture it made: all fang and claw. But, without intending any disrespect, I should hardly like to build my church on *lamb en casserole*.'

Sbirro rose and laid a hand gently on his shoulder. 'So perspicacious,' he said. 'Sometimes when you have nothing to do, nothing, perhaps, but sit for a very little while in a dark room and think of this world – what it is and what it is going to be – then you must turn your thoughts a little to the significance of the Lamb in religion. It will be so interesting. And now' – he bowed deeply to both men – 'I have held you long enough from your dinner. I was most happy' – he nodded to Costain – 'and I am sure we will meet again.' The teeth gleamed, the eyes glittered, and Sbirro was gone down the aisle of tables.

Costain twisted around to stare after the retreating figure. 'Have I offended him in some way?' he asked.

Laffler looked up from his plate. 'Offended him? He loves that kind of talk. Lamb Amirstan is a ritual with him; get him started and he'll be back at you a dozen times worse than a priest making a conversion.'

Costain turned to his meal with the face still hovering before him. 'Interesting man,' he reflected. 'Very.'

It took him a month to discover the tantalizing familiarity of that face, and when he did he laughed aloud in his bed. Why, of course! Sbirro might have sat as the model for the Cheshire cat in *Alice*!

He passed this thought on to Laffler the very next evening as they pushed their way down the street to the restaurant against a chill, blustering wind. Laffler only looked blank.

'You may be right,' he said, 'but I'm not a fit judge. It's a far cry back to the days when I read the book. A far cry, indeed.'

22

As if taking up his words, a piercing howl came ringing down the street and stopped both men short in their tracks. 'Someone's in trouble there,' said Laffler. 'Look!'

Not far from the entrance to Sbirro's two figures could be seen struggling in the near darkness. They swayed back and forth and suddenly tumbled into a writhing heap on the sidewalk. The piteous howl went up again, and Laffler, despite his girth, ran towards it at a fair speed with Costain tagging cautiously behind.

Stretched out full-length on the pavement was a slender figure with the dusky complexion and white hair of one of Sbirro's servitors. His fingers were futilely plucking at the huge hands which encircled his throat, and his knees pushed weakly up at the gigantic bulk of a man who brutally bore down with his full weight.

Laffler came up, panting. 'Stop this!' he shouted. 'What's going on here?'

The pleading eyes, almost bulging from their sockets, turned towards Laffler. 'Help, sair. This man – drunk –'

'Drunk, am I, ya dirty –' Costain saw now that the man was a sailor in a badly soiled uniform. The air around him reeked with the stench of liquor. 'Pick me pocket and then call me drunk, will ya!' He dug his fingers in harder, and his victim groaned.

Laffler seized the sailor's shoulder. 'Let go of him, do you hear! Let go of him at once!' he cried, and the next instant was sent careening into Costain, who staggered back under the force of the blow.

The attack on his own person sent Laffler into immediate and berserk action. Without a sound he leaped at the sailor, striking and kicking furiously at the unprotected face and flanks. Stunned at first, the man came to his feet with a rush and turned on Laffler. For a moment they stood locked together, and then, as Costain joined the attack, all three went sprawling to the ground. Slowly Laffler and Costain got to their feet and looked down at the body before them.

'He's either out cold from liquor,' said Costain, 'or he struck his head going down. In any case, it's a job for the police.'

'No, no, sair!' The waiter crawled weakly to his feet and stood, swaying. 'No police, sair. Mr Sbirro do not want such.

You understand, sair.' He caught hold of Costain with a pleading hand, and Costain looked at Laffler.

'Of course not,' said Laffler. 'We won't have to bother with the police. They'll pick him up soon enough, the murderous sot. But what in the world started all this?'

'That man, sair. He make most erratic way while walking, and with no meaning I push against him. Then he attack me, accusing me to rob him.'

'As I thought.' Laffler pushed the waiter gently along. 'Now go on in and get yourself attended to.'

The man seemed ready to burst into tears. 'To you, sair, I owe my life. Is there anything I can do –'

Laffler turned into the areaway that led to Sbirro's door. 'No, no, it was nothing. You go along, and if Sbirro has any questions send him to me. I'll straighten it out.'

'My life, sair,' were the last words they heard as the inner door closed behind them.

'There you are, Costain,' said Laffler, as a few minutes later he drew his chair under the table, 'civilized man in all his glory. Reeking with alcohol, strangling to death some miserable innocent who came too close.'

Costain made an effort to gloss over the nerve-shattering memory of the episode. 'It's a neurotic cat that takes to alcohol,' he said. 'Surely there's a reason for that sailor's condition.'

'Reason? Of course there is. Plain atavistic savagery!' Laffler swept his arm in an all-embracing gesture. 'Why do we all sit here at our meat? Not only to appease physical demands, but because our atavistic selves cry for release. Think back, Costain. Do you remember that I once described Sbirro as the epitome of civilization? Can you now see why? A brilliant man, he fully understands the nature of human beings. But unlike lesser men he bends all his efforts to the satisfaction of our innate natures without resultant harm to some innocent bystander.'

'When I think back on the wonders of lamb Amirstan,' said Costain, 'I quite understand what you're driving at. And, by the way, isn't it nearly due to appear on the bill of fare? It must have been over a month ago that it was last served.'

The waiter, filling the tumblers, hesitated. 'I am so, so

24

sorry, sair. No special this evening.'

'There's your answer,' Laffler grunted, 'and probably just my luck to miss out on it altogether the next time.'

Costain stared at him. 'Oh, come, that's impossible.'

'No, blast it.' Laffler drank half his water at a gulp, and the waiter immediately refilled the glass. 'I'm off to South America for a surprise tour of inspection. One month, two months, Lord knows how long.'

'Are things that bad down there?'

'They could be better.' Laffler suddenly grinned. 'Mustn't forget it takes very mundane dollars and cents to pay the tariff at Sbirro's.'

'I haven't heard a word of this around the office.'

'Wouldn't be a surprise tour if you had. Nobody knows about this except myself – and now you. I want to walk in on them completely unsuspected. Find out what flimflammery they're up to down there. As far as the office is concerned, I'm off on a jaunt somewhere. Maybe recuperating in some sanatorium from my hard work. Anyhow, the business will be in good hands. Yours, among them.'

'Mine?' said Costain, surprised.

'When you go in tomorrow you'll find yourself in receipt of a promotion, even if I'm not there to hand it to you personally. Mind you, it has nothing to do with our friendship, either; you've done fine work, and I'm immensely grateful for it.'

Costain reddened under the praise. 'You don't expect to be in tomorrow. Then you're leaving tonight?'

Laffler nodded. 'I've been trying to wangle some reservations. If they come through, well, this will be in the nature of a farewell celebration.'

'You know,' said Costain slowly, 'I devoutly hope that your reservations don't come through. I believe our dinners here have come to mean more to me than I ever dared imagine.'

The waiter's voice broke in. 'Do you wish to be served now, sair?' and they both started.

'Of course, of course,' said Laffler sharply. 'I didn't realize you were waiting.'

'What bothers me,' he told Costain as the waiter turned away, 'is the thought of the lamb Amirstan I'm bound to miss. To tell you the truth, I've already put off my departure a

25

week, hoping to hit a lucky night, and now I simply can't delay any more. I do hope that when you're sitting over your share of lamb Amirstan, you'll think of me with suitable regrets.'

Costain laughed. 'I will indeed,' he said as he turned to his dinner.

Hardly had he cleared the plate when a waiter silently reached for it. It was not their usual waiter, he observed; it was none other than the victim of the assault.

'Well,' Costain said, 'how do you feel now? Still under the weather?'

The waiter paid no attention to him. Instead, with the air of a man under great strain, he turned to Laffler. 'Sair,' he whispered. 'My life. I owe it to you. I can repay you!'

Laffler looked up in amazement, then shook his head firmly. 'No,' he said. 'I want nothing from you, understand? You have repaid me sufficiently with your thanks. Now get on with your work and let's hear no more about it.'

The waiter did not stir an inch, but his voice rose slightly. 'By the body and blood of your God, sair, I will help you even if you do not want! *Do not go into the kitchen, sair.* I trade you my life for yours, sair, when I speak this. Tonight or any night of your life, do not go into the kitchen at Sbirro's!'

Laffler sat back, completely dumbfounded. 'Not go into the kitchen? Why shouldn't I go into the kitchen if Mr Sbirro ever took it into his head to invite me there? What's all this about?'

A hard hand was laid on Costain's back, and another gripped the waiter's arm. The waiter remained frozen to the spot, his lips compressed, his eyes downcast.

'What is all *what* about, gentlemen?' purred the voice. 'So opportune an arrival. In time, as ever, I see, to answer all the questions, hurr?'

Laffler breathed a sigh of relief. 'Ah, Sbirro, thank heaven you're here. This man is saying something about my not going into your kitchen. Do you know what he means?'

The teeth showed in a broad grin. 'But of course. This good man was giving you advice in all amiability. It so happens that my too emotional chef heard some rumour that I might have a guest into his precious kitchen, and he flew into a fearful rage. Such a rage, gentlemen! He even threatened to give notice on

26

the spot, and you can understand what that would mean to Sbirro's, hurr? Fortunately, I succeeded in showing him what a signal honour it is to have an esteemed patron and true connoisseur observe him at his work first hand, and now he is quite amenable. Quite, hurr?'

He released the waiter's arm. 'You are at the wrong table,' he said softly. 'See that it does not happen again.'

The waiter slipped off without daring to raise his eyes, and Sbirro drew a chair to the table. He seated himself and brushed his hand lightly over his hair. 'Now I am afraid that the cat is out of the bag, hurr? This invitation to you, Mr Laffler, was to be a surprise; but the surprise is gone, and all that is left is the invitation.'

Laffler mopped beads of perspiration from his forehead. 'Are you serious?' he said huskily. 'Do you mean that we are really to witness the preparation of your food tonight?'

Sbirro drew a sharp fingernail along the tablecloth, leaving a thin, straight line printed in the linen. 'Ah,' he said, 'I am faced with a dilemma of great proportions.' He studied the line soberly. 'You, Mr Laffler, have been my guest for ten long years. But our friend here –'

Costain raised his hand in protest. 'I understand perfectly. This invitation is solely to Mr Laffler, and naturally my presence is embarrassing. As it happens I have an early engagement for this evening and must be on my way anyhow. So you see there's no dilemma at all, really.'

'No,' said Laffler, 'absolutely not. That wouldn't be fair at all. We've been sharing this until now, Costain, and I won't enjoy this experience half as much if you're not along. Surely Sbirro can make his conditions flexible, this one occasion.'

They both looked at Sbirro, who shrugged his shoulders regretfully.

Costain rose abruptly. 'I'm not going to sit here, Laffler, and spoil your great adventure. And then too,' he bantered, 'think of that ferocious chef waiting to get his cleaver on you. I prefer not to be at the scene. I'll just say good-bye,' he went on, to cover Laffler's guilty silence, 'and leave you to Sbirro. I'm sure he'll take pains to give you a good show.' He held out his hand, and Laffler squeezed it painfully hard.

'You're being very decent, Costain,' he said. 'I hope you'll continue to dine here until we meet again. It shouldn't be too long.'

Sbirro made way for Costain to pass. 'I will expect you,' he said. '*Au 'voir.*'

Costain stopped briefly in the dim foyer to adjust his scarf and fix his homburg at the proper angle. When he turned away from the mirror, satisfied at last, he saw with a final glance that Laffler and Sbirro were already at the kitchen door: Sbirro holding the door invitingly wide with one hand, while the other rested, almost tenderly, on Laffler's meaty shoulders.

The memory of Bertha's fifth birthday party had left a nasty taste in Aunt Emily's mouth – especially the fate of poor Miss Twomey.

AFTER ALL THESE YEARS

Michael Gilbert

'It happened a long time ago, when I was only a girl,' said Great-Aunt Emily. 'In fact, it was the year I came out, because I remember I was staying with my sister Alice and her husband, Bill, in their house in Stanhope Gate.'

'Bill?' said Bohun, casting his mind through the ranks of his great-uncles. 'That was the one in phosphates who had a weakness for Gaiety Girls.'

'*Any* girls,' said Emily. 'However – *de mortuis –*'

'Alice must have been a good deal older than you, though,' said Bohun. 'She had quite a family by then, hadn't she?'

'Only four then. Bertha, Tom, Augusta, and Brian. It all happened on June tenth.'

'You've a remarkably accurate memory,' said Bohun approvingly. He was an accurate man himself.

'There's no question of accuracy. I remember it *because* it happened on June tenth. It was Bertha's birthday. She was five. Alice always had a tea-party on her children's birthdays. And a big cake – she used to ice it herself – and animal biscuits for the children and sandwiches for the grown-ups.'

'Grown-ups were invited too?'

'Oh, certainly. Miss Twomey was one of them.'

'She was the one who –?'

'That's right. She died – the next morning. In terrible agony. Poor woman.' Emily pursed her lips. The horror of it was still with her after all those years. She added, 'She was a harpist, you know. Quite famous in her way.'

Bohun refrained from a facetious comment. Indeed, he looked unusually serious. 'Who else was at the party?' he said. 'Tell it all to me.'

29

'I remember it,' said Emily, 'as if it were yesterday. There were six of us grown-ups – Alice, myself, and poor Miss Twomey, the Vicar of All Souls Lavender Hill – and a splendid man, though he afterwards became an agnostic and sold sewing machines in America – and his wife, rather a dull little woman, and Mrs Armstrong.'

'And she was *not* a dull little woman.'

'Far from it,' said Emily. Her voice had acquired the detached coldness which the older generation reserved for Certain Topics and Certain People.

'A merry widow?' suggested Bohun.

'Well,' said Aunt Emily, 'we must speak no evil of her either. She's dead. In fact she died soon after the party I was telling you about. She slipped, on a very wet night, and fell under a horse-bus. Alice was walking with her at the time, and it was a great shock to her.'

Bohun preserved in his own mind a picture of his Great-Aunt Alice. She had been very old, and he had been very young. But he had not been deceived. An amiable-looking woman of mild disposition and gentle manners, but under it all a character and determination beside which concrete was soft and steel yielding.

'Tell me more about the birthday party,' he said. 'A lot more.'

'Let me see, then,' said Emily. 'I've told you who were there—the six of us grown-ups and the four children. I think I can even remember how we sat. The Vicar on my right. His wife on his right. Mrs Armstrong on my left. Then Miss Twomey.'

'Where was Alice?'

'She hardly had time to sit down. At the moment I visualize her' – Emily screwed up her birdlike eyes – 'she is cutting the cake. A lovely birthday cake. I don't think she made it herself – one didn't in those days, you know. But she'd certainly iced it, and very pretty it was. In the middle was the name *Bertha* in green icing – green was the child's favourite colour. Then on the bottom edge *Five Years Old* in blue – and on the top edge the year, in red figures.'

'Remarkable,' said Bohun. 'Remarkable.'

Emily accepted this as a tribute to her memory. 'But of

course,' she explained, 'we all talked about that tea a good deal afterwards. The inquest, you know.'

'Tell me about that.'

'Poor Miss Twomey. Three hours later – while she was changing for dinner. The most agonizing cramps and – er – other things. Acute arsenic poisoning. She died at dawn.'

'And the tea-party naturally came under suspicion.'

'Well, it couldn't have had anything to do with it,' said Emily. 'How could it? That was the whole point. Cook was furious. She had made all the sandwiches herself. And the cake. Everyone ate the sandwiches and the cake. And they ate nothing else.'

'I see,' said Bohun. 'That did make it awkward. Had Miss Twomey had anything else to eat recently?'

'She had luncheon alone, in a station restaurant.' Emily's tone expressed very clearly what she thought of people who ate in station restaurants. 'It was impossible to prove anything, but it was just when Home Rule was becoming troublesome again, and one of the waiters was an Irishman.'

'Did Mrs Armstrong take sugar in her tea?' asked Bohun.

'Mrs Armstrong?' Emily brought her mind back with some difficulty to the gay widow. 'No. I don't think she did. Nor milk either. Why do you ask?'

'Fascinating,' said Bohun. 'Fascinating. After all these years. By the way, I don't think you told me. Was it eighteen-ninety-six or nineteen-six? No. Come to think of it, it could hardly have been as late as nineteen-six. Bertha must be well over sixty.'

'As a matter of fact,' said Emily, 'it *was* eighteen-ninety-six. What horrible ideas are you turning over in that head of yours?'

'I was thinking,' said Bohun, 'that you never know when you stand in the greatest danger. The Mafeking celebrations? Zeppelins? Buzz bombs? Traffic? Don't let them kid you. You'll never be nearer death than you were at tea that afternoon in eighteen-ninety-six.'

'Now you must explain what you mean – at once!'

'It's very simple,' said Bohun. 'Dear Aunt Alice. A tigress in defence of her mate. She must have known – or suspected – more than you thought about Bill and Mrs Armstrong.'

31

'Yes, there was something in it, I believe. But when Mrs Armstrong had her accident –'

'Accident my foot!' said Bohun. 'Alice pushed her good and hard. It was her second attempt – after the first had misfired, don't you see, and carried off poor Miss Twomey.'

'Really!' said Emily. Curiosity struggled with repugnance. 'How did she manage it?'

'The only way she could pick on one individual – particularly if that individual was awkward enough not to take sugar in her tea. That would have been simple, of course, because she could have impregnated a lump and popped it into her cup when she served her. However, she didn't do too badly.'

'You are being irritating and obscure,' said Emily. 'How?'

'The icing. It must have been. First she'd spread the white icing over the whole cake. Then she'd get one of those nice little icing-gun gadgets and put on the words and letters. Only right at the end, when she was putting on the last number of the year eighteen-ninety-six, she recharged the gun with a special dollop of red icing plus arsenic. That was the only poisonous part of the whole cake, you see – *the final number in the date – the number six.*'

'Then when – Oh, yes. I see.'

Even after the years Emily turned pale.

'That's right,' said Bohun. 'You've spotted it. After she'd cut the slices she got them turned round. Mrs Armstrong got the nine. Miss Twomey got the six ... You know, it might have been any of you.'

'It might, indeed,' said Aunt Emily.

She recovered herself. 'Anyway,' she said, 'Alice is dead now. And you've no proof. And it all happened a very long time ago.'

Finally, firmly, she buried it – after all these years.

*He was a successful architect with a wife and a grown-up son –
but he also had a passion for young girls. And it was this that
led to a killing which shocked America . . .*

THE MURDER OF STANFORD WHITE

Edgar Lustgarten

It happens every week. A young married couple go into a café
and settle themselves at a table, and then he sees someone he
hates the sight of, and who, he is absolutely certain, hates the
sight of him. A man who was a boy friend of his wife's, or
what they used to call her 'steady'. He is just thinking about
this when they catch each other's eye, and there's something of
an atmosphere.

Different husbands, and different boy friends will handle it
different ways. Some will be icily polite – empty smile, eyebrows slightly lifted. Some will deliberately pretend not to
have noticed, and will work hard, not noticing. But whatever
they do, in the ordinary way, it will pass off peacefully.

I say in the ordinary way . . . I mean when they are ordinary
people, who can be relied upon to behave in ordinary style.

But the whole point about that Thaw case is that it did
revolve round such a situation but the people concerned were
not ordinary at all. They were three exceedingly unusual
characters: that is how such a violent climax was reached.
They were also three exceedingly conspicuous characters: that
is why the case excited world-wide interest – and why this
interest still exists after seventy years.

Perhaps, then, it is best to start with these three characters,
to look them over as they are sitting in a glossy New York
night-spot – sitting there in the last few minutes before a deed
is done that brings either death or disaster to them all on that
night of 25 June 1906.

The man by himself, with an arm negligently resting across
his chair – a tall fellow, sandy, middle-aged – is America's
greatest architect, Stanford White. He was alone that night

33

from choice, for there are many people who would count it a privilege to keep him company. And it is not just that they admire him, natural that they should a man who has planned so many splendid buildings, a man who had made a million out of talent and hard work. But Stanford White was greatly liked as such as well as much admired; he had the kind of qualities which made him likeable – kind, considerate, generous almost to a fault.

But although he was 52, with a wife and grown-up son, he had a weakness – that was the charitable term. To put it more harshly he had a vice, the vice of seducing, by means of his charm, wealth, and his prestige, pretty teenage girls. It is that which attracts him to places like this night-spot – Madison Square Roof Garden, where they stage a youthful dancing troupe. It is that which makes him such a patron of the Broadway musical plays, and, especially, a patron of the chorus. It is that which explains his link with Evelyn Thaw.

She is the second major character, and was also at the Roof Garden, with three men at a table near the front, a lovely young creature with deep blue eyes, gleaming long black hair, and a slender figure. She had an air of fresh and dewy innocence about her that had hardly changed at all in the four years that had passed since Stanford White eagerly sought out her acquaintance when she first was in a chorus, and not yet 17.

She had led a tough life before she reached the chorus, years as a child shifting from town to town with a widowed mother who had no money, mostly hungry, sometimes without a place to sleep.

Harry K. Thaw is the third character. He married Evelyn a couple of months previously, after going round with her for two years. He is a stocky, plump fellow, rather obviously showing off both to his wife and his two men companions. As a husband Thaw has one unarguable asset: he is rich, heir to a railroad millionaire, but that concludes the list of his attractions. That he is an idle playboy who has reached the age of 34 without ever doing any work – the railroad millions were to blame for that. But he was also a bully and a brute; his temper was uncontrollable – or he simply did not bother to control it – and wherever he went he left a trail of scandal, in New York, London, and Paris, a trail of immorality with persons of both sexes, immorality of such a character that he was constantly forced to buy off blackmailers. He was called 'Mad Harry' and detested even by the toadies who were his only friends.

The Thaws and Stanford White were barely 20 yards apart, but never a sign, not so much as a nod is exchanged between the tables. There is no hint that Evelyn Thaw and Stanford White were once great chums, not a hint that Harry Thaw is well aware of it, not a hint that anyone recognizes anyone. It does not mean that they have not noticed. This is one of those affairs – at the moment – when everyone is engaged in *not* noticing.

Perhaps Evelyn Thaw feels awkward, nonetheless, uncomfortable, and embarrassed sitting there, a newly married lady with her husband, and her old admirer sitting across the way. Or maybe – no one knows – she does not care, and she is only bored with the show.

'Let's go somewhere else,' she says.

'All right,' Thaw agrees, 'let's go.'

The party gets up and moves towards the nearest exit, first Evelyn, then the two guests, and Thaw bringing up the rear . . . or so the others think – they do not look round, taking it for granted he is following.

It is only when they get into the foyer that they find they are three instead of four.

'Why, now,' says Evelyn, and she walks back to look into the Roof Garden through the open door, 'Where's Harry?'

He is standing over the wholly unsuspecting Stanford White. He suddenly draws a pistol and takes careful aim, shooting White through the brain, shooting him through the mouth, and shooting him a third time. Harry now holds the pistol up by the muzzle, as if to show he has accomplished all he intended and that no one need have any cause for alarm. He is pale and tense, but seeming somehow gratified – an odd exception in that horror-stricken room.

Evelyn shrieks from the door: 'My God, what have you done!'

'Probably saved your life.'

She comes over. She looks at the attendants who are hurrying to seize Thaw; she looks at the gun which he readily gives up; she looks at the red pool already forming round Stanford

35

White's body on the floor.

'I'll stick by you, Harry,' she says, 'I'll stick by you, but, my God, you're in an awful mess . . .'

In the succeeding days and weeks the prominent lawyers that Harry Thaw engaged must have thought Evelyn's remark an under-statement.

There can seldom have been a clearer act of murder committed before so many pairs of eyes. Thaw had no conceivable prospect of a clean acquittal; no jury could return a simple verdict of Not Guilty, no counsel could so much as dare to ask for one. There was only one possible plea, a long shot – insanity, *temporary* insanity if they could bring it off; that is to say, mad enough at the time of the crime not to be held responsible, but sane enough at the time of the trial not to be detained. But where was the evidence, what facts could be produced to show that Mad Harry had been literally mad?

Along this line the lawyers got to work. They dug up every available detail from Thaw's past. They dug up every available detail, too, from Stanford White's past. They had long and repeated conferences with their imprisoned client's young and lovely wife. And out of all these conferences, and out of all this probing, a defence of sorts was finally evolved.

What it amounted to was this – that Thaw had been born with what they called a psychopathic temperament . . . in simple terms, he had always been slightly unbalanced, not mad in the ordinary sense but a man who, under a heavy mental strain, might be *driven* while the strain lasted, into madness. It meant that when Thaw had first asked Evelyn to become his wife, she had refused and she had given him a reason – she was not worthy to become his wife, she said, because in her trustfulness and youth and innocence she had once been drugged and then despoiled by Stanford White. On pressure from Thaw who was distraught with grief and rage, she had told him the whole story, exactly what had happened; this story had so preyed on Thaw's mind, he had become so obsessed with the wrong that had been done to this pure young girl he loved, and with the wrongs that might have been done to others like her in the future, that he eventually worked himself into the delusion that providence had chosen him to destroy Stanford White.

It was a far-fetched defence, not at all an easy matter to establish. But if they *did* establish it, they were safely home. The rule about insanity in American criminal law, broadly, is the same as it is in British law. A person is only held insane if he did not know what he was doing, or *else*, if he did not know that what he was doing was *wrong*. Now, according to the defence's picture of his state of mind, Thaw knew what he was doing, knew, and shot to kill; but so far from knowing it was wrong, he was convinced that it was right.

As soon as this line of defence had been adopted the Thaw millions were employed to drive it home. A gigantic newspaper campaign was organized, a campaign which had a twofold object, to make Thaw out as a kind of modern Galahad, a virtuous champion of mistreated womanhood, and to make Stanford White out as a vile, black-hearted monster, luring pretty girls to his den to be devoured. In the court, when the trial opened on 23 January 1907, psychiatrists stood by to testify that on the night of the shooting, Thaw had been in the legal sense, insane.

But in the last resort the trial result does not depend on the Thaw millions, on psychiatrists, or on newspaper campaigns. It depends on that story about herself that Evelyn is supposed to have told Harry Thaw, and it depends on whether the jury *believe* that she did tell it to him, and on how moved they are when they hear it themselves ... they cannot be expected to believe a man has been driven mad by a girl's story if *they* can listen to her telling it without a pang.

What it all amounts to is this: the fate of Harry Thaw depends on his wife, and when her name is called by Mr Delmas, his defence counsel, the critical moment of the trial has been reached.

Shyly she walks up to the witness-stand and takes the oath.

She wears a plain dark blue frock, with a broad white collar, and hardly looks grown up, more like a wide-eyed, lovely child. And children have a way of arousing sympathy in their helplessness, and their lack of worldly guile, which appeals to the protective instinct in everyone.

Evelyn makes that appeal before she says a word, adds to it

as she answers the first few friendly questions. She had got them, every one eating out of her hand by the time Mr Delmas brings her to the vital point.

'What exactly did you tell Harry Thaw to explain why you had rejected his proposal?'

'I told him everything.'

'Concerning you and Stanford White?'

'Yes.'

'Proceed, please, Mrs Thaw.'

'I told him that I had first met Mr White when I went to a lunch party with a young lady friend.' She seems hardly old enough for lunch parties today, let alone four whole years ago. 'Mr White was very nice to me and I liked him very much. He asked where l lived, and a day or two later he called to see my mother. After that, he often had me out to parties; but there were always other people there and it was perfectly all right.'

'Did there come an occasion when no one else was there?'

'Yes.'

'Proceed, please, Mrs Thaw.'

'It happened this way.' She has gone very pale; her lips are quivering, but she speaks out bravely. 'Mr White had sent me a note asking me to a party, but when I arrived at the studio I found him there alone.'

'Yes?'

'I said I'd better go home, but he said no, we'd have some food anyhow. So we had some food, and then he said he'd like to show me the other rooms, the ones I hadn't seen, because there were some beautiful things in them.'

'Yes?'

'So we went round these rooms, and there were some beautiful things, and while I was looking at a picture he poured me out a glass of champagne, and he said, now, drink that down.'

'Yes?'

'Well, the next thing was a sort of pounding started in my ears and, almost at once, everything got black.'

It is all she can do to keep her voice up now, all she can do to tell them of her awakening. She describes in whispers how, when she recovered consciousness she found herself unclothed, found she had been ravished.

A wave of pity and a wave of anger sweep the court. That a

fragile child like this should be outraged by a beast . . .

The jury – a jury wholly composed of men – see how Thaw is sobbing, and perhaps they think to themselves, well, yes, it isn't any wonder, if he was a little bit unbalanced anyhow, to learn that such a thing had happened to this child he worshipped, it *was* enough to send him round the bend.

It looks set fair for an insanity verdict, it looks as though the murderer is going to dodge the chair, when Mr Delmas, well content, says formally, 'Your witness,' and District Attorney Jerome, gets up to cross-examine.

Not a pleasant job for him, to attack this girl. Everyone will resent it; everyone will be hostile. But Mr Jerome regards this as a clear case of murder, and he is not in the mood for pulling any punches. He is all out to show that Evelyn is a fake and a liar, that they cannot attach the smallest weight to anything she says.

He strikes his first blow without speaking – just hands the witness a single sheet of paper, waits while she looks at it, watches her face fall.

'Did you write that letter?'

She seems bewildered as if it were impossible to say.

'Did you write that letter?'

'I . . . think so . . . yes.'

'Is it addressed to the Mercantile Trust Company?'

'Yes.'

'Does it relate to a weekly sum of twenty-five dollars being paid to you through that Company by Mr Stanford White?'

'Yes.'

'Was that being paid to you in the year 1902?'

'Yes.'

'Months after this drugging episode you have described?'

'Yes.'

'And you were accepting it?'

Evelyn doesn't answer. She puckers her forehead, more than ever like a child.

'Your suggestion is that you were betrayed, after being drugged by Stanford White?'

'Yes.'

Mr Jerome leans forward, hands on hips, jaw set.

'Did you not from that time on see him frequently?'

'I saw him.'

'Frequently?'

'Yes.'

'Every week for a considerable period, wasn't it?'

'Yes.'

'Sometimes two or three times a week?'

'Yes.'

'Sometimes every day?'

Again she does not answer.

'Sometimes every day?'

'Yes,' she says.

Mr Jerome pauses for a moment to give the court a breathing space to reflect on what is happening.

'And on these frequent occasions when you saw him, often you would actually go to his studio, would you not?'

'Yes.'

'When you got there, to the studio, didn't you remember the horrible things that had happened to you there?'

'I tried *not* to remember,' Evelyn says.

She is on the verge of tears. But for Mr Jerome so far it has been merely a preamble. Now he lets fly with the real thunderbolt.

'On these visits to the studio, after the drugging episode, was there not impropriety between you and Stanford White?'

The tears begin to flow.

'Was there not?'

The tears flow faster.

'Sometimes.'

'So that after this dreadful act of Stanford White's you continued to maintain relations with him?'

'For a short time only.'

'Of your own free will?'

'Yes.'

Once more Mr Jerome leans forward in that menacing attitude.

'Did you tell your husband about *that* when he proposed?'

She breaks down completely and half the crowd in court promptly break down with her. Thaw, in particular, bellows

40

like a bull. It is several minutes before the District Attorney can go on.

'Do you remember the Lederer divorce case?' he then asks.

'Yes.'

Evelyn is at last calm again.

'That was before your marriage, wasn't it?'

'Yes.'

'Were you cited in it as a co-respondent?'

'Yes.'

'Do you know a Mr Garland?'

'Yes.'

'Did you meet him when you were in *Floradora*?'

'Yes.'

'Did you spend most of your Sundays on his yacht?'

'With my mother.'

She does her best to make it sound respectable.

'But your mother wasn't very pleased with Mr Garland's attentions to you, was she?'

'Well ... Perhaps not,' Evelyn says.

'Was Mr Garland awaiting a divorce?'

'I didn't know that then.'

'You knew when you were named in it,' Mr Jerome says grimly.

The final item in the list, in some respects, the most disgraceful of the lot – disgraceful, when remembering the defence that Harry Thaw was so appalled at the idea of anyone corrupting Evelyn's innocence that a mere report of it was enough to rob him of his reason.

Mr Jerome continues:

'Your birthday falls on Christmas Day, doesn't it?'

'It does.'

'Your nineteenth birthday – was that on Christmas Day of nineteen hundred and two?'

'Yes.'

'More than two years before you married Harry Thaw?'

'Yes.'

'H'm. On that Christmas Eve, the eve of your nineteenth birthday, did you go out to a restaurant, you and Harry Thaw?'

'Yes, I think we did.'

'When you left that restaurant, did you go with Harry Thaw

41

to an apartment in the Sixties – somewhere opposite the west side of the Park?'

'Yes, I think we did.'

'Whose apartment was it?'

'It was Harry's – it was his.'

Mr Jerome assumes his favourite posture.

'And you remained there all night, didn't you, with him?'

Evelyn sees – Mr Jerome intends that she should see – familiar faces behind him in the court: night porters, bell-boys, and perhaps detectives?

'You remained there all night, didn't you, with him?'

She dare not answer no – and she dare not answer yes. So she stands there silent, exposed on every count – exposed as a girl who quite deliberately traded her attractions, exposed as a girl both willing and able to perform a part . . .

Perhaps this seems to be a handy place to stop, after that classical example of the power and the value of cross-examination. It might seem we might very well take all the rest for granted; anybody can anticipate what is coming, the total collapse of Thaw's false defence, total failure of his plea that he was mad, verdict of Guilty, and a well-merited finale in the electric chair. That is how the Thaw case should have worked out in theory. But it is not how it worked out in fact.

The jury disagreed, seven to five, split about evenly; seven for straight verdict of murder against Thaw, five for finding him insane. On what grounds, on what reason – that is anybody's guess.

Disagreement meant a second trial. The whole thing, the whole routine, was tapped out once again in January 1908 – the plea of insanity, the hired psychiatrists, the innocent performance by Evelyn Thaw.

The second jury *could* agree; they agreed that Thaw was not responsible for that cold-blooded murder because, they were unanimous, at the time he was insane.

Presently they let him out (after a series of appeals between 1908 and 1912, which were dismissed and after an escape to Canada in 1913, and deportation back to the U.S.A., when he was pronounced sane on 11 January 1914), and that was all the punishment, the full scale of the punishment, ever imposed on Harry Thaw for killing Stanford White.

42

It seems that he had the good luck to strike juries who were more impressed by pretty faces than by evidence. For there is not the slightest doubt that he owed his escape to Evelyn, as she was very much aware.

'Harry Thaw,' she said some time afterwards, 'hid behind my skirts right through two dirty trials' and the pity is that he hid successfully.

The little Mediterranean port was already a powder keg of political intrigue – but it didn't deter Sabina from carrying out her plan . . .

DEATH AT THREE-THIRTY

Dennis Wheatley

The blue waters of the Mediterranean lap the tumble-down quays of Decastzban. It is a little old town, old when Rome was young, smelly, picturesque; nestling at the foot of craggy, sun-scorched mountains.

Its normally sleepy Plaza was thronged with a murmuring crowd; the Dictator had honoured the small port with a one-night visit and was to leave again for the capital that afternoon.

From the entrance of the old 'Three Angels' Hotel a girl suddenly appeared. Soldiers held back the crowd as she hurried to a waiting car. Some trunks were strapped upon its grid and a tall gaunt man sat hunched in the passenger seat.

Police Chief Sperantze waved her forward. He knew Sabina Tovorri; had known her since she was a little girl. Who did not know her haughty profile and regal carriage in Decastzban? Her family had possessed great estates in the neighbourhood – until the Revolution. Since, she had made good as a journalist on the local paper; her foreign education had helped her in that – and her looks. Sperantze was mildly surprised that she neglected to give him her usual smile. Her olive face was clouded and the corners of her shapely mouth turned down. He assumed, quite wrongly, that the 'Great Man' had refused her an interview.

As Sabina wriggled into the driver's seat, the porter came running from the hotel. Over his outstretched arm was slung a camera and in his hand he held a small square package. '*Contessa!*' he cried. '*Contessa*, you have forgotten this!'

She gave him one startled glance, jammed her small foot on the accelerator and the car, gathering speed, raced away down the troop-lined street.

The man beside her had noticed nothing. He turned his gaunt face towards her and stared for a moment at the finely cut features, pale under their tan. His eyes were dull, half-filmed like those of a snake or drug-taker, but his question was curt. 'Well?'

'An utter failure,' she almost choked. 'We might have known.'

'What! He refused to see you after all?'

'No, I saw him; and he was charming. Whatever he may have done he has an air, that one, and his eyes. Wise, understanding, kind. I felt like a sneak thief trying to pick the pocket of a saint.'

'You little fool.' The gaunt man's mouth worked furiously. 'How like a woman to fall for that mountebank. I warned you to keep your eyes away from him because his gaze is known to be hypnotic. Yet you must stare at him so that scruples overcame your determination at the last moment.'

'They might have!' she exclaimed bitterly. 'He's not evil – an unscrupulous brigand – as I've always been taught to believe. I know that now – but there *was* no last moment. Your agents are hopelessly incompetent, Korto. They should have told you – we should have realized, ourselves. His people are prepared for such attempts, I had no chance to leave the parcel in his room. Before I entered it everything was taken from me. The bomb, my camera, even my bag – and when I came out I was too dazed to think . . .'

Sabina lied unconsciously. She had been thinking, hard, fast, furiously, from the very second she had been compelled to relinquish her belongings. A wiry, forceful-looking young officer had courteously but firmly relieved her of them in the ante-room. She had recognized him at the first glance. It was Ruran: her childhood friend and girlhood lover. No! That was not true. He had kissed her once, only once, on a hot summer night heavy with thunder. The storm had broken and driven them indoors. Next day he had gone off to begin his military service.

So much had happened since; a dozen different men had occupied her interest; there had been the Revolution and the confiscation of her father's property; the new necessity to carve a career for herself. She had scarcely given Ruran a thought in half a dozen years, but no woman ever forgets the first time she receives a kiss and gives it back with meaning.

She did not think he had recognized her. The formalities had only occupied a matter of seconds before she was ushered into the Dictator's room. The people at the hotel knew her real name, but that under which she wrote her articles would have conveyed nothing to Ruran. Vaguely she remembered hearing that he had become one of the Dictator's most vigorous supporters, but to meet him face to face after all those years at such a tense moment had thrown her completely off her balance.

'What happened to the bomb?' asked Korto suddenly.

'It's still there. The porter came after me with it, but I lost my head and drove away.'

'Good,' he said quietly. 'With luck it may still settle one or two of those swine even if we've failed to get the arch-traitor himself.'

She swung upon him furiously. 'D'you think I'll chance it killing innocent people?' As she spoke she swung the car into the kerb and braked viciously, bringing it to a halt outside a small pâtisserie.

'What are you going to do?' he grunted, grabbing at her wrist.

Her eyes snapped at him. 'Telephone, of course. Tell them to put it out of action. It's only ten past three and the thing's not timed to explode until half past.'

'Listen,' his voice was urgent. 'Our getaway's all fixed. I hate to exercise pressure on you yet again, but I still have your father's papers. He doesn't like being poor, but he'll like prison far less. I told you what I'd do if you double-crossed me; and I'll do it yet if you get us caught through telephoning some damn-fool warning.'

With a sudden unexpected wrench, Sabina tore her arm away and flung herself out of the car. He made a swift movement to follow her, then thought better of it. Three minutes later she rejoined him, and the car sped on through the narrow twisting streets towards the west gate of the old town.

'Hell!' exclaimed Korto as they came in sight of the ancient arch flanked by squat battlemented towers. 'See where your crazy warning's landed us. They've telephoned the garrison.'

A double file of carabineers barred their progress. Korto's hand slid up to his armpit holster, but he withdrew it as a young officer, flourishing an automatic, jumped on the running board.

'Turn your car round,' he snapped at Sabina. 'You're wanted at Headquarters – quick now.'

Sick with fear and apprehension, she obeyed. If only she had waited to telephone until they were outside the town – but it was too late to think of that now. Tales of the Dictator's prisons flashed through her mind. She would probably suffer unspeakable degradation – unless they shot her – which was even more likely. In a mist of misery she automatically steered the car back to the 'Three Angels' and noticed subconsciously that the clock in the Plaza showed it to be twenty past three.

The Lieutenant shepherded them straight upstairs to the ante-room. Ruran sat there behind a desk table; on it reposed her bag, camera and the package containing the infernal machine: a small alarm clock attached by a fuse to a pound of gelignite and set to go off at three-thirty exactly.

Ruran dismissed the Lieutenant of Carabineers with a nod, glanced at Korto, and signed to two troopers standing at the door. 'Take this man away. Put him below in the courtyard and keep him under observation from the gateway. No one is to be allowed to speak to him or go near him.'

With a baleful glance at Sabina, Korto turned, but Ruran called after him. 'Here, take this trash away – your girl friend's not likely to need it from now on.'

He held out the camera and handbag. With a sullen shrug Korto took them and left the room beween his guards. Ruran and Sabina were alone.

'Have you anything to say?' His eyes were hard as rocks, his voice flinty.

'You – you don't remember me?' Sabina loathed herself even as she spoke for attempting to soften him by recalling their old friendship, yet they were the only words she could think of.

'Perfectly,' he replied coldly. 'You are Sabina Tovorri, daughter of Count Tovorri, the Liberal leader whose estates were confiscated for having opposed my great Master's ordi-

47

nances for saving our country from anarchy. Now, it seems, you have turned anarchist yourself. What have you to say about this?' He tapped the square package on the desk before him.

Sabina stared at it in sudden horror. 'Good God, you haven't opened it?' she gasped. 'It – it's timed to go off at half past three.'

'So you told the porter on the telephone,' Ruran observed. 'It is now twenty-three minutes past. His Excellency is not original in desiring that, wherever possible, punishment should fit the crime. I shall not touch the infernal thing, but propose to leave you with it.'

Her eyes flickered towards the window, but he caught her glance. 'Oh, no!' he smiled sardonically, as he stood up. 'I do not intend that you should throw it outside and kill somebody else.'

With a swift movement he opened the top drawer of the desk, slipped the package inside and, locking the drawer, pocketed the key. 'It will shatter the desk, of course, but I doubt if it will kill you. Your chance of surviving will be slightly better than His Excellency's would have been.' Before Sabina had time to collect her wits he had gone, locking the door behind him.

With a gasp of dismay she flung herself on the heavy desk and wrenched at the drawer. A brass handle came away in her hand, grazing her knuckles. Her eyes distended by terror, she stared frantically round for some implement with which she might force the lock. It was a sparsely furnished hotel sitting-room and she could see nothing which would serve her purpose. She ran to the window, but a wire mosquito screen was nailed across it. As she stared out she saw Korto, the cause of her desperate plight, sitting hunched up on the edge of a fountain in the empty courtyard. By banging on the wire she endeavoured to attract his attention, but he was sunk in torpid gloom. A clock showed above the stables opposite; it was twenty-six minutes past three. Swinging round she attacked the drawer again with renewed frenzy. For three ghastly minutes, each of which seemed an age, she stabbed at the lock with the splintered end of a bone paper-knife. Her hands were bruised and bleeding. She glimpsed the clock again, it was twenty-nine minutes past. In another moment the desk would shatter in a searing sheet of flame. Its jagged splinters would pierce her flesh. She would be stunned, perhaps killed, by the force of the explosion. Wildly she stared round for cover; but the room held no cupboards, only the desk and a few chairs.

Suddenly the door opened. Ruran and the 'Great Man' stood there.

'Your Excellency,' said Ruran, 'you have met this lady as a journalist; I now wish to present her as the Countess Tovorri. Her father's estates were confiscated, you will remember, but today she has rendered you a great service. She warned us by telephone that the anarchist Korto was about to attempt your assassination with a bomb.'

'Korto!' exclaimed the Dictator. 'Where is he?'

'Down there in the courtyard,' said Ruran pointing.

For one second Sabina withdrew her terrified gaze from the desk. The clock above the stable stood at half past three. There was a blinding flash, a cloud of smoke, windows rattled violently; and when they could see again, Korto's mangled body lay on the flagstones by the fountain.

A few minutes later Ruran was giving Sabina a badly needed cognac; his eyes had softened to their old friendliness and humour.

'I had to give you a lesson,' he said softly, 'but I have memories too. It was quite simple to transfer the bomb from the package to your camera case before you came in and send Korto out there with it.'

Mr Schmidt's attractive wife Rosie had two weaknesses – men and drink. But perhaps the tragic consequence of her over-indulgence was not entirely her fault . . .

THE CASE OF
THE UNHAPPY PIANO-TUNER

Julian Symons

Mr Schmidt the piano-tuner sat opposite Francis Quarles in the detective's office overlooking Trafalgar Square. Quarles was a big man, rather dandyishly dressed in a white silk shirt, a brown polka-dotted bow tie and a double-breasted fawn gaberdine suit. The piano-tuner was a shabby little man with the large pleading eyes of a spaniel. He had heard that Quarles could work miracles, Mr Schmidt said. Could he work the miracle of saving a marriage?

Generally Quarles would have turned away such a character as Mr Schmidt before he had spoken half a dozen sentences, but in this case some deep unhappiness in the little man's brown eyes made him listen while the piano-tuner told his sordid and pathetic story, picking nervously during the telling of it at the handle of the little black bag that contained his tools. Mr Schmidt was an Austrian refugee from Nazism who had come to England in 1938. In Austria he had been a man of independent means. In England he obtained a precarious living as a piano-tuner, helped by the money which he had been able to bring out of Austria. For several years Mr Schmidt had lived rather miserably as a single man. Then in 1946 he had married a young woman in a grocer's shop named Rosie, and since then he had been even more miserable.

Mr Schmidt had married Rosie looking for a good gentle wife who would make a home for him. Rosie had married Mr Schmidt under the impression that he was comparatively well-to-do. He had boasted to her foolishly enough of the money he had been able to bring out of Austria, and told her that they would be able to have a home of their own. This was literally true. Mr Schmidt had just enough money to buy a small house in Camden Town after they were married, and with the fatuity of the newly-married he bought it in his wife's name.

When Rosie discovered that her husband's considerable fortune had existed only in her imagination she behaved badly to him. But then Mr Schmidt, Quarles reflected, was the kind of man whose pathetic feebleness invited bad behaviour. They made a comic pair in the photograph that Schmidt showed the detective. Rosie, a coarsely handsome girl with a magnificent figure and the fine shoulders of a horse, was a full head taller than her husband. She had circled Schmidt's waist with one large proprietorial arm.

When deprived of her hopes for the life of a lady of leisure Rosie showed her weaknesses. She had only two, but they were not unimportant, for one was drink and the other was men. Because Schmidt was unable to support them by his earnings as a piano-tuner they were obliged to take lodgers, and with these lodgers Rosie had a succession of affairs. She showed, indeed, by Schmidt's account, signs of something approaching nymphomania. 'Anybody, she would be after *anybody*,' the little piano-tuner said earnestly. 'Believe it, neighbours tell me she make love with the milkman.' Quarles repressed a desire to laugh. There was something almost irresistibly comic, as well as pathetic, in the little man's story.

At present the Schmidts had two lodgers. One was an Indian student named Karaka who seemed indifferent to Rosie's advances. The other, an Australian building foreman named Jim Keeley, was only too susceptible. What with the lodger and the drinking – Mr Schmidt put his hands to his head in despair.

'Surely you can stop her drinking by paying the household bills yourself?'

'I have cut off her allowance.' Mr Schmidt made an emphatic gesture. 'Still she gets it, I do not know how.'

'What does she drink?'

'Whisky. She has it always in the house.'

'An expensive taste. Does she get it through the lodger – what's his name, Keeley?'

'Perhaps. I do not think so. He has said to me it is a pity she drinks so much. And he has been there only three months. She

51

is drinking for a long time before that.'

The climax to the Schmidts' married life had come the night before, when the piano-tuner returned home to find his wife in Keeley's arms. Mr Schmidt had attacked Keeley. The building foreman, a big bull-necked man, had pushed him away contemptuously. Rosie, half-drunk – the bottle of whisky on the table was empty – had said: 'All right, I may as well tell you. I've told everybody else. I'm leaving you, see. I'm going to live with Jim.' She added contemptuously: 'I want a *man* to look after me.' She had then torn off her wedding ring, and thrown it at Schmidt. As a final blow she told him that she was going to sell the house. The money, she said, would be some compensation for her four years of marriage.

When the little man had finished Quarles said, with a mixture of contempt and sympathy: 'You need a divorce lawyer, not a detective.' He explained carefully, while the piano-tuner sat nursing his little black bag, that there was nothing a detective could do for him. What had he expected?

Mr Schmidt was staring at the floor. He muttered: 'Could you not – make him go away? This Keeley?'

'If I could, what would be the use? There would always be somebody else.'

'Yes,' Mr Schmidt sighed. 'Always somebody else.' He picked up his greasy brown hat and said: 'What do I owe?'

'No payment for no service,' Quarles said. 'By the way, about that whisky –'

'The whisky, yes?' Mr Schmidt turned eagerly at the door.

'Nothing,' Quarles said. What good could it do Mr Schmidt to know the probable source of Rosie's whisky?

Quarles expected to hear nothing more of Mr Schmidt and his matrimonial difficulties. That evening, however, he picked up the telephone to hear the harsh voice of his friend Inspector Leeds. The Inspector was elaborately casual. 'Did a little pip-squeak come to see you today – name of Schmidt, piano-tuner, about forty-five years old? Ah, that's what he said. In trouble with his wife.'

'What's happened to him?'

'What do you think?'

Quarles made a guess. 'Suicide?'

'Murder.'

'He's dead?'

'Got it wrong for once, Quarles,' the Inspector said in a voice that sounded like grit being shaken through a sieve. 'It's his wife that's dead. Poisoned. And we're holding him for it.'

It amused Inspector Leeds that Quarles should have entertained a murderer unawares, and he pointed out gleefully to the detective that he would no doubt be called as a witness. The Inspector was only too delighted to recount the events in the last day of Rosie's life.

The Schmidts gave their lodgers bed and breakfast and that morning the atmosphere at the breakfast table according to Karaka, the Indian student, was very strained indeed. Karaka left at eight-thirty and when he said 'Good-bye,' Mr and Mrs Schmidt were sitting silent at the table. Their other lodger Keeley had not then come down. Karaka said that he knew nothing of Rosie's intention to leave home and live with Keeley. At eight-forty-five when, by Schmidt's own account, he also left, Keeley had still not come down. At nine-thirty the baker Danny Williams called at the tradesman's entrance to the house, approached by a blind alley at the back. Rosie seemed, he said, very excited. 'No bread,' she said to him. 'No bread today or tomorrow or the next day, Danny.' She flashed her hand at him, and he saw that she was not wearing her wedding ring. 'I'm a free woman, Danny,' she said. 'Free as air from now on.' She said much the same to the milkman Joe Foster when he called about eleven, and he also noticed her ringless hand. Curiously enough, however, after her refusal of the bread, she ordered a pint of milk which he gave to her. She took it from him and put it down in the kitchen, where it was found unopened.

And what of Keeley? Was he in the house at those times? Neither the baker nor the milkman could be sure, although they agreed that Rosie had a great air of expectancy and excitement. Keeley, in fact, had vanished. He had not been in to his job that morning and he had not been seen to leave the Schmidts' house.

At six o'clock little Schmidt had returned home. He found his wife's body, contorted in the agony of death, on the floor. On the table was a freshly opened bottle of whisky and an empty glass. The whisky was loaded with cyanide, and the glass contained traces of it. Rosie's clothes – and Keeley's – were packed ready for departure. She had been dead for some hours.

When they had reached this point Quarles said to the Inspector: 'Why should it be Schmidt? Why not Keeley?'

'Why should it be Keeley? She was going off to live with him. Schmidt was losing his wife and his home. I shouldn't be surprised if Keeley's dead too and buried somewhere in nice little Mr Schmidt's cellar or backyard. But I'll tell you the real clincher of the case. The whisky.'

'What about the whisky?'

'Schmidt was a non-drinker and non-smoker. Two days before his wife died he did what he'd never done before – bought her a bottle of whisky.'

The police didn't find Keeley's body in the backyard or the cellar – a slight flaw which did not much affect the Inspector's cheerfulness. Quarles, interested in the case almost against his will, saw the little piano-tuner in jail. Schmidt's explanation of the whisky was simple and – like the rest of the story – slightly pathetic. It was a gesture on his part to his wife, he explained. He had felt that he was losing her, and in an attempt to compete with Keeley had bought her a bottle of whisky. Naturally he denied tampering with it, and he believed that this was the empty bottle on the table when she declared her intention of leaving him.

There was, anyway, no proof that this bottle of whisky was the one from which Rosie had taken her fatal drink, as the Inspector readily conceded while waving a hand at the exhibits on the table. 'It's got no prints on it but Rosie's,' he said. 'And why should it have? It would have been wrapped in paper.'

Quarles looked at the wide range of neatly ticketed finger-printed objects on the table. There was the whisky bottle and glass, which bore only Rosie's fingerprints, a silver cigarette case with a number of prints on it (but not Schmidt's) and the tray on which the whisky had been standing, which bore the prints of Rosie and some unknown person presumed to be Keeley. From the kitchen there was the unopened bottle of milk which bore only the prints of Joe Foster, and the plates and cups from breakfast. There were four cups, three of them with the prints of Schmidt, Rosie and Karaka respectively.

The fourth cup again bore unidentified prints. Quarles paused before it. 'Presumably Keeley again,' he said.

The Inspector said grandly: 'I daresay. Make what you can of that lot.'

'Thanks,' said Quarles. 'I will.'

But before he could do anything about it Keeley was found working on a building site near Birmingham, and brought in for questioning. In front of hard-eyed Inspector Leeds and watchful Quarles the building foreman told his story. He had had this job near Birmingham all fixed for some time, he said. It was just a question of when Rosie would come with him. When she had her row with Schmidt they arranged that they would leave on the following day. Keeley therefore deliberately stayed in bed until Karaka and Schmidt had left the house. Then he got up, had breakfast, and left at about ten o'clock to make arrangements about tickets and luggage. He returned just before twelve to find Rosie dead, and experienced a few minutes of utter panic. Back in Australia, Keeley revealed under questioning, he had served a prison sentence for violent assault. He was terrified of being mixed up in a murder case, and with no thought except to save himself from possible arrest he cleared out.

'Well,' said Quarles, 'that clears up the case.' He looked like an enormous cat that had lapped a bowlful of cream.

'What do you mean?'

Quarles told him.

'The thing that struck me when Schmidt told me his story,' Quarles said to an interested audience that included the two lodgers, the little piano-tuner, the milkman and the baker, 'was – where did Rosie get her whisky. She had been getting it for a long time before Keeley came, so it wasn't through him. She didn't get it through an ordinary wine and spirit merchant, because she had no money. It was delivered to the house, then – but who delivered it? A friend? Not an ordinary friend, obviously, or Schmidt would have heard about him. No, the whisky must have been delivered by someone with whom she was friendly – with whom she was carrying on an affair, in fact – and yet *whose visits to the house would pass unnoticed*. Do I make myself plain?'

Somebody sighed. Keeley wiped his forehead.

'So much for the source of the whisky. And then the evidence. There was one curious point. When Danny Williams the baker called at half past nine Rosie Schmidt said that she didn't want any bread, that she wouldn't want any tomorrow or the next day. But when Joe Foster called at eleven Rosie took a pint of milk. Now, why did she do that?'

Joe Foster, a heavy-browed man with an underslung jaw, shook his head in bewilderment. Danny Williams said: 'She'd changed her mind about going away perhaps?'

'That's a possibility, although we don't know of anything that could have made her change it,' Quarles said. He added pleasantly: 'Or it could be that she was dead when Joe called.'

The milkman gaped: 'What do you mean?'

'*You* were the one who supplied her with whisky,' Quarles said. 'It had to be a tradesman who called at the house regularly and could give it to her unobserved. You were the only one who had a motive.'

'What motive?'

'Schmidt gave it to me when he told his story. "Neighbours tell me she make love with the milkman," ' he said. 'That sounded like a joke, and maybe it was a bit of a joke to Rosie, but it wasn't a joke to you. And you knew she was leaving the district and going off with Keeley. Rosie said to Schmidt, "I've told everybody else," when she told him the news. What did she mean by that? She hadn't told Karaka or the neighbours. She meant everybody who'd be interested. She meant you. And when you understood that she was serious about going off with Keeley you gave her a pleasant little parting gift – a bottle of whisky laced with cyanide. You gave it to her the previous day, and when you called on the milk round at eleven o'clock she was dead.'

Foster crossed his arms. 'She took in a bottle of milk from me that morning. That's my story and I'm sticking to it.'

'And that's the story that'll hang you, Joe,' Quarles said amiably. 'Because you slipped up badly there. You said in your evidence that you gave her the pint of milk. She took it from you and put it down in the kitchen.'

'That's right.'

'Then how did it happen,' Quarles asked, 'that there were only your fingerprints on the bottle?'

The MP for Minchcombe East was furious when he was told
police had searched the murder suspect's bicycle shed without a
warrant. And PC Potts had a lot of explaining to do . . .

A NICE CUP OF TEA

Herbert Harris

With a twinkle in his eye that was faintly malicious, the
Sergeant said, 'Jim Brady's in there, sir . . . waiting to see
you.'

Inspector Drew of Scotland Yard's Murder Squad,
frowned. 'Brady? Who's he?'

'Member of Parliament,' the Sergeant said. 'Sits for Minchcombe East. A fighting champion of the underdog. Talks
about the liberty of the individual and all that.'

'I suppose he's griping about something?' Drew prompted.

'It's about Finney, sir. Finney's complained about his
bicycle shed being searched while he was out.'

The Inspector looked surprised. 'Who did it – one of *my*
blokes?'

'No, sir. One of ours. Potts. Rather an eager beaver.'

'You're telling me,' Drew muttered. He was visited by a
sudden mental vision of Potts of the Minchcombe force – a
very young constable with a very pink face and very ginger
hair, the sort of chap old-fashioned detective-story writers
used for comic relief. He *would* have a name like Potts, Drew
thought.

'Of course, sir,' the Sergeant said anxiously, 'he'll have to
be told that going off on his own and searching a private citizen's bicycle shed without an official warrant is bound to get
the local hotheads talking about police persecution.'

'Oh, blast,' murmured Inspector Drew and went in to face
the Member for Minchcombe East.

Brady, stocky, florid, and forthright, jumped up. 'Ah, you'd
be Inspector Drew? I daresay you know who I am?'

'I've just found out,' Drew answered a little crossly.

'Well, it's about this man Finney, the one you chaps have been hounding,' Brady said. 'He's the son of an ex-mayor, you know. He's entitled to his freedom, like the rest of us.'

Brady leaned forward. 'I know you Yard chaps have your work cut out and I've no wish to be obstructive, but there's such a thing as the liberty of the individual. This man Finney hasn't been charged with anything . . .'

'I'm hoping he will be,' Drew put in.

'He's not been charged with anything,' Brady persisted, 'and, of course, he's right in saying that policemen have no right to climb over the wall into his garden and rifle his bicycle shed.'

'I know nothing about that,' Drew answered, 'but I'm hoping to find out shortly. May I ask what else you learned from Finney?'

'Nothing that you don't already know, I expect,' Brady said. 'His uncle, John Marchant, was battered to death in his house at Whitford. And because Finney stood to inherit a good deal of money, he's Number One suspect.'

'Correct,' the Inspector nodded. 'And the day Marchant was murdered, his nephew Finney was away for the whole day – on one of his bicycle jaunts. He left home after breakfast and didn't return until evening.'

'But Whitford is fifty miles from Winchcombe,' Brady said.

'That's true,' Drew replied, 'and Finney has been a racing cyclist. He can take such distances in his stride. There is one big snag from my point of view.'

'Ah' – Brady allowed himself a smug smile.

'When he started out,' Drew said grimly, 'he told his landlady he was bound for Liffley, which is entirely the opposite direction from Whitford.'

'And he did actually cycle towards Liffley?' Brady prompted.

'Yes, sir, but he could have doubled back and gone to Whitford after all,' Drew pointed out. 'Our problem is that not a soul has come forward to say they saw Finney that day.'

'What about his girl – Verity somebody – who says that Finney visited her at Liffley?' Brady wanted to know.

'Verity!' exploded Drew, and laughed. 'In my opinion she's a slut and a liar. Don't forget Finney has come into money from Marchant's death. If you want to believe Marchant was coshed by an intruder, you can. Frankly, I don't.'

'You've got to prove Finney was *in* Whitford,' Brady said. 'He claims he hasn't been near Whitford for years.'

The Sergeant pushed his head round the door. 'Potts is here, sir,' he announced. 'He'd be obliged if you could see him right away, as he has to go to the assizes to give evidence in an accident case.'

'Tell him to come in!' Drew said with a heavy sigh.

Potts entered diffidently, his helmet under one arm, and bobbed his ginger head nervously at the Yard man and the MP.

Drew said, 'You know what you've done, don't you? You've got the citizens of Minchcombe calling us Gestapo.'

The constable's boyish skin became pinker. 'I realize I was a bit hasty, sir, and that I might have cut across what you were doing like. But you weren't available, see. There was this shed door unlocked and Finney nowhere in sight . . .'

'Look,' Drew said impatiently, 'one of my chaps went over Finney's shed with a toothcomb – and a search warrant, I might add. He also examined the bike. Might I ask what you expected to find that a member of the Murder Squad didn't?'

Potts swallowed. 'Well, it's like this, sir. I was struck by an idea, see. It arose out of my missus being partial to a cup of tea, and her brother Ted – who's an analytical chemist – talking about how tea varies according to where you drink it, on account of the water being different from place to place . . .'

Four keen eyes were trained on him. He eased his collar.

'I remembered the bottle of water Finney carried on his bike, and I thought there might be some water left in it and that I ought to get hold of it before he threw it away, see. So I nipped into his shed and got the water bottle – which I see now was the wrong thing to do, sir – but there *was* some water in it, and I got my brother-in-law Ted to test it . . .'

He paused, cleared his throat, and went on, 'Ted said there was fluoride in it – I think that's the name, sir – the stuff that certain authorities put in the water to stop people's teeth decaying . . .'

'Well?' snapped the Inspector.

'Ted says there are very few districts in Britain where

59

they've started to put fluoride in the water supply, sir. I questioned my brother-in-law as to what these districts were, sir, and he stated that the nearest place to here, sir, was Whitford.'

'Well, I'm damned!' Drew muttered incredulously, and hurled a look of triumph at MP Brady.

Potts shifted his helmet from one arm to the other. 'I'm prepared to accept a reprimand, of course, sir.'

'Of course,' said the Inspector. But the Member for Minchcombe East didn't see him wink.

Daffy was the apple of her father's eye ... and she knew there was nothing he wouldn't do for her.

THE WHISPERING

Christianna Brand

She leaned against the counter and the empty glass made a tiny chattering against the mahogany with the shaking of her ringless left hand. They were whispering about her over there in the corner. She said so to the barman. 'They're whispering about me over there.'

'Oh, for Pete's sake!' he said. 'You always think people are whispering.'

'Why do they whisper? Why don't they just talk to me straight out?'

'Perhaps they don't wish to talk to you straight out,' he said, 'or any other way. And I'll be frank with you – neither do I.'

Tears welled up into her large blue eyes. She said with maudlin dignity: 'In future I'll go to some other bar.'

'You do that,' he said, 'God knows we're fed up with you in here.'

But she stayed. She always stayed. Where ever else she went, it would be the same. 'It was all such a long time ago,' she said to the man. 'Why should they whisper still?'

But they whispered: and the whispering grew and grew.

Such a long time ago ...

Of course Simon should never have taken her there in the first place. But she'd begged and pleaded and he never could resist her. 'You know I'd take you if I could, Daffy. I'd do anything for you, you know I would, I'd die for you ...'

And so would they all, all the others, all the boys – they'd lie down and die for Daffy Jones. And not only the young ones. 'My Pa,' Daffy used to say, 'he'd go out and get himself

61

run over if it would do me any good. No, honestly he would – he'd die for me.' His Daffodil, he called her, his Golden Daffodil.

Talk about daffy! Simon thought – but there it was, she did remind one of a daffodil, so slender and fresh in the little narrow green frocks she so often wore, with that bell of bright yellow hair.

'All the same, Daffy, I couldn't take you to the Blue Bar. It's just what it says, it's off-colour, it's an awful place. I couldn't.'

But it sounded thrilling and the other girls at school would have fits when they heard she'd been there. 'Oh, Simon, don't be so stuffy! Please.'

'Honestly, I couldn't. What would your father say? He'd have a heart attack.'

'My father has heart attacks the whole time,' she said.

'Well, I didn't mean that. I mean he'd do hand-springs.'

'If my father did hand-springs he'd have a heart attack,' she said laughing, 'so it comes to the same thing.'

'I just meant that he wouldn't like it. He'd murder me!'

Daffy was his cousin, her father was his Uncle John.

'It's a dreadful, sordid place, sailors and tarts and people like that, everybody drunk or hashed up, some of them even on the hard stuff.'

He had, in fact, been there only once himself, taken by two much older boys who had left school – his own school. He went to boarding school; not Daffy's. It had shocked and scared him; scared him even more to think it might ever come out that he had been there.

And she recognised that. She was a fly one, little Daffy Jones.

She said: 'But *you* go there,' and added with the smallest slyest of meaningful glances, 'what would *your* Pa say?'

So he took her. Never mind the threat implicit, he loved her, he had always loved her, always, since they'd been small children together: Daffy so fresh and dewy-eyed, Daffy irre-sistible.

'Gosh!' she said when they got there, 'isn't it frightful? Fancy you!'

'Oh, well,' he said, casually sophisticate, 'one grows up.'

But when his neighbour on the close-packed bench against the greasy wall offered him a drag, he said at once: 'No thanks.'

'Oh, do!' said Daffy. 'I'd love to have a try.' Not for nothing was she known at school, with double meaning, as the Sex-Pot, but he was not to know that. 'Only I don't like sharing,' she said to the man.

'Plenty more where that came from,' said the man, producing a handful of ready-rolled untidy cigarettes. He suggested to Simon, 'Only it'll cost you bread, man, bread.'

Of all the phoneys! But poor Simon fell for it all like a ton of bricks and forked out twice as much for the stuff as Daffy could have got it for, any day, from the school gardener.

'Do let me have a – a drag, do they call it? – Simon. I'd love to try it.'

The stuff takes you different ways. Simon it wafted into a beautiful dream, sitting huddled on the bench gazing before him into a brilliance where beautiful people danced and hugged and did beautiful things, right out there in the open before everyone. He awoke to the sound of her screeching. She was shaking him, screaming at him.

'Look at me! Look what he did to me.'

She looked beautiful, he thought, standing there with her dress half ripped off her body, showing the lovely white nakedness underneath, her hair all torn and tousled, her eyes so strangely bright – she must have been having a beautiful, beautiful time.

'You look beautiful, Daffy,' he said. 'Did you have a good time?'

'Good? It was horrible. Look what he did to me!'

'You shouldn't have gone with him if you didn't like it.'

But she had liked it. For most of the time. She had never before been with a real, grown-up man. But then . . .

'He wanted it all wrong,' she said. 'I thought he was going mad. I didn't know what he was up to.' She went into details. 'So I tried to make him stop because, after all, there are limits; and he went berserk – it was absolutely frightful.'

And indeed when he looked at her again, fighting his way up out of his euphoric self-absorption, she did perhaps look rather a mess.

'I'd better take you home. We'd better both go home.'
Lovely, blissful home, warm bed, comfortable dreams ...

She was hugging together her ripped dress, trying to comb out her torn and tangled hair, scrabbling in her handbag for lipstick and little tubes of shiny eye make-up: spitting into an oblong box of mascara, thickening her lashes with great blobs of it, with some vague idea of getting back to normal, making herself 'look good'.

'What'll I tell them? How'll I explain to Mummy and Daddy? They'll go mad.'

'Tell them what happened,' he said comfortably. 'You couldn't help it. Say he made a pass at you and, of course, you wouldn't and he beat you up.'

'They'll say what was I doing here?' Out of her anxiety, grew belligerence. 'You should never have brought me to a place like this.'

He protested: 'You made me bring you.'

'You, my own cousin! What will my Pa say?' Her father was a simple man: simple and gentle. But when he saw her like this, his little pet, his darling, his innocent flower ... 'He'll murder you,' she said.

'*You* went with the man. I told you not to.'

'You should have stopped me.'

'How could I?' he said, simply. 'I was stoned.'

'Well, you shouldn't have got stoned and let me.' She sat hunched up beside him on the bench. Now and again, vaguely, curious glances swept over them and swept on. She looked a bit young for the Blue Bar – too young and too – well, different – to have been outside, having it rough with that sailor chap they called The Butcher; for that matter, *both* of them looked much too young, two silly kids out of place, from another world. Still, that was their affair. She, in her turn, looked back at them: dirty, raddled women, too remote from long-past youth and beauty to be of use to anyone but the rough, drunken, drug-soaked degenerates that would come to such a place.

'Simon, if my father knew! Swear you won't ever tell him I was here.'

'What shall we say to them, then?'

'Say that we ... say we were walking along, say we were

coming home from the Singing Café, that's harmless enough, along the river path. And just by that bench, the bench in front of Mardon's hotel, say it was there; we must stick to the same story exactly – say there were these three boys and they jumped up and started making passes at me. And you fought them off – I'll say you were terribly brave – but it was three to one and one of them got me away. Here, pull out your tie, mess up your clothes, look as if you'd been in a fight.' But he'd have no scratches and bruises, no black eyes, he wouldn't look a bit as if he'd been in a fight; and what was more, he didn't look as though he were taking in a word she said. Anyone would see that he was stoned, even her innocent father would recognize that much. He'll be at the zombie stage, she said to herself, he'll never stick to anything. She said : 'No, after all, skip it. I'd better go alone.'

Her light summer coat covered her ripped clothes. She got home at last, going the direct way, not along the river path. It was late, but the later she got home, the more likely her father would be anxiously waiting to see that she was safe. And, sure enough, at the first scrape of her key in the lock, the landing light went on and he was creeping downstairs so as not to wake her mother, wrapped in his old brown checked dressing-gown, the tassel of his cord following him with tiny muffled bumps from step to step.

'Daffy? Where've you been? You're awfully late.'

The coat covered her clothes but the pale, bruised face told its own story and the torn, tousled yellow hair. She had been thinking all the way home what best to say. His face, always so thin and worn, now turning to a bad colour she too well knew, gave her her cue. She tumbled into his arms. 'Oh, Daddy!'

'What is it, darling, what's happened? Oh, my God – you haven't been...? They haven't...?' He led her, as she sobbed and shuddered, into the sitting-room, lowered her on to the sofa, fell on his knees before the electric fire to switch it on, as though offering a prayer to it for warmth and comfort for her; came back to sit beside her on the sofa, circling her shoulders with a trembling arm.

'Don't cry, sweetheart. You're safe now, sweetheart. Tell Daddy, darling, it'll be better when you've told.' But he left her again for a moment, ran to the door, called up the stairs :

'Hester!', darted back to the cupboard, found brandy and a glass. 'Here, darling, try, just a sip. Then you can tell me.'

His hand was shaking as he held the glass, his face was a terrible colour, that ugly blue-grey, rather frighteningly patched with a dusky red. He fumbled almost surreptitiously in the breast pocket of his pyjamas, shook a small pill into his hand and swallowed it.

She sobbed and shivered and at last burst out with it all. 'Oh, Daddy! It was Simon.'

'Simon?' he said; stupefied at the sound of that name.

'On that bench by the river, Daddy. You know, the bench in front of Mardon's Hotel –'

'Mardon's?' he said. 'That's not on your way home.'

'No, but he – he wanted to go there. So we went and then we stopped and sat on the bench and we were just looking at the river and talking – at least I was just talking; and then ...' She buried her face against his shoulder. 'Don't make me tell!'

'Oh, my God, Daffy!' he said; and you could sense his reaction to her plea, humble and gentle: it's her mother she needs, not me. He left her again for a moment and went out into the hall, calling more urgently up from the foot of the stairs. 'Hester! Wake up, come down! Hester, it's Daphne: come down.'

And she came, hurry-scurrying, anxious, trembling, her dressing-gown clutched with a shaking hand tight up against her throat as though to shut out some bitter cold wind in that well-warmed house.

'What is it, my darling, what's happened? Oh, God, darling! – your face, all those marks – your hands, your hair.' And she cried out, as the father had cried out, voicing the nameless fear never far from their hearts: 'You haven't ...? They haven't ...?'

'It was Simon,' she said dully.

'Simon? What Simon? Which Simon?'

'Simon, our Simon.' 'You did mean your cousin, Simon, Daffy?'

'Mummy, I *tried* not to let him.'

The mother could not – would not – take it in. 'Simon? He's only a boy, he's only seventeen.'

66

'Boys of seventeen nowadays . . .' said her husband.

'But Simon? – he's her own cousin, he's like her brother.'

'No, Mum,' said Daphne. 'He isn't. He's never been.' But how would she, innocent blossom, have recognised that? 'I mean, he was always sort of – sloppy, sort of lovey-dovey, you know.' And she searched in her keen little mind for a phrase from her mother's own courting days. 'I mean he's always sort of carried the torch for me.'

'But, Daffy, what happened?'

What had happened? He hadn't taken her to that place, no; for any investigation might produce someone who had observed her, going off outside, so flirtatious and willing, with the sailor, Butch. But Simon would soon admit that they had been there: would confess to having taken her there – to having given way to her entreaties and taken her there. And to having smoked that wicked pot and so been unable to control her when she had insisted upon leaving him. Simon in his silly innocence would give it all away. Well, then, Simon must be discredited in advance. 'He was stoned, Daddy. He didn't know what he was doing. He was stoned out of his mind.'

They picked up these dreadful expressions from the television. 'You mean he'd been drinking?'

'He was on hash. On hashish. Of course, I didn't know. I couldn't understand him. He kept talking about some awful place, some sort of dance place, you know, where sailors went with women, awful women, and everyone was on hash or something, even on the hard stuff; Simon told me that, he said lots of them were "on the hard stuff". He said he'd take me there, he wanted to take me there. I believe in the end,' said Daffy carefully, 'he almost thought he *had* taken me there, he was in a sort of dream, a sort of nightmare, he thought he was there, he thought I was one of those – those women . . .' She broke off, shuddering and whimpering; looking into their white, stricken faces, searching for any sign of doubt. But there was none. Simon could protest and deny but would be obliged to admit that he had been under the influence of an unfamiliar drug – he was far too stupid and honest not to tell the truth; and might, in the end, even be brought to half believe in her story himself. No one in that place was likely to have taken any notice of them; let alone to admit to having stood by and watched her, so young and obviously unaccustomed, being taken out to be raped and beaten up by the man even they called The Butcher.

'We were going to the folk-singing café – you know, you all sit round and have coffee and listen to the singing. Well, we did go and we were sitting at the back of the café, away from the stage, and suddenly the man next to Simon passed him a cigarette and Simon said "Thank you" and smoked it and then he said had the man got any more that he wouldn't mind selling him, because he'd run out; and the man said, "It'll cost you bread, man," but, of course, that can mean only "you'll have to pay for them". At least, that's what I thought; but anyway, he sold Simon a few loose ones and Simon was smoking away and he seemed to go a bit dreamy, not to say zombie, but of course I thought it was only the music. But on the way home, we went and sat on the bench like I told you, Daddy...'

'She didn't want to go,' he said quickly to her mother.

'It wouldn't matter, darling, if you did,' said her mother, gently. 'I mean, just sitting on a bench in the moonlight just...' You could see her thinking that one mustn't be square and narrow-minded, things had changed these days. 'Just doing a bit of necking, darling.'

Honestly, thought Daffy, they were so naive it was almost sickening. She said: 'Oh, yes, I know, Mummy; but actually I was tired. I wanted to come home. And then he – he was so strange and insistent and then he started trying to kiss me and then – then...'

'Oh, Daphne, he didn't –?' Her mother sat staring at her, one hand fisted against her mouth as though to plug in the little moaning, whimpering sounds that would force their way out. Her father was silent and his silence was worse than the whimpering.

Into that frightening silence, she began to gabble; and with the gabbling, memories came flooding back. 'Then he ... I fought and struggled...' Real memories, genuinely terrifying, genuinely vile, the shock and horror of that onslaught by a man savage with drink and frustration of a perverted passion. The earlier passages of her acquiescence were passed over: the rest, with genuine sobbings and bleatings, blurted out in a genuine sickness of frightened and disgusted recollection. The thin summer coat had all this time remained wrapped about her. Now she stood up and let it fall.

That slender white body like a lily, swaying within its ragged enfolding leaf of the little green dress: livid weals scoring the delicate skin, throat, arms, breast, great patches of red which tomorrow would be purple bruises, dried blood where filthy nails had scratched: marks of teeth on a soft round shoulder ... The mother gave one horror-stricken glance and fell back, half fainting, into her corner of the sofa. The father said, in a high, harsh, scraping voice: 'Daffy. You must answer. Did he? Did Simon—'

If any investigation arose, it could be proved all too surely that here was no dear little virgo intacta. She collapsed, sobbing afresh. 'Oh, Daddy, please! Don't ask me.'

But he repeated it, sick, dull, with that horrible grey-blue look on his face, though now, thanks to the medicine, the flush had died down. 'I must ask you, Daffy. Did he...? Dear God! – Daffy, did Simon succeed in – raping you?'

She lifted her head and looked back into his face; the small flower-face looking back into the haggard thin face with that blue-grey, ash-grey skin. She bit on an already bleeding lip and turned away her head.

A simple man: with a serious heart condition, perhaps with but little time left to live. A man with one passion, with one hope, one idea, one total, blinding perfection of happiness in his life – so young, so fresh, untouched by the dirty world about her, so starry innocent – his golden girl, his golden Daffodil ... A gentle man who for the rest of his life had retained the symbol of the hideous years of enforced ungentleness: his old Army revolver. He went to it now: went with a sort of automatism, turned back to that symbol of the red rage that had in those bad days consumed him at the sight of friends and comrades lying shattered into hideous stillness at the hands of the enemy; the red rage that then – as now again it must – had borne him on the only wings that would carry him to the duty that must be done: the wings of an unthinking, revengeful fury. Like an automaton, he loaded the gun with a single shot, left the house, walked the short distance to his brother's home: stood in the darkness outside the white painted door and called out, sharp and harsh, hardly knowing that he lifted his voice: 'Simon! Come out here!'

The front door opened. Framed in the light from the hall, still reeling a little, shocked, sickened by the memories which, with a terrifying clarity, were now returning, the boy stood there and looked out into the night. Looked out and saw where the stream of light caught the barrel of the revolver in a black gleam: and cried out: 'It wasn't my fault, Uncle John! She *made* me take her there.'

Like a man deaf and dumb, he lifted the gun, took aim at the boy's left breast and fired; and stood quietly aside through the ensuing uproar till the police came to take him away.

And so the Golden Daffodil – the press had latched on to her pet name in one minute flat – was on all the front pages. Only Mummy – true to form – had fought off the reporters and photographers and there was always the same photograph and it was an awful thing – taken quite early on the following morning when she was still drenched in tears about poor Simon being dead and poor Daddy being in prison; no make-up, hair in the most frightful mess because, of course, there'd been no time to go to Freesia's to get it done; face patched with bruises, and still in one's dressing-gown, though, fortunately the lovely new one that had been Mummy's last birthday present. And things were slightly dicey. Policemen kept coming and asking her questions – or policewomen, rather: it was all so delicately handled that really it almost made Daffy giggle – though of course it was too awful about Daddy and Simon. Mummy made her stay in bed and she lay propped up on pillows and wanly lived again through the recital of Simon's attack and Daddy's reaction to what she had told him about it. That all went all right, went fine, and after all now at least Simon could never contradict her. But after that ...

First Maureen and Lindy turned up. Allowed to visit her after anxious telephone calls between the Mums.

'You won't – well, tell them anything about all *that*, darling? They might not understand. Of course they're older than you are, but still ...'

So it all had to be told in whispers; not about the Blue Bar, of course, best to keep that entirely to oneself – it was quite rivetting enough just pinned on to poor Simon (who ever would have thought that a proper little cousin of Daffy's would have had such kinky ideas?). But when she mentioned Mardon's bench, Maureen responded immediately: 'You can't have been on that bench, because *we* were. We were there half the night with the Frazer boys.'

She didn't think of the come-back quick enough. She drew a red herring. "I didn't know you even knew the Frazer boys.'

'Good lord, Daffy, Maureen and Roddy Frazer have been having it off for weeks. Haven't you, Maureen?'

'He's terrific,' said Maureen.

'Eddie's not too bad,' said Lindy. 'But inexperienced.' She wouldn't have bothered with him, she added, but they wanted to make up a foursome.

'I went with him once and I thought he was absolutely dreary.'

'Oh, well, we know your standards, Daffy,' said Lindy laughing.

'But, anyway, why all this drama with your cousin, Simon? Why not just let him?' And she laughed again and said that heaven knew, kinky or not, Daffy hadn't exactly had anything to lose by it.

'He happens to be dead,' said Daphne stiffly; drawing the subject ever further from the bench by the river.

'Oh, well, yes we know that, darling; and of course it's too frightful. And about your father and all that. My God, it's frightful!'

'Why on earth did you have to go and tell your father, Daph?'

'He caught me sneaking in. I was in such a mess, I had to say something. And anyway, I was pretty steamed up. I did have an awful time. I mean, look at these bruises.'

'I can't see why you should struggle? Why not just let him get on with it?'

'Well, good heavens, he was like a sex maniac! He'd been smoking all evening and heaven knows what this pusher at the bar, well I mean in the café, had sold him. He was stoned clean, he just did his nut. Of course I couldn't tell my parents I'd let him. I had to say he'd forced me.'

'Good lord – poor Simon.'

'Yes, but he did knock me about. Of course it's awful about

71

Daddy shooting him, but still he did knock me about.'

'All the same, Daphne, it wasn't on that bench outside Mardon's,' said Maureen, coming back to cases. 'Because we were there ourselves.'

'I didn't say the bench outside Mardon's. I said it wasn't the one outside Mardon's. The one we went to was the one further down, by the warehouse. You know I always go to the warehouse one, at least I always used to with Tom.'

'What's Tom going to say about all this poor-little-raped-virgin stuff, when it comes out?'

'For that matter, Daffy, what's everyone going to say? I mean, everyone knows about *you*.'

'Well, then everyone will just have to shut up, won't they?' said Daffy. She gave them that sly little sideways glance of hers, the meaningful glance that had finally blackmailed poor Simon into giving way and taking her to the Blue Bar. 'Otherwise I might start talking in self-defence. I mean, if they knew how everyone at school was doing it, not to mention the pot and all the rest of it – if they knew the temptations I'd had and the example that had been set me by – by older girls than me: well, I wouldn't be so much to blame, would I? So everyone had better just shut up, hadn't they? And I didn't say I was down by the river near Mardon's, I said "we were on that bench, not the Mardon's one but the other bench". Or would you like to get up in court when they're trying my father for murder and say that you know I wasn't at the Mardon's bench because you were there yourselves all night having it off with a couple of boys?'

'My God, that young Daphne, she's a cool one!' said Maureen to Linda as they hastily went away. (All the same, she *had* said she'd been outside Mardon's.)

Daphne herself was not too pleased with the way she had handled it. She should have thought of that threat earlier. Because one day she was going to have to face Daddy and she'd definitely told Daddy that she'd been by the Mardon's bench; and he'd commented that that wasn't on the way home – he wouldn't forget that, you couldn't just slur it over with *him*. Had Mummy heard? No, she hadn't come downstairs by then. So only Daddy would know. A thought flicked through her mind and flicked out again. If Daddy knew she'd told one lie, would he begin to wonder if, after all, Simon had been innocent?

If Daddy should give her away! If everyone got to know that she'd gone to that place, that she'd been with that sailor, that she'd lied about poor Simon and lied and lied and lied ... If all the newspapers, cooing now about poor little innocent-injured Golden Daffodil – if they knew that she was just a sexy trollop who could give lessons to any of the boys at school and *had* given lessons to most of them! If they knew that she'd let Daddy go off and murder Simon – murder him! – was letting Daddy now face the rest of his life in prison, all because of her lies ... And Mummy, poor Mummy, having to live on, with all the family knowing that Daddy had killed Simon, her own cousin, his own nephew, his own brother's son – had actually shot and killed him: because of her lies ...! If Daddy were ever to give her away!

But he wouldn't. How could he ever harm her, his Golden Daffodil? He'd die to protect her. Daddy would *die* for her.

And it wasn't only Maureen and Lindy. Now a man came forward and told the police that he'd recognized her picture in the paper as that of a girl he'd seen that night at the Blue Bar, a disreputable haunt of sailors in the bad part of town.

The police had informed the solicitor who was looking after Daddy's defence and he came to see her. Could this man's story possibly be true?

'Of course not,' said Daffy, opening the large blue eyes. 'I never even heard of such a place.'

'You were at the folk-singing café all through the evening?'

'Yes, till we went home by the river. Of course we were.'

'Did you see anyone who might confirm that?'

'What, you mean at the café? No, we didn't see anyone we knew. We were near the back and they keep the lights very low because of the singing.'

'One man did speak to you?'

'Yes, but he was a pusher. *He* wouldn't come forward, would he?'

No flies on little Miss Jones, reflected the solicitor. He suggested: 'Your cousin, however, had wanted to take you to some place like this bar? You told your father so.'

'Oh, yes, but ...' She thought it all out rapidly. It was get-

73

ting rather scarey. 'Perhaps the man saw Simon there on some other night,' she suggested, 'and just mixed up the nights. He used to take other girls there – or anyway to some place.'

'It was your picture the man recognized.'

'He couldn't from the papers, that was the most awful thing. He probably recognized Simon's and remembered seeing him there on some other night with some other girl and then associated the other girl with me.' It sounded pretty good, but it wouldn't deceive Daddy; Daddy would think it too much of a coincidence, after all she'd told him about Simon wanting to take her to just such a place. And the thought flicked in and out again. If Daddy realized that all along Simon had been innocent of any assault on her – would he really stand by her still? Would he let Simon be blamed for the rest of his life – well, for the rest of his death, then: wouldn't that seem even worse to Daddy? – that Simon was dead and unable to defend himself, that all Simon's family, Daddy's own family, his brothers and sisters and Granny and everyone – should live on, believing that dead Simon had been so vile, when all the time he'd been innocent? Of course she could admit to having been to the Blue Bar – to having allowed Simon to inveigle her to that awful place and then been ashamed to admit it; it need make no difference to the story of his subsequent attack on the river bank. But then if more people came forward, if people remembered how she'd gone off with the sailor of her own accord – indeed against Simon's rather woozy protestations. Nothing to do but deny it; deny it all.

'Don't tell Daddy about it,' she said. 'It simply isn't true that the man could have seen me there; it would only upset him.'

It upset the solicitor also. He thought to himself: 'If this damn' little bitch has been lying all this time!' But it was necessary to take the story to her father.

The sad, grey man caged up in the prison hospital awaiting his trial said at once: 'Of course it isn't true.'

'The man's very sure. He says he remarked at the time how ill-suited they were to such a place.'

'No, no, he *wanted* to take her –' But that didn't make sense. A thought, a memory, came to his mind, terrifying in its intensity. But he thrust it aside. 'Surely this – mistake of this man's needn't come out in court?'

'I don't think so, no. They were obliged to inform us. But it's no good to the prosecution. You're pleading guilty, so that's all there is to it. And for the defence –'

'I don't want any defence. I've told you. I killed the boy for what he did to my child. I don't want any defence.'

'It's just a matter of mitigating circumstances. But anyway,' said the lawyer, 'this wouldn't help us either, so I think we'll just drop the whole matter.' Hardly a mitigating circumstance if the boy turned out to have been shot for something he had never done.

The lawyer went away. But the memory came back. That cry, only half heard, all unattended to. 'It wasn't my fault, Uncle John. She *made* me take her there.' Dear God! If Simon had been innocent after all!

Goodness, the photographers outside the court! It was like being a film star. And of course her hair was done now and Freesia, quite thrilled, had made a special job of it and it looked terrific. And the bruises on her face had faded. Pity she couldn't have used her proper make-up but it would be best, they'd said, to appear very young and fresh and innocent, not to say generally gormless: so that Daddy couldn't be blamed too much for what he'd done. And, indeed, in the witness box she looked like a flower, the light shining down from the canopy above, on the careful halo of golden hair: the golden, Golden Daffodil.

Your name is Daphne Jones? Of such and such an address? And you are sixteen years of age . . .?

Only sixteen years of age.

Only sixteen; and had been with every boy in the top form at school, with or without drugs for extra kicks.

'Yes, sixteen last birthday.'

'Now, don't upset yourself, Miss Jones – or Daphne, may I call you Daphne? I just wanted to ask you to tell us very simply in your own words what happened that night, the night your cousin died.'

(*It wasn't my fault, Uncle John. She made me take her there.*)

75

Best to cover all tracks. They weren't going to use it in court, she knew that now; but best to cover all tracks: the man might talk to the paper afterwards, one never knew.

'He wanted to take me to a dance place he knew about. He used to go there, he used to take other girls. But it sounded like a horrible place so I wouldn't go.'

'You went instead to –?'

'We went to the Singing Café and then we came home by the path along the river bank –'

'Would that be your direct way home?'

'No, he just wanted to come that way. He made me come that way.' But she saw from beneath her eye-lashes the suddenly tightened grip of the two thin hands clasped on the edge of the dock and she knew that that had been a mistake. Daddy would know better; Simon had never in all his life made her do anything against her will – it had been all the other way.

'He wasn't like his usual self,' she said quickly. 'He'd been smoking this pot.'

'And then I think you came to a certain bench –?'

'Yes,' she said, quickly again, running it on into the next sentence, 'and then we sat down and we were looking at the river –'

It made no difference whatever to the case against John Jones, which bench it had been. But something had to be said in the wretched man's defence and if one could spin it out a little more, Counsel felt, it would look a bit more like earning one's fee. He humped himself over, leaning on both fisted hands, looking earnestly down at a map laid out before him.

'That would be the bench outside Dent's warehouse – here?'

'Yes,' she said, slurring it over quickly again, into the following words, 'and we sat there –'

She saw the quick upwards jerk of the bowed head. He called out sharply from the dock, called out sharply in that high, harsh too-well-remembered voice he had spoken in that night, just before Simon died. 'You told me it was Mardon's bench.'

Shushing from the Clerk of the Court and ushers; a glance of compassionate severity from the Bench. But now she knew that Daddy knew. There was nothing to be done about that –

nothing. She must concentrate on convincing the court that she spoke the truth. She explained it all away in her frank little, rather charmingly garrulous way.

'I keep just saying that it wasn't the bench by Mardon's but then people seem to remember that I said the word "Mardon's" and they think I said it *was*. But it wasn't. It was the warehouse bench. He took me to the warehouse bench.'

'Very well. In fact, which bench it was doesn't really matter. But something happened there which you later told your father? Now – what did you tell him? Tell us, please, just as you told it to him.'

So she told it all again: lived yet again through that horrible half hour with the sailor, Butch – lived through the last half of the time anyway: the less said about the first ten minutes the better, but the rest she lived through as she had lived through it many times already – each time ascribing her injuries, as now, to her cousin. Lived through it: poured it all out, the filth, the bestiality, the brutality, the dress half torn away, the terrible bruising ... They listened breathlessly and, as her voice fell silent in the hushed court, she knew that she had won – had won for herself but had won for Daddy also – if only he would accept it. A father – hearing that story poured out through bruised and bleeding lips, seeing the white young face ugly with bruising, the bitten and broken skin, the torn, dishevelled hair – whatever the father had subsequently done, must be condoned to the fullest limit of the law's discretion. Poor little injured blossom, poor smirched and broken golden Daffodil! Not a man in court but knew – but hoped with all his heart – that he would have done the same. Not a man in court who did not feel sick to the pit of his stomach at the wrongs that had been done to this lovely child. Not one man.

Or only one.

He had to be helped to the witness box; and now the light shone down, not upon yellow halo and pale, uplifted face but on a bowed head whose face and hair seemed almost of a uniform grey. He fumbled his way through the oath. He said: 'I have to tell. I have to say ...'

From the body of the court where now she sat with her mother, she shot up to her feet.

She cried out, sick, faltering, terrified, hardly knowing what

77

she was doing: 'Daddy!' And on a note of pleading, again, 'Daddy!'

Hushing and shushing. Throughout it he stood there looking back into her terrified face: a long, long, searching look. If that boy had all along been innocent...! He looked into her sick white face and knew that she had lied to him. He had killed – murdered – an innocent child.

Her mother saw the first signal: the terrible purple red flush rising up over the ashy grey; and into the silence she, also, cried out. 'John! Your pills!' and besought the stern face a thousand miles away up there on the Bench: 'He's going to have a heart attack. He must take his pills.'

He stood there, reeling, his hand going slowly, automatically to his breast pocket, his eyes still fixed on the young, scared, pleading face across the courtroom. An usher proffered the glass of water, all eyes were riveted on the scene where he stood there in the witness box. Across the turned heads she stared back at him. Daddy would never give her away. Daddy would rather die than do harm to his golden Daffodil.

Over the turned white wigs, the averted faces – begging, beseeching, almost imperceptibly she shook her head.

The hand reaching for the life-saving drug, dropped to his side. Daddy would die for her.

And he died. Like a ruined building, slowly toppling, crumbling with horrible acceleration tumbling at last into a crumpled heap on the floor of the witness box, out of their sight. The heart for so long a traitor to its own harbouring body, looked into the fair face of treachery and broke and bled: and beat no more.

The photographs on the front pages of the evening papers were teriffic! Freesia's hair-do was wonderful, just like a halo. It made her look like an angel, honestly it did.

But by the next morning the whispering had begun. And it grew and it grew and it grew ...

© *Christianna Brand 1976*

Walter was intrigued by Reggie's idea of a literary competition to find the perfect murder – more so when he realized that nobody was better qualified than himself ...

THE LAST OF THE MIDNIGHT GARDENERS

Tony Wilmot

Walter Oates said: 'That's the third midnight gardener this week.' He threw the typescript into his Out tray and yawned. 'Do we have any appointments this afternoon, Edna?'

Miss Tewsland, his secretary, smiled; she wasn't quite sure what he meant, but she had learned that if anything was guaranteed to exasperate a fiction editor it was contributors who sent in stories involving characters Mr Oates called 'midnight gardeners'.

She checked the appointments book. 'None ... Walter,' she cooed.

Walter nodded, pleased. Edna always showed plenty of leg whenever she leaned across her desk; it was one of the things he liked about her.

'Well, then, why don't we take the afternoon off. I know a cosy little bistro in Soho ...'

The phone rang. Miss Tewsland answered it and handed him the receiver, mouthing: 'Your wife.'

Walter said: 'Hello, dear. Yes, it *is* rather a busy time right now. No, dear, I don't know what time I'll be home.' He caught the expression in Miss Tewsland's eyes. 'But I expect I'll be late.'

Walter hung up and winked at Miss Tewsland; he was looking forward to a leisurely lunch. And afterwards ... well, Miss Tewsland's flat was only a taxi-ride from the bistro ... and she was always the soul of discretion.

At his club next day Walter was buttonholed by his barrister friend, Reggie. 'We need your professional opinion, old boy.

About the *modus operandi* of murder.'

Groaning inwardly, Walter joined Reggie's group; he would much rather be thinking about Miss Tewsland.

'We were saying, Walter, how so many wife murderers are mild-mannered, insignificant little chaps. But I don't suppose the fellows who write for your crime magazine bother about that. I bet their murderers have more than a touch of James Bond. Am I right?'

'Sorry to disappoint you, Reggie. The characters are just like their creators. They're all bank clerks, civil servants, insurance men ...

'They live in suburbia and suffer in silence for years. Then one day something snaps. They do in the wife and bury her in the cabbage patch – usually in the middle of the night. Ridiculous, of course. Which is why I call them midnight gardeners. Police would rumble them in ten seconds flat.'

Over a brandy Reggie said: 'Well then, there's an idea for your magazine, Walter. A competition for the perfect murder – told in story form. The rules would be simple: no psychopaths, no crimes of passion, no killing in self defence.

'It must be murder premeditated. With a logical motive. And it must be foolproof, so that even if the police suspected, they'd never be able to prove it.'

Jane, Walter's wife, said: 'You ought to relax more. Bringing all that work home.'

Walter merely grunted. Since the announcement of the competition entries had been pouring in. But none even came close to being feasible *and* foolproof. Too many weed killers, barbiturate overdoses, electric shocks in the bath.

'What about that one, dear ... a man uses a blade of ice as a knife.'

'Old hat,' Walter snapped. Jane had never taken any real interest in crime stories; nurse-and-doctor romances were more her line.

'Why don't you write one yourself?' she said.

Walter stared. 'Me?'

'Why not? You know all the plots inside out. I'm sure you could think up something original.'

He shook his head. "It wouldn't be ethical. I'm one of the judges.'

'That's easily remedied: stand down.'

The more Walter thought about it, the more he liked the idea. He certainly knew every murder method, from rare South American poisons with 'no known antidotes' to air embolism by injection. And it wouldn't actually be cheating. Indeed, he'd be doing his readers a service ... Reggie would stand in for him on the panel of judges; he would ring him in the morning.

That night, typing up the story, he lost all track of time and it was past 3 am when he'd sewn up all the loose ends. He typed a pseudonym on the title page and left it ready for posting.

At the club, members were telling one another incredulously: 'Heard about old Walter? He's snuffed it.'

Even the old codgers dozing in the library roused themselves to hear how his wife had found him dead in bed. She'd been unable to wake him when she took him his early morning cup of tea and, thinking he'd had a stroke, had phoned the doctor.

'Poor old Walter,' Reggie murmured. 'He was the last person I'd have thought would have heart trouble.'

'Well, that's what they think it was,' the club secretary said. 'The actual cause of death is a mystery, I'm told; but the pathologist definitely rules out foul play.

'His wife said he'd been burning the midnight oil a lot lately. Overdid it, I suppose. Must have been quite a shock for her.'

Jane was lolling in a chair on the sundeck, carrying out doctor's orders. He'd told her she needed a complete change, to get over the shock. 'A Mediterranean cruise for you, Mrs Oates. And don't be in a hurry to pick up the threads again.'

Walter hadn't been wealthy, she reflected; but with his life insurance and the sale of the house ... It had hurt, at first, finding out about Miss Tewsland. Now it didn't seem to matter.

Gino, a young Italian steward, had been flirting with her for days. She had almost forgotten what it was like ... having a man look at her that way.

'Why don't you bring a bottle of champagne to my cabin, Gino.'

'Si, Signora.'

'And Gino – bring *two* glasses.'

'Pronto, Signora,' he smiled.

In her shoulder-bag was a typescript. She took it out and tore it up; then she dropped the pieces over the side of the ship.

Too bad about Walter, she thought. He would have won the competition hands down. His method was diabolically clever, yet so simple. It was a pity she couldn't tell anybody. She might need to use it again...

*When one of the regulars at the Gallant Endeavour restaurant
ordered an uncharacteristic meal of tomato soup, beefsteak and
kidney pudding and blackberry tart, Hercule Poirot was immediately intrigued ...*

FOUR-AND-TWENTY BLACKBIRDS

Agatha Christie

Hercule Poirot was dining with his friend, Henry Bonnington
at the Gallant Endeavour in the King's Road, Chelsea.

Mr Bonnington was fond of the Gallant Endeavour. He
liked the leisurely atmosphere, he liked the food which was
'plain' and 'English' and 'not a lot of made up messes.' He
liked to tell people who dined with him there just exactly
where Augustus John had been wont to sit and to draw their
attention to the famous artists' names in the visitors' book. Mr
Bonnington was himself the least artistic of men – but he took
a certain pride in the artistic activities of others.

Molly, the sympathetic waitress, greeted Mr Bonnington as
an old friend. She prided herself on remembering her customers' likes and dislikes in the way of food.

'Good evening, sir,' she said, as the two men took their seats
at a corner table. 'You're in luck today – turkey stuffed with
chestnuts – that's your favourite, isn't it? And ever such a nice
Stilton we've got! Will you have soup first or fish?'

Mr Bonnington deliberated the point. He said to Poirot
warningly as the latter studied the menu:

'None of your French kickshaws now. Good well-cooked
English food.'

'My friend,' Hercule Poirot waved his hand, 'I ask no better! I put myself in your hands unreservedly.'

'Ah – hruup – er – hm,' replied Mr Bonnington and gave
careful attention to the matter.

These weighty matters, and the question of wine, settled,
Mr Bonnington leaned back with a sigh and unfolded his nap-
kin as Molly sped away.

'Good girl, that!' he said approvingly. 'Was quite a beauty once – artists used to paint her. She knows about food, too – and that's a great deal more important. Women are very unsound on food as a rule. There's many a woman if she goes out with a fellow she fancies – won't even notice what she eats. She'll just order the first thing she sees.'

Hercule Poirot shook his head.

'*C'est terrible.*'

'Men aren't like that, thank God!' said Mr Bonnington complacently.

'Never?' There was a twinkle in Hercule Poirot's eye.

'Well, perhaps when they're very young,' conceded Mr Bonnington. 'Young puppies! Young fellows nowadays are all the same – no guts – no stamina. I've no use for the young – and they,' he added with strict impartiality, 'have no use for me. Perhaps they're right! But to hear some of these young fellows talk you'd think no man had a right to be *alive* after sixty! From the way they go on, you'd wonder more of them didn't help their elderly relations out of the world.'

'It is possible,' said Hercule Poirot, 'that they do.'

'Nice mind you've got, Poirot, I must say. All this police work saps your ideals.'

Hercule Poirot smiled.

'*Tout de même,*' he said. 'It would be interesting to make a table of accidental deaths over the age of sixty. I assure you it would raise some curious speculations in your mind.'

'The trouble with you is that you've started going to look for crime – instead of waiting for crime to come to you.'

'I apologize,' said Poirot. 'I talk what you call "the shop". Tell me, my friend, of your own affairs. How does the world go with you?'

'Mess!' said Mr Bonnington. 'That's what's the matter with the world nowadays. Too much mess. And too much fine language. The fine language helps to conceal the mess. Like a highly-flavoured sauce concealing the fact that the fish underneath it is none of the best! Give me an honest fillet of sole and no messy sauce over it.'

It was given him at that moment by Molly and he grunted approval.

'You know just what I like, my girl,' he said.

'Well, you come here pretty regular, don't you, sir? I ought to know what you like.'

Hercule Poirot said:

'Do people then always like the same things? Do they not like a change sometimes?'

'Not gentlemen, sir. Ladies like variety – gentlemen always like the same thing.'

'What did I tell you?' grunted Bonnington. 'Women are fundamentally unsound where food is concerned!'

He looked round the restaurant.

'The world's a funny place. See that odd-looking old fellow with a beard in the corner? Molly'll tell you he's always here Tuesdays and Thursday nights. He has come here for close on ten years now – he's a kind of landmark in the place. Yet nobody here knows his name or where he lives or what his business is. It's odd when you come to think of it.'

When the waitress brought the portions of turkey he said:

'I see you've still got Old Father Time over there?'

'That's right, sir. Tuesdays and Thursdays, his days are. Not but what he came in here on a *Monday* last week! It quite upset me! I felt I'd got my date wrong and that it must be Tuesday without my knowing it! But he came in the next night as well – so the Monday was just a kind of extra, so to speak.'

'An interesting deviation from habit,' murmured Poirot. 'I wonder what the reason was?'

'Well, sir, if you ask me, I think he'd had some kind of upset or worry.'

'Why did you think that? His manner?'

'No, sir – not his manner exactly. He was very quiet as he always is. Never says much except good evening when he comes and goes. No, it was his *order*.'

'His order?'

'I dare say you gentlemen will laugh at me,' Molly flushed up, 'but when a gentleman has been here for ten years, you get to know his likes and dislikes. He never could bear suet pudding or blackberries and I've never known him take thick soup – but on that Monday night he ordered thick tomato soup, beefsteak and kidney pudding and blackberry tart! Seemed as though he just didn't notice *what* he ordered!'

85

'Do you know,' said Hercule Poirot, 'I find that extra-ordinarily interesting.'

Molly looked gratified and departed.

'Well, Poirot,' said Henry Bonnington with a chuckle. 'Let's have a few deductions from you. All in your best manner.'

'I would prefer to hear yours first.'

'Want me to be Watson, eh? Well, old fellow went to a doctor and the doctor changed his diet.'

'To thick tomato soup, steak and kidney pudding, and blackberry tart? I cannot imagine any doctor doing that.'

'Don't believe it, old boy. Doctors will put you on to anything.'

'That is the only solution that occurs to you?'

Henry Bonnington said:

'Well, seriously, I suppose there's only one explanation possible. Our unknown friend was in the grip of some powerful mental emotion. He was so perturbed by it that he literally did not notice what he was ordering or eating.'

He paused a minute and then said:

'You'll be telling me next that you know just *what* was on his mind. You'll say perhaps that he was making up his mind to commit a murder.'

He laughed at his own suggestion.

Hercule Poirot did not laugh.

He has admitted that at that moment he was seriously worried. He claims that he ought then to have had some inkling of what was likely to occur.

His friends assure him that such an idea is quite fantastic.

It was some three weeks later that Hercule Poirot and Bonnington met again – this time their meeting was in the Tube.

They nodded to each other, swaying about, hanging on to adjacent straps. Then at Piccadilly Circus there was a general exodus and they found seats right at the forward end of the car – a peaceful spot since nobody passed in or out that way.

'That's better,' said Mr Bonnington. 'Selfish lot, the human race, they won't pass up the car however much you ask 'em to!'

Hercule Poirot shrugged his shoulders.

86

'What will you?' he said. 'Life is too uncertain.'

'That's it. Here today, gone tomorrow,' said Mr Bonnington with a kind of gloomy relish. 'And talking of that, d'you remember that old boy we noticed at the Gallant Endeavour? I shouldn't wonder if *he'd* hopped it to a better world. He's not been there for a whole week. Molly's quite upset about it.'

Hercule Poirot sat up. His green eyes flashed.

'Indeed?' he said. 'Indeed?'

Bonnington said:

'D'you remember I suggested he'd been to a doctor and been put on a diet? Diet's nonsense of course – but I shouldn't wonder if he had consulted a doctor about his health and what the doctor said gave him a bit of a jolt. That would account for him ordering things off the menu without noticing what he was doing. Quite likely the jolt he got hurried him out of the world sooner than he would have gone otherwise. Doctors ought to be careful what they tell a chap.'

'They usually are,' said Hercule Poirot.

'This is my station,' said Mr Bonnington. 'Bye, bye. Don't suppose we shall ever know now how the old boy was – not even his name. Funny world!'

He hurried out of the carriage.

Hercule Poirot, sitting frowning, looked as though he did not think it was such a funny world.

He went home and gave certain instructions to his faithful valet, George.

Hercule Poirot ran his finger down a list of names. It was a record of deaths within a certain area.

Poirot's finger stopped.

'Henry Gascoigne. Sixty-nine. I might try him first.'

Later in the day, Hercule Poirot was sitting in Dr Mac-Andrew's surgery just off the King's Road. MacAndrew was a tall red-haired Scotsman with an intelligent face.

'Gascoigne?' he said. 'Yes, that's right. Eccentric old bird. Lived alone in one of those derelict old houses that are being cleared away in order to build a block of modern flats. I hadn't attended him before, but I'd seen him about and I knew who he was. It was the dairy people got the wind up first. The milk bottles began to pile up outside. In the end the people next door sent word to the police and they broke the door in and found him. He'd pitched down the stairs and broken his neck. Had on an old dressing-gown with a ragged cord – might easily have tripped himself up with it.'

'I see,' said Hercule Poirot. 'It was quite simple – an accident.'

'That's right.'

'Had he any relations?'

'There's a nephew. Used to come along and see his uncle about once a month. Lorrimer, his name is, George Lorrimer. He's a medico himself. Lives at Wimbledon.'

'Was he upset at the old man's death?'

'I don't know that I'd say he was upset. I mean, he had an affection for the old man, but he didn't really know him very well.'

'How long had Mr Gascoigne been dead when you saw him?'

'Ah!' said Dr MacAndrew. 'This is where we get official. Not less than forty-eight hours and not more than seventy-two hours. He was found on the morning of the sixth. Actually, we got closer than that. He'd got a letter in the pocket of his dressing-gown – written on the third – posted in Wimbledon that afternoon – would have been delivered somewhere around nine-twenty pm. That puts the time of death at after nine-twenty on the evening of the third. That agrees with the contents of the stomach and the processes of digestion. He had had a meal about two hours before death. I examined him on the morning of the sixth and his condition was quite consistent with death having occurred about sixty hours previously – round about ten pm on the third.'

'It all seems very consistent. Tell me, when was he last seen alive?'

'He was seen in the King's Road about seven o'clock that same evening, Thursday the third, and he dined at the Gallant Endeavour restaurant at seven-thirty. It seems he always dined there on Thursdays. He was by way of being an artist, you know. An extremely bad one.'

'He had no other relations? Only this nephew?'

'There was a twin brother. The whole story is rather curious. They hadn't seen each other for years. It seems the other brother, Anthony Gascoigne, married a very rich woman and gave up art – and the brothers quarrelled over it. Hadn't seen each other since, I believe. But oddly enough, *they died on the same day*. The elder twin passed away at three o'clock on the afternoon of the third. Once before I've known a case of twins dying on the same day – in different parts of the world! Probably just a coincidence – but there it is.'

'Is the other brother's wife alive?'

'No, she died some years ago.'

'Where did Anthony Gascoigne live?'

'He had a house on Kingston Hill. He was, I believe, from what Dr Lorrimer tells me, very much of a recluse.'

Hercule Poirot nodded thoughtfully.

The Scotsman looked at him keenly.

'What exactly have you got in your mind, M. Poirot?' he asked bluntly. 'I've answered your questions – as was my duty seeing the credentials you brought. But I'm in the dark as to what it's all about.'

Poirot said slowly:

'A simple case of accidental death, that's what you said. What I have in mind is equally simple – a simple push.'

Dr MacAndrew looked startled.

'In other words, murder! Have you any grounds for that belief?'

'No,' said Poirot. 'It is a mere supposition.'

'There must be something –' persisted the other.

Poirot did not speak. MacAndrew said:

'If it's the nephew, Lorrimer, you suspect, I don't mind telling you here and now that you are barking up the wrong tree. Lorrimer was playing bridge in Wimbledon from eight-thirty till midnight. That came out at the inquest.'

Poirot murmured:

'And presumably it was verified. The police are careful.'

The doctor said:

'Perhaps you know something against him?'

'I didn't know that there was such a person until you mentioned him.'

'Then you suspect somebody else?'

'No, no. It is not that at all. It's a case of the routine habits

of the human animal. That is very important. And the dead
M. Gascoigne does not fit in. It is all wrong, you see.'

'I really don't understand.'

Hercule Poirot murmured :

'The trouble is, there is too much sauce over the bad fish.'

'My dear sir?'

Hercule Poirot smiled.

'You will be having me locked up as a lunatic soon, *Monsieur le Docteur*. But I am not really a mental case – just a
man who has a liking for order and method and who is worried
when he comes across a fact *that does not fit in*. I must ask you
to forgive me for having given you so much trouble.'

He rose and the doctor rose also.

'You know,' said MacAndrew, 'honestly I can't see anything
the least bit suspicious about the death of Henry Gascoigne. I
say he fell – you say somebody pushed him. It's all – well – in
the air.'

Hercule Poirot sighed.

'Yes,' he said. 'It is workmanlike. Somebody has made the
good job of it!'

'You still think –?'

The little man spread out his hands.

'I'm an obstinate man – a man with a little idea – and
nothing to support it! By the way, did Henry Gascoigne have
false teeth?'

'No, his own teeth were in excellent preservation. Very
creditable indeed at his age.'

'He looked after them well – they were white and well
brushed?'

'Yes, I noticed them particularly. Teeth tend to grow a little
yellow as one grows older, but they were in good condition.'

'Not discoloured in any way?'

'No. I don't think he was a smoker if that is what you
mean?'

'I did not mean that precisely – it was just a long shot –
which probably will not come off! Good-bye, Dr MacAndrew,
and thank you for your kindness.'

He shook the doctor's hand and departed.

'And now,' he said, 'for the long shot.'

*

At the Gallant Endeavour, he sat down at the same table which he had shared with Bonnington. The girl who served him was not Molly. Molly, the girl told him, was away on a holiday.

It was only just seven and Hercule Poirot found no difficulty in entering into conversation with the girl on the subject of old Mr Gascoigne.

'Yes,' she said. "He'd been here for years and years. But none of us girls ever knew his name. We saw about the inquest in the paper, and there was a picture of him. "There," I said to Molly. "If that isn't our 'Old Father Time'" as we used to call him.'

'He dined here on the evening of his death, did he not?'

'That's right. Thursday, the third. He was always here on a Thursday. Tuesdays and Thursdays – punctual as a clock.'

'You don't remember, I suppose, what he had for dinner?'

'Now let me see, it was mulligatawny soup, that's right, and beefsteak pudding or was it the mutton – no pudding, that's right, and blackberry and apple pie and cheese. And then to think of him going home and falling down those stairs that very same evening. A frayed dressing-gown cord they said it was as caused it. Of course, his clothes were always something awful – old-fashioned and put on anyhow, and all tattered, and yet he *had* a kind of air, all the same, as though he was *somebody*! Oh, we get all sorts of interesting customers here.'

She moved off.

Hercule Poirot ate his filleted sole. His eyes showed a green light.

'It is odd,' he said to himself, 'how the cleverest people slip over details. Bonnington will be interested.'

But the time had not yet come for leisurely discussion with Bonnington.

Armed with introductions from a certain influential quarter, Hercule Poirot found no difficulty at all in dealing with the coroner for the district.

'A curious figure, the deceased man Gascoigne,' he observed. 'A lonely, eccentric old fellow. But his decease seems to arouse an unusual amount of attention?'

He looked with some curiosity at his visitor as he spoke.

Hercule Poirot chose his words carefully.

'There are circumstances connected with it, Monsieur, which make investigation desirable.'

'Well, how can I help you?'

'It is, I believe, within your province to order documents produced in your court to be destroyed, or to be impounded – as you think fit. A certain letter was found in the pocket of Henry Gascoigne's dressing-gown, was it not?'

'That is so.'

'A letter from his nephew, Dr George Lorrimer?'

'Quite correct. The letter was produced at the inquest as helping to fix the time of death.'

'Which was corroborated by the medical evidence?'

'Exactly.'

'Is that letter still available?'

Hercule Poirot waited rather anxiously for the reply.

When he heard that the letter was still available for examination he drew a sigh of relief.

When it was finally produced he studied it with some care. It was written in a slightly cramped handwriting with a stylographic pen.

It ran as follows:

Dear Uncle Henry,

I am sorry to tell you that I have had no success as regards Uncle Anthony. He showed no enthusiasm for a visit from you and would give me no reply to your request that he would let bygones be bygones. He is, of course, extremely ill, and his mind is inclined to wander. I should fancy that the end is very near. He seemed hardly to remember who you were.

I am sorry to have failed you, but I can assure you that I did my best.

Your affectionate nephew,
George Lorrimer

The letter itself was dated 3rd November. Poirot glanced at the envelope's postmark – 4.30 pm 3 Nov.

He murmured:
'It is beautifully in order, is it not?'

Kingston Hill was his next objective. After a little trouble, with the exercise of good-humoured pertinacity, he obtained an interview with Amelia Hill, cook-housekeeper to the late Anthony Gascoigne.

Mrs Hill was inclined to be stiff and suspicious at first, but the charming geniality of this strange-looking foreigner would have had its effect on a stone. Mrs Amelia Hill began to unbend.

She found herself, as had so many other women before her, pouring out her troubles to a really sympathetic listener.

For fourteen years she had had charge of Mr Gascoigne's household – *not* an easy job! No, indeed! Many a woman would have quailed under the burdens *she* had had to bear! Eccentric the poor gentleman was and no denying it. Remarkably close with his money – a kind of mania with him it was – and he as rich a gentleman as might be! But Mrs Hill had served him faithfully, and put up with his ways, and naturally she'd expected at any rate a *remembrance*. But no – nothing at all! Just an old will that left all his money to his wife and if she predeceased him then everything to his brother, Henry. A will made years ago. It didn't seem fair!

Gradually Hercule Poirot detached her from her main theme of unsatisfied cupidity. It was indeed a heartless injustice! Mrs Hill could not be blamed for feeling hurt and surprised. It was well known that Mr Gascoigne was tight-fisted about money. It had been said that the dead man had refused his only brother assistance. Mrs Hill probably knew all about that.

'Was it that that Dr Lorrimer came to see him about?' asked Mrs Hill. 'I knew it was something about his brother, but I thought it was just that his brother wanted to be reconciled. They'd quarrelled years ago.'

'I understand,' said Poirot, 'that Mr Gascoigne refused absolutely?'

'That's right enough,' said Mrs Hill with a nod. ' "*Henry?*" he says, rather weak like. "*What's this about Henry? Haven't*

*seen him for years and don't want to. Quarrelsome fellow,
Henry."* Just that.'

The conversation then reverted to Mrs Hill's own special
grievances, and the unfeeling attitude of the late Mr Gascoigne's solicitor.

With some difficulty Hercule Poirot took his leave without
breaking off the conversation too abruptly.

And so, just after the dinner hour, he came to Elmcrest,
Dorset Road, Wimbledon, the residence of Dr George Lorrimer.

The doctor was in. Hercule Poirot was shown into the
surgery and there presently Dr George Lorrimer came to him,
obviously just risen from the dinner table.

'I'm not a patient, Doctor,' said Hercule Poirot. 'And my
coming here is, perhaps, somewhat of an impertinence – but
I'm an old man and I believe in plain and direct dealing. I do
not care for lawyers and their long-winded roundabout
methods.'

He had certainly aroused Lorrimer's interest. The doctor
was a clean-shaven man of middle height. His hair was brown
but his eyelashes were almost white which gave his eyes a pale,
boiled appearance. His manner was brisk and not without
humour.

'Lawyers?' he said, raising his eyebrows. 'Hate the fellows!
You rouse my curiosity, my dear sir. Pray sit down.'

Poirot did so and then produced one of his professional
cards which he handed to the doctor.

George Lorrimer's white eyelashes blinked.

Poirot leaned forward confidentially. 'A good many of my
clients are women,' he said.

'Naturally,' said Dr George Lorrimer, with a slight twinkle.

'As you say, naturally,' agreed Poirot. 'Women distrust the
official police. They prefer private investigations. They do not
want to have their troubles made public. An elderly woman
came to consult me a few days ago. She was unhappy about a
husband she'd quarrelled with many years before. This husband of hers was your uncle, the late Mr Gascoigne.' George
Lorrimer's face went purple.

'My uncle? Nonsense! His wife died many years ago.'

'Not your uncle, *Mr Anthony* Gascoigne. Your uncle, Mr

94

Henry Gascoigne.'

'Uncle Henry? But *he* wasn't married?'

'Oh yes, he was,' said Hercule Poirot, lying unblushingly. 'Not a doubt of it. The lady even brought along her marriage certificate.'

'It's a lie!' cried George Lorrimer. His face was now as purple as a plum. 'I don't believe it. You're an impudent liar.'

'It is too bad, is it not?' said Poirot. 'You have committed murder for nothing.'

'Murder?' Lorrimer's voice quavered. His pale eyes bulged with terror.

'By the way,' said Poirot, 'I see you have been eating blackberry tart again. An unwise habit. Blackberries are said to be full of vitamins, but they may be deadly in other ways. On this occasion I rather fancy they have helped to put a rope round a man's neck – your neck, Dr Lorrimer.'

'You see, *mon ami*, where you went wrong was over your fundamental assumption.' Hercule Poirot, beaming placidly across the table at his friend, waved an expository hand. 'A man under severe mental stress doesn't choose that time to do something that he's never done before. His reflexes just follow the track of least resistance. A man who is upset about something *might* conceivably come down to dinner dressed in his pyjamas – but they will be his *own* pyjamas – not somebody else's.

'A man who dislikes thick soup, suet pudding, and blackberries suddenly orders all three one evening. *You* say, because he is thinking of something else. But *I* say that a man who has got something on his mind will order automatically the dish he has ordered most often before.

'*Eh bien*, then, what other explanation could there be? I simply could not think of a reasonable explanation. And I was worried! The incident was all wrong. It did not fit! I have an orderly mind and I like things to fit. Mr Gascoigne's dinner order worried me.

'Then you told me that the man had disappeared. He had missed a Tuesday and a Thursday the first time for years. I liked that even less. A queer hypothesis sprang up in my mind.

If I were right about it *the man was dead*. I made inquiries. The man *was* dead. And he was very neatly and tidily dead. In other words the bad fish was covered up with the sauce!

'He had been seen in the King's Road at seven o'clock. He had had dinner here at seven-thirty – two hours before he died. It all fitted in – the evidence of the stomach contents, the evidence of the letter. Much too much sauce! You couldn't see the fish at all!

'Devoted nephew wrote the letter, devoted nephew had beautiful alibi for time of death. Death very simple – a fall down the stairs. Simple accident? Simple murder? Everyone says the former.

'Devoted nephew only surviving relative. Devoted nephew will inherit – but is there anything *to* inherit? Uncle notoriously poor.

'But there is a brother. And brother in his time had married a rich wife. And brother lives in a big rich house on Kingston Hill, so it would seem that rich wife must have left him all her money. You see the sequence – rich wife leaves money to Anthony, Anthony leaves money to Henry, Henry's money goes to George – a complete chain.'

'All very pretty in theory,' said Bonnington. 'But what did you do?'

'Once you *know* – you can usually get hold of what you want. Henry had died two hours after a *meal* – that is all the inquest really bothered about. But supposing that meal was not dinner, but *lunch*. Put yourself in George's place. George wants money – badly. Anthony Gascoigne is dying – but his death is no good to George. His money goes to Henry, and Henry Gascoigne may live for years. So Henry must die too – and the sooner the better – but his death must take place *after* Anthony's, and at the same time George must have an alibi. Henry's habit of dining regularly at the restaurant on two evenings of the week suggest an alibi to George. Being a cautious fellow, he tries his plan out first. *He impersonates his uncle on Monday evening at the restaurant in question.* It goes without a hitch. Everyone there accepts him as his uncle. He is satisfied. He has only to wait till Uncle Anthony shows definite signs of pegging out. The time comes. He writes a letter to his uncle on the afternoon of the second November but dates it the third. He comes up to town on the afternoon of the third, calls on his uncle, and carries his scheme into action. A sharp shove and down the stairs goes Uncle Henry. George hunts about for the letter he has written, and shoves it in the pocket of his uncle's dressing-gown. At seven-thirty he is at the Gallant Endeavour, beard, bushy eyebrows all complete. Undoubtedly Mr Henry Gascoigne is alive at seven-thirty. Then a rapid metamorphosis in a lavatory and back full speed in his car to Wimbledon and an evening of bridge. The perfect alibi.'

Mr Bonnington looked at him.

'But the postmark on the letter?'

'Oh, that was very simple. The postmark was smudgy. Why? It had been altered with lamp black from second November to third November. You would not notice it *unless you were looking for it*. And finally there were the blackbirds.'

'Blackbirds?'

'Four-and-twenty blackbirds baked in a pie! Or blackberries if you prefer to be literal! George, you comprehend, was after all not quite a good enough actor. Do you remember the fellow who blacked himself all over to play Othello? That is the kind of actor you have got to be in crime. George *looked* like his uncle and *walked* like his uncle and *spoke* like his uncle and had his uncle's beard and eyebrows, but he forgot to *eat* like his uncle. He ordered the dishes that he himself liked. Blackberries discolour the teeth – the corpse's teeth were not discoloured, and yet Henry Gascoigne ate blackberries at the Gallant Endeavour that night. But there were no blackberries in the stomach. I asked this morning. And George had been fool enough to keep the beard and the rest of the make-up. Oh! plenty of evidence once you look for it. I called on George and rattled him. That finished it! He had been eating blackberries again, by the way. A greedy fellow – cared a lot about his food. *Eh bien*, greed will hang him all right unless I am very much mistaken.'

A waitress brought them two portions of blackberry and apple tart.

'Take it away,' said Mr Bonnington. 'One can't be too careful. Bring me a small helping of sago pudding.'

Martin Retsov knew everything there was to know about horses — but the one thing he lacked was a partner in crime. Then he chanced upon the hitch-hiker ...

NIGHTMARE

Dick Francis

For three years after his father died Martin Retsov abandoned his chosen profession. To be successful he needed a partner, and partners as skilled as his father were hard to find. Martin Retsov took stock of his bank book, listed his investments and decided that with a little useful paid employment to fill the days he could cruise along comfortably in second gear, waiting for life to throw up a suitable replacement.

A day's travel put him a welcome distance from the scene of his unhappier memories, although they themselves journeyed along with him, as inescapable as habit.

Thoroughbred Foodstuffs gave him a month's trial as a salesman and, when the orders swelled everywhere in his wake, a permanent post. Martin Retsov relaxed behind the wheel of the company's Chrysler and drifted easily around his new area, visiting stud farms and racing stables and persuading their managers that even if Thoroughbred Foodstuffs were no better than anyone else's, at least they were no worse.

The customers of Thoroughbred Foodstuffs saw a big man in his late thirties with a rugged, slightly forbidding face and a way of narrowing his eyes to dark-lashed slits. The frank, open and sincere stock-in-trade expression of a salesman was nowhere to be seen, nor was there any obvious honey in his voice. The one factor which brought out the handshakes, the fountain pens and the cheque books was his formidable knowledge of horses. He could sum up a horse in a glance and make helpfully constructive suggestions in a throwaway fashion, never taking credit although it was due.

'I expect you've tried remedial shoeing,' he would say casually, or 'Don't you find vitamin B-12 injections help build bone?'

Second time around, he was greeted as a trusted friend. He prospered.

All the same, he was in trouble. There was no peace in his sleep. When he slept, he woke always from a nightmare, heart thumping, skin prickling with cold instant sweat. Always a dream variation on the same theme – the violent, untimely death of his father. Sometimes he saw the face, dead but still talking, with blood gushing out of the mouth. Sometimes he saw the wheel, the great fat black sharp-treaded tyre biting into the soft bulging belly. Sometimes he felt he was inside his father's body, slipping and falling behind the loaded motor horsebox and having the life crushed out of him in one great unimaginable explosion of agony. Sometimes, but not so often, he saw the face of the other man who had been there, the callous man in the dark clothes, looking coldly down at his dying father and giving him no comfort, saying not a word.

Every morning Martin Retsov stood wearily under the shower, rinsing the stickiness from his body and wishing he could as easily sponge his subconscious mind. Every day, sliding into the Chrysler, he shed his night self and looked to the future. He saw foals born, watched them grow, traced their fortunes at auction and beyond. He could have told the trainers, better than they knew themselves, the breeding, history, career and fate of every horse he reached with Thorough-bred food.

After nearly three years he had made many acquaintances: he was not a man to make friends. He knew every horse over a wide stretch of country and hundreds which had been sold out of it. He was the most efficient salesman in his company. And even his nightmares were at last becoming rarer.

One evening in early spring he picked up Johnnie Duke. A hitch-hiker, a tall thin fair-haired youth looking not much above twenty, wearing faded jeans and an old leather jacket and carrying a few extra clothes in a canvas hold-all. Martin Retsov, in an expansive mood, took him to be a college kid on vacation and agreed to drop him forty miles down the road in the next town.

'Haven't I seen you before?' he asked, half puzzled, as the young man settled into the front seat beside him.

'Shouldn't think so.'

'Well . . .' He thought it over. "I've seen you. Day or two ago. Where would that be?'

The young man took his time over answering. Then he said, 'I hitch up and down this road pretty regular. Maybe you saw me thumbing.'

Martin Retsov nodded several times. "Yes. That's it.' He relaxed in his seat, glad to have resolved the small mystery. He liked to be sure of things. 'That's where I've seen you. On the road. More than once.'

The young man nodded briefly and said he was glad Martin had stopped for him as he had a date with his girl.

'I don't often stop for hitchers,' Martin Retsov said, and thought, with amusement, that three easy years must have softened him.

They drove amicably together for five miles and passed alongside the white railed paddocks of a prosperous stud farm. Martin Retsov cast a rapid assessing eye over the small groups of animals grazing the new spring grass in the evening sunshine but kept his thoughts unspoken.

It was Johnnie Duke who said: 'It's odd you never get a piebald thoroughbred.'

'You know about horses?' Martin Retsov asked, surprised.

'Sure. I was raised with them.'

Martin Retsov asked him where, but the young man evasively said he'd had some trouble back home and left in a hurry, and he didn't exactly want to talk about it. Martin Retsov smiled. He dropped Johnnie Duke in the next town and drove on towards his destination, and it was only when he stopped to fill up his tanks that the remains of the smile vanished as smartly as investors in a depression.

Johnnie Duke had stolen his billfold. Martin Retsov kept it in the inside pocket of his jacket, and his jacket, owing to the efficiency of the heater, had been lying along the back seat of the car. He remembered Johnnie Duke putting his hold-all on the floor behind the front seats, and he remembered him leaning over to pick it up.

Martin Retsov's rugged face hardened to something his

customers had never seen, and the eyes slitted as narrow and glittery as ice chips. The sum of money he had lost was small compared with the affront to his self-respect.

For several days he drove round his area searching for Johnnie Duke, remembering details about him from their drive together ... the hesitation when Martin Retsov said he'd seen him before ... the refusal to say where he'd come from ... the slickness with which he'd spotted and extracted the billfold.

Martin Retsov searched for him with a hard face but without success and finally, after two or three weeks, accepted that the young man had gone away to another district where irate victims in Chryslers were not looking out for him sharp-eyed.

Regularly, once a month, Martin Retsov called at the furthest stud farm in his area, and it was as he left there, early one evening, that he again saw Johnnie Duke. Standing by the roadside, lifting his thumb, hesitating perhaps when he saw the Chrysler.

Martin Retsov drove up fast beside him, braked to a wheel-locked standstill, opened his door and stood up smoothly outside it. For a big man he moved like oiled machinery, precise and efficient: and he held a gun.

'Get in the car,' he said.

Johnnie Duke looked at the barrel pointing straight at his stomach and turned a little pale. He swallowed, his larynx making a sharp convulsive movement, and slowly did as he was told.

'I'll pay back the money,' he said anxiously, as Martin Retsov slid on to the seat beside him. The gun was held loosely now, pointing at the floor, but both were aware that this could change.

'I should hand you to the police,' Martin Retsov said.

The young man dumbly shook his head.

'Or you could do a little job for me instead.'

The young man looked at Martin Retsov's slitted eyes and visibly shivered. 'Is this blackmail?' he said.

'I'll pay you, if you're any good.'

'Doing what?'

'Stealing horses,' Martin Retsov said.

He made his plans as meticulously as in the old days with his father, untraceably buying a two-horse trailer and a car to pull it, and hiding them away in a city lock-up garage. He decided against the large type of motor horsebox he had used with his father; mostly because of the nightmares about those wheels. Besides, he was not sure if his new apprentice would be suitable for long-term planning. They would do one trial run; a test, Martin Retsov thought, before he offered a steady partnership for the future.

Johnnie Duke greeted Martin Retsov's announcement of his chosen profession with a huge, welcoming and relieved grin.

'Sure,' he said. 'I can steal horses. Which ones?'

'It's not so easy round here,' Martin Retsov said. 'Training stables and stud farms have good security arrangements.' But he knew them all: he had been assiduously studying them for three years.

He gave Johnnie Duke a list of things to buy and some money for himself. Two days later they inspected the resulting mole-grip wrenches and steel-cutting saw.

Martin Retsov said: 'We will go ahead tomorrow night.'

'So soon?'

Martin Retsov smiled. 'We are taking two brood mares. One is near to foaling. We want her safely away before that happens.'

Johnnie Duke looked at him in long surprise. 'Why don't we take good fast racers?' he said.

'They're too easily identified. Tattoo marks and registrations see to that. But foals, now. New-born foals. Who's to say which is which? So we take a top-class mare, now in foal by the best sires, and we drive her a long way away, and sell her at the end of the journey to some owner or trainer who is glad to get a fabulously bred foal for a fraction of what it would cost at auction.

'The star foal is swopped soon after birth with any other one handy, and is registered and tattooed in its new identity. Its new owner knows what he's really got, so after racing it he keeps it for stud. Some of my clients in the past have made millions out of these foals. I always collect a small percentage.'

Johnnie Duke listened with his mouth open.

'This is not casual thieving,' Martin Retsov said with a certain pride. 'This is like taking the Mona Lisa.'

'But what happens to the brood mare afterwards? And to the other foal?'

'Some of my clients have consciences. For these, for a consideration, I collect the mare and foal and dump them in any convenient field. If the owner of the field is honest, she gets identified and sent home.'

Johnnie Duke did not ask what happened when the client had no conscience. He swallowed.

'Do you already have a buyer for the two we're taking tomorrow?' he asked.

'Of course. You don't steal a da Vinci on spec.'

Martin Retsov laughed at the idea, showing a strong row of teeth. 'When we've got the mares I'll tell you where to go. You will go alone. And you will bring back the money.'

Johnnie Duke was again surprised. 'Can you trust me?' he asked.

'I want to find out.'

The following day, at dusk, they collected the newly bought car and hitched on the trailer. Martin Retsov had difficulty manoeuvring the two linked vehicles in the small courtyard which enclosed the lock-up garages and Johnnie Duke, trying to be helpful, went to the rear of the trailer to report how much space there was for reversing.

'Get away from there,' Martin Retsov said sharply. 'Get away at once.' He stood up out of the car and Johnnie Duke saw that he was shaking.

'I was only . . .' he began.

'You are never to go behind the trailer. Understand? Never.'

'Well, all right. If you say so.'

Martin Retsov took several deep breaths and wiped the palms of his hands down his trousers. He was horrified at the strength of his own reaction. Three years, he thought, had hardly blunted the terror at all. He wondered whether, if his nerves were so jumpy, it might not be better to abandon the whole project. He wondered whether the fact that it had taken him three years to get back to his business meant that deep down he was afraid to.

He licked his lips. His heart-beat settled. This time there would be no ambush when he took the horses. The last time his potential client had betrayed him to the police, but this time it was perfectly safe. This client had bought three top-grade foals in the past and had been delighted to hear he could now have two more.

Martin Retsov eased himself back into the car and Johnnie Duke climbed in beside him.

'What's the matter?' he asked.

'I saw an accident once. Man fell behind a horsebox.'

'Oh.'

Martin Retsov shut his mouth on the untellable details, but they rolled on inexorably through his mind. The ambush. Police spotlights suddenly shining out before his father was safe up beside him in the horsebox's cab. He'd had to reverse a yard or two to get a clear run at the only space left between the police cars and the fence ... he'd thrown the lever, stamped on the accelerator, shot backwards ... he would never forget his father's scream ...

Just one scream, cut short. He'd jumped from the cab and seen the tyre cutting into the stomach. Seen the blood pouring out of the dying mouth ... and the other man, the policeman, standing there looking down, doing nothing to help.

'Help him,' he had said, frantically.

'Help him yourself.'

He had leapt back to the cab, climbed panic-stricken into the driving seat, knowing even as he pushed at the gear lever that his father was dead. He had rolled the horsebox forward off the crushed body ... and he kept on going. He took the police by surprise. He drove the horsebox at 65 mph for two miles and long before they caught up he had abandoned it and taken to the woods.

The police had not known his name, which he prudently never divulged to his clients. All they had had was one quick sight of him in extremis, which was not enough, and evasion and escape had, in the end, proved the smallest of his personal problems. He had never forgotten the face of the policeman who had looked down at his father. A senior policeman, wearing authority and insignia. He saw him too often in his uneasy dreams.

Martin Retsov shook off the regretted past and applied his concentration to the theft in hand. He had expected to feel the old anticipation, the old excitement, the pleasing raising of the pulse. He felt none of these things. He felt old.

'Come on,' said Johnnie Duke, 'or it will be light again before I deliver the goods.'

Martin Retsov nodded unwillingly and committed them both to the enterprise. Half an hour later, when they pulled up in a dark side road, he had succeeded in thrusting his soul's shadows back into their cupboard and was approaching the next half hour with cool practicality.

They stepped quietly from the car and let down the ramp of the trailer. The night closed around them; small sounds, light sighing wind, stars showing in sparkling bunches between grey drifting clouds. Traffic on the high road half a mile away swept past now and then, more a matter of flashing lights than of noise. Martin Retsov waited for his eyes to grow used to the dark and then put his hand lightly on the young man's arm.

'This way,' he said. His voice was a gentle whisper and, when he moved, his feet were soundless on the grass verge.

Johnnie Duke followed him, marvelling at the big man's silence and easy speed.

'Where are we?' he whispered. 'Whose horses are we taking?'

'Never you mind.'

They came to a gate, padlocked. The wrenches and the saw made it easy. They slid through into the field. Martin Retsov whistled gently in the dark, a seductive gypsy trill in the teeth. He pulled out a handful of Thoroughbred horse nuts and called persuasively into the blackness ahead. 'Come on then, girl. Come on.'

There was a soft, warm whinny and movement somewhere out beyond sight. Then they came, slowly, inquiringly, moving towards the human voices. They ate the nuts held out to them and made no fuss when the two men took hold of their head-collars.

'You go ahead,' Martin Retsov said softly to Johnnie Duke. 'I'll be right behind you.'

105

They went sweetly, the two big mares, out of the gate and down the road to the transport. Easy as ever, thought Martin Retsov, once you knew what to take.

Johnnie Duke led his mare into the trailer and fastened her there.

And that was where the nightmare began again. That was when the lights shone out, blinding Martin Retsov. That was when the man stepped out to confront him. The same man. The face from the dreams. Same callous face, dark clothes, high-ranking insignia.

'Martin Retsov,' he was saying, 'I arrest you . . .'

Martin Retsov was not listening. He was thinking wildly that it simply couldn't be true. His client would never betray him. Never.

Two constables took the mare from his unresisting charge and put handcuffs on him.

'How did you get here?' he asked.

The high-ranking policeman said. 'We've been looking for you for three years. A few weeks ago we found you. But we had no conclusive evidence against you. So we've been keeping an eye on you ever since.'

Johnnie Duke came out of the trailer, and Martin Retsov thought it was hard on the boy, being caught on his first big job. The policeman walked over to him, looking satisfied. He brought out no handcuffs. He patted the boy on the shoulder.

'Well done, Sergeant Duke,' he said.

The benevolent Mr Croon was always thinking up money-making schemes for others to invest in. But, as Simon Templar observed, it was only Mr Croon who stood to gain ...

THE UNBLEMISHED BOOTLEGGER

Leslie Charteris

Mr Melford Croon considered himself a very prosperous man. The brass plate outside his unassuming suite of offices in Gray's Inn Road described him somewhat vaguely as a 'Financial Consultant'; and while it is true that the gilt-edged moguls of the city had never been known to seek his advice, there is no doubt that he flourished exceedingly.

Out of Mr Croon's fertile financial genius emerged, for example, the great Tin Salvage Trust. In circulars, advertisements, and statements to the Press, Mr Croon raised his literary hands in horror at the appalling waste of tin that was going on day by day throughout the country. 'Tins,' of course, as understood in the British domestic vocabulary to mean the sepulchres of Heinz's 57 Varieties, the Crosse & Blackwell vegetable garden, or the Campbell soup kitchen, are made of thin sheet steel with the most economical possible plating of genuine tin; but nevertheless (Mr Croon pointed out) tin was used. And what happened to it? It was thrown away.

The garbage man removed it along with the other contents of the ashcan, and the municipal incinerators burnt it. And tin was a precious metal – not quite so valuable as gold and platinum, but not very far behind silver. Mr Croon invited his readers to think of it. Hundreds of thousands of pounds being poured into garbage dumps and incinerators every day of the week from every kitchen in the land. Individually worthless 'tins' which in the accumulation represented an enormous potential wealth.

The great Tin Salvage Trust was formed with a capital of nearly a quarter of a million to deal with the problem. Barrows would collect cans from door to door. Rag-and-bone men

107

would lend their services. A vast refining and smelting plant would be built to recover the pure tin. Enormous dividends would be paid. The subscribers would grow rich overnight.

The subscribers did not grow rich overnight; but that was not Mr Croon's fault. The Official Receiver reluctantly had to admit it, when the Trust went into liquidation eighteen months after it was formed. The regrettable capriciousness of fortune discovered and enlarged a fatal leak in the scheme; without quite knowing how it all happened, a couple of dazed promoters found themselves listening to sentences of penal servitude; and the creditors were glad to accept one shilling in the pound. Mr Croon was overcome with grief – he said so in public – but he could not possibly be blamed for the failure. He had no connection whatever with the Trust, except as Financial Consultant – a post for which he received a merely nominal salary. It was all very sad.

In similar circumstances, Mr Croon was overcome with grief at the failures of the great Rubber Waste Products Corporation, the Iron Workers' Benevolent Guild, the Small Investors' Co-operative Bank, and the Consolidated Albion Film Company. He had a hard and unprofitable life; and if his mansion flat in Hampstead, his Rolls-Royce, his shoot in Scotland, his racing stable, and his house at Marlow helped to console him, it is quite certain that he needed them.

'A very suitable specimen for us to study,' said Simon Templar.

The latest product of Mr Croon's indomitable inventiveness was spread out on his knee. It took the form of a very artistically typewritten letter, which had been passed on to the Saint by a chance acquaintance.

Dear Sir,

As you cannot fail to be aware, a state of Prohibition exists at present in the United States of America. This has led to a highly profitable trade in the forbidden alcoholic drinks between countries not so affected and the United States.

A considerable difference of opinion exists as to whether this traffic is morally justified. There can be no question, however, that from the standpoint of this country it cannot

108

be legally attacked, nor that the profits, in proportion to the risk, are exceptionally attractive.

If you should desire further information on the subject I shall be pleased to supply it at the above address.

Yours faithfully,
Melford Croon

Simon Templar called on Mr Croon one morning by appointment; and the name he gave was not his own. He found Mr Croon to be a portly and rather pale-faced man, with the flowing iron-grey mane of an impresario; and the information he gave – after a few particularly shrewd inquiries about his visitor's status and occupation – was very much what the Saint had expected.

'A friend of mine,' said Mr Croon – he never claimed personally to be the author of the schemes on which he gave Financial Consultations – 'a friend of mine is interested in sending a cargo of wines and spirits to America. Naturally, the expenses are somewhat heavy. He has to charter a ship, engage a crew, purchase the cargo, and arrange to dispose of it on the other side. While he would prefer to find the whole of the money – and, of course, reap all the reward – he is unfortunately left short of about two thousand pounds.'

'I see,' said the Saint.

He saw much more than Mr Croon told him, but he did not say so.

'This two thousand pounds,' said Mr Croon, 'represents about one-fifth of the cost of the trip, and in order to complete his arrangements my friend is prepared to offer a quarter of his profits to anyone who will go into partnership with him. As he expects to make at least ten thousand pounds, you will see that there are not many speculations which offer such a liberal return.'

If there was one role which Simon Templar could play better than any other, it was that of the kind of man whom financial consultants of every size and species dream that they may meet one day before they die. Mr Croon's heart warmed towards him as Simon laid on the touches of his self-created character with a master's brush.

'A very charming man,' thought the Saint as he paused on

the pavement outside the building which housed Mr Croon's offices.

Since at various stages of the interview Mr Croon's effusive bonhomie had fairly bubbled with invitations to lunch with Mr Croon, dine with Mr Croon, shoot with Mr Croon, watch Mr Croon's horses win at Goodwood with Mr Croon, and spend week-ends with Mr Croon at Mr Croon's house on the river, the character which Simon Templar had been playing might have thought that the line of the Saint's lips were unduly cynical; but Simon was only thinking of his own mission in life.

He stood there with his walking cane swinging gently in his fingers, gazing at the very commonplace street scene with thoughtful blue eyes, and became aware that a young man with the physique of a pugilist was standing at his shoulder. Simon waited.

'Have you been to see Croon?' demanded the young man suddenly.

Simon looked around with a slight smile.

'Why ask?' he murmured. 'You were outside Croon's room when I came out, and you followed me down the stairs.'

'I just wondered.'

The young man had a pleasantly ugly face with crinkly grey eyes that would have liked to be friendly; but he was very plainly nervous.

'Are you interested in bootlegging?' asked the Saint; and the young man stared at him grimly.

'Listen, I don't know if you're trying to be funny, but I'm not. I'm probably going to be arrested this afternoon. In the last month I've lost about five thousand pounds in Croon's schemes – and the money wasn't mine to lose. You can think what you like. I went up there to bash his face in before they get me, and I'm going back now for the same reason. But I saw you come out, and you didn't look like a crook. I thought I'd give you a word of warning. You can take it or leave it. Good-bye.'

He turned off abruptly into the building, but Simon reached out and caught him by the elbow.

'Why not come and have some lunch first?' he suggested. 'And let Croon have his. It'll be so much more fun punching him in the stomach when it's full of food.'

He waved away the young man's objections and excuses without listening to them, hailed a taxi and bundled him in. It was the kind of opportunity that the Saint lived for, and he would have had his way if he was compelled to kidnap his guest for the occasion. They lunched at a quiet restaurant in Soho; and in the persuasive warmth of half a litre of Antinori Chianti and the Saint's irresistible personality the young man told him what he knew of Mr Melford Croon.

'I suppose I was a complete idiot – that's all. I met Croon through a man I used to see in the place where I always had lunch. It didn't occur to me that it was all a put-up job, and I thought Croon was all right. I was fed to the teeth with sitting about in an office copying figures from one book to another, and Croon's stunts looked like a way out. I put three thousand quid into his Consolidated Albion Film Company: it was only on paper, and the way Croon talked about it made me think I'd never really be called on for the money. They were going to rent the World Features studio at Teddington – the place is still on the market. When Consolidated Albion went smash I had to find the money, and the only way I could get it was to borrow it out of the firm. Croon put the idea into my head, but – Oh, hell! It's easy enough to see how things have happened after the damage is done.'

He had borrowed another two thousand pounds – without the cashier's knowledge – in the hope of retrieving the first loss. It had gone into a cargo of liquor destined for the thirsty States. Six weeks later Mr Croon broke the news to him that the coastal patrols had captured the ship.

'And that's what'll happen to any other fool who puts money into Croon's bootlegging,' said the young man bitterly. 'He'll be told that the ship's sunk, or captured, or caught fire, or grown wings and flown away. He'll never see his money back. My God – to think of that slimy swab trying to be a bootlegger! Why, he told me once that the very sight of a ship made him feel sick, and he wouldn't cross the Channel for a thousand pounds.'

'What are you going to do about it?' asked the Saint, and the young man shrugged.

'Go back and try to make him wish he'd never been born – as

I told you. They're having an audit today at the office, and they can't help finding out what I've done. I stayed away – said I was ill. That's all there is to do.'

Simon took out his chequebook and wrote a cheque for five thousand pounds.

'Whom shall I make it payable to?' he inquired, and his guest's eyes widened.

'My name's Peter Quentin. But I don't want any of your damned –'

'My dear chap, I shouldn't dream of offering you charity.' Simon blotted the pink slip and scaled it across the table. 'This little chat has been worth every penny of it. Besides, you don't want to go to penal servitude at your age. It isn't healthy. Now be a good fellow and dash back to your office – square things up as well as you can –'

The young man was staring at the name which was scribbled in the bottom right-hand corner of the paper.

'Is that name Simon Templar?'

The Saint nodded.

'You see, I shall get it all back,' he said.

He went home with two definite conclusions as a result of his day's work and expenses: first, that Mr Melford Croon was in every way as undesirable a citizen as he had thought, and second, that Mr Melford Croon's contribution to the funds of righteousness was long overdue. Mr Croon's account was, in fact, exactly five thousand pounds overdrawn; and that state of affairs could not be allowed to continue.

Nevertheless, it took the Saint twenty-four hours of intensive thought to devise a poetic retribution; and when the solution came to him it was so simple that he had to laugh.

Mr Croon went down to his house on the river for the week-end. He invariably spent his week-ends there in the summer, driving out of London on the Friday afternoon and refreshing himself from his labours with three happy days of rural peace. Mr Croon had an unexpected appetite for simple beauty and the works of nature: he was rarely so contented as when he was lying out in a deck-chair and spotless white flannels, directing his gardener's efforts at the flower-beds, or sipping an iced whisky-and-soda on his balcony while he watched supple young athletes propelling punts up and down the stream.

This week-end was intended to be no exception to his usual custom. He arrived at Marlow in time for dinner, and prepared for an early night in anticipation of the tireless revels of a mixed company of his friends who were due to join him the next day. It was scarcely eleven o'clock when he dismissed his servant and mixed himself a final drink before going to bed.

He heard the front door-bell ring, and rose from his armchair grudgingly. He had no idea who could be calling on him at that hour; and when he had opened the door and found that there was no one visible outside he was even more annoyed.

He returned to the sitting-room, and gulped down the remainder of his nightcap without noticing the bitter tang that had not been there when he poured it out. The taste came into his mouth after the liquid had been swallowed, and he grimaced. He started to walk towards the door, and the room spun around. He felt himself falling helplessly before he could cry out.

When he woke up, his first impression was that he had been buried alive. He was lying on a hard narrow surface, with one shoulder squeezed up against a wall on his left, and the ceiling seemed to be only a few inches above his head. Then his sight cleared a little, and he made out that he was in a bunk in a tiny unventilated compartment lighted by a single circular window. He struggled up on one elbow, and groaned. His head was one reeling whirligig of aches, and he felt horribly sick.

Painfully he forced his mind back to his last period of consciousness. He remembered pouring out that last whisky-and-soda – the ring at the front door – the bitter taste in the glass ... Then nothing but an infinity of empty blackness ... How long had he been unconscious? A day? Two days? A week? He had no means of telling.

With an agonizing effort he dragged himself off the bunk and staggered across the floor. It reared and swayed sickeningly under him, so that he could scarcely keep his balance. His stomach was somersaulting nauseatingly inside him. Somehow he got over to the one window: the pane was frosted over, but outside he could hear the splash of water and the shriek of wind. The explanation dawned on him dully – he was in a ship.

Mr Croon's knees gave way under him, and he sank moaning to the floor. A spasm of sickness left him gasping in a clammy sweat. The air was stiflingly close, and there was a smell of oil in it which made it almost unbreathable. Stupidly, unbelievingly, he felt the floor vibrating to the distant rhythm of the engines. A ship! He'd been drugged – kidnapped – shanghaied! Even while he tried to convince himself that it could not be true, the floor heaved up again with the awful deliberateness of a seventh wave; and Mr Croon heaved up with it . . .

He never knew how he managed to crawl to the door between the paroxysms of torment that racked him with every movement of the vessel. After what seemed like hours he reached it, and found strength to try the handle. The door failed to budge. It was locked. He was a prisoner – and he was going to die. If he could have opened the door he would have crawled up to the deck and thrown himself into the sea. It would have been better than dying of that dreadful nausea that racked his whole body and made his head swim as if it were being spun on the axle of a dynamo.

He rolled on the floor and sobbed with helpless misery. In another hour of that weather he'd be dead. If he could have found a weapon he would have killed himself. He had never been able to stand the slightest movement of the water – and now he was a prisoner in a ship that must have been riding one of the worst storms in the history of navigation. The hopelessness of his position made him scream suddenly – scream like a trapped hare – before the ship slumped suckingly down into the trough of another seventh wave and left his stomach on the crest of it.

Minutes later – it seemed like centuries – a key turned in the locked door, and a man came in. Through the bilious yellow mists that swirled over his eyes, Mr Croon saw that he was tall and wiry, with a salt-tanned face and far-sighted twinkling blue eyes. His double-breasted jacket carried lines of dingy gold braid, and he balanced himself easily against the rolling of the vessel.

114

'Why, Mr Croon – what's the matter?'

'I'm sick,' sobbed Mr Croon, and proceeded to prove it.

The officer picked him up and laid him on the bunk.

'Bless you, sir, this isn't anything to speak of. Just a bit of a blow – and quite a gentle one for the Atlantic.'

Croon gasped feebly.

'Did you say the Atlantic?'

'Yes, sir. The Atlantic is the ocean we are on now, sir, and it'll be the same ocean all the way to Boston.'

'I can't go to Boston,' said Mr Croon pathetically. 'I'm going to die.'

The officer pulled out a pipe and stuffed it with black tobacco. A cloud of rank smoke added itself to the smell of oil that was contributing to Croon's wretchedness.

'Lord, sir, you're not going to die!' said the officer cheerfully. 'People who aren't used to it often get like this for the first two or three days. Though I must say, sir, you've taken a long time to wake up. I've never known a man be so long sleeping it off. That must have been a very good farewell party you had, sir.'

'Damn you!' groaned the sick man weakly. 'I wasn't drunk – I was drugged!'

The officer's mouth fell open.

'Drugged, Mr Croon?'

'Yes, drugged!' The ship rolled on its beam ends, and Croon gave himself up for a full minute to his anguish. 'Oh, don't argue about it! Take me home!'

'Well, sir, I'm afraid that's –'

'Fetch me the captain!'

'I am the captain, sir. Captain Bourne. You seem to have forgotten, sir. This is the *Christabel Jane*, eighteen hours out of Liverpool with a cargo of spirits for the United States. We don't usually take passengers, sir, but seeing that you were a friend of the owner, and you wanted to make the trip, why, of course we found you a berth.'

Croon buried his face in his hands.

He had no more questions to ask. The main details of the conspiracy were plain enough. One of his victims had turned on him for revenge – or perhaps several of them had banded together for the purpose. He had been threatened often before.

115

And somehow his terror of the sea had become known. It was poetic justice – to shanghai him on board a bootlegging ship and force him to take the journey of which he had cheated their investments.

'How much will you take to turn back?' he asked; and Captain Bourne shook his head.

'You still don't seem to understand, sir. There's ten thousand pounds' worth of spirits on board – at least, they'll be worth ten thousand pounds if we get them across safely – and I'd lose my job if I –'

'Damn your job!' said Melford Croon.

With trembling fingers he pulled out a chequebook and fountain-pen. He scrawled a cheque for fifteen thousand pounds and held it out.

'Here you are. I'll buy your cargo. Give the owner his money and keep the change. Keep the cargo. I'll buy your whole damned ship. But take me back. D'you understand? Take me back –'

The ship lurched under him again, and he choked. When the convulsion was over the captain was gone.

Presently a white-coated steward entered with a cup of steaming beef-tea. Croon looked at it and shuddered.

'Take it away,' he wailed.

'The captain sent me with it, sir,' explained the steward. 'You must try to drink it, sir. It's the best thing in the world for the way you're feeling. Really, sir, you'll feel quite different after you've had it.'

Croon put out a white, flabby hand. He managed to take a gulp of the hot soup; then another. It had a slightly bitter taste which seemed familiar. The cabin swam around him again, more dizzily than before, and his eyes closed in merciful drowsiness.

He opened them in his own bedroom. His servant was drawing back the curtains, and the sun was streaming in at the windows.

The memory of his nightmare made him feel sick again, and he clenched his teeth and swallowed desperately. But the floor underneath was quite steady. And then he remembered something else, and struggled up in the bed with an effort which threatened to overpower him with renewed nausea.

'Give me my chequebook,' he rasped. 'Quick – out of my coat pocket –'

He opened it frantically and stared at a blank stub with his face growing haggard.

'What's today?' he asked.

'This is Saturday, sir,' answered the surprised valet.

'What time?'

'Eleven o'clock, sir. You said I wasn't to call you –'

But Mr Melford Croon was clawing for the telephone at his bedside. In a few seconds he was through to his bank in London. They told him that his cheque had been cashed at ten.

Mr Croon lay back on the pillows and tried to think out how it could have been done.

He even went so far as to tell his incredible story to Scotland Yard, though he was not by nature inclined to attract the attention of the police. A methodical search was made in Lloyd's Register, but no mention of a ship called the *Christabel Jane* could be found.

Which was not surprising, for *Christabel Jane* was the name temporarily bestowed by Simon Templar on a dilapidated Thames tug which had wallowed very convincingly for a few hours in the gigantic tank at the World Features studio at Teddington for the filming of storm scenes at sea, which would undoubtedly have been a great asset to Mr Croon's Consolidated Albion Film Company if the negotiations for the lease had been successful.

Victor was eleven and longed to be able to grow up. But it seemed his mother wanted him to stay young for ever . . .

THE TERRAPIN

Patricia Highsmith

Victor heard the elevator door open, his mother's quick footsteps in the hall, and he flipped his book shut. He shoved it under the sofa pillow, and winced as he heard it slip between sofa and wall and fall to the floor with a thud. Her key was in the lock.

'Hello, Veector-r!' she cried, raising one arm in the air. Her other arm circled a big brown-paper bag, her hand held a cluster of little bags. "I have been to my publisher and to the market and also to the fish market,' she told him. 'Why aren't you out playing? It's a lovely, lovely day!'

'I was out,' he said. 'For a little while. I got cold.'

'Ugh!' She was unloading the grocery bag in the tiny kitchen off the foyer. 'You are seeck, you know that? In the month of October, you are cold? I see all kinds of children playing on the sidewalk. Even I think that boy you like. What's his name?'

'I don't know,' Victor said.

His mother wasn't really listening, anyway. He pushed his hands into the pockets of his too small shorts, making them tighter than ever, and walked aimlessly around the living room, looking down at his heavy, scuffed shoes. At least, his mother had to buy him shoes that fit him, and he rather liked these shoes, because they had the thickest soles of any he had ever owned, and they had heavy toes that rose up a little, like mountain climbers' shoes.

Victor paused at the window and looked straight out at a toast-coloured apartment building across Third Avenue. He and his mother lived on the eighteenth floor, just below the top floor where the penthouses were. The building across the street was even taller than this one. Victor had liked their Riverside

118

Drive apartment better. He had liked the school he had gone to there better. Here they laughed at his clothes. In the other school they had got tired of laughing at them.

'You don't want to go out?' asked his mother, coming into the living-room wiping her hands briskly on a wadded paper bag. She sniffed her palms. 'Ugh! That stee-enk!'

'No, Mama,' Victor said patiently.

'Today is Saturday.'

'I know.'

'Can you say the days of the week?'

'Of course.'

'Say them.'

'I don't want to say them. I know them.' His eyes began to sting around the edges with tears. 'I've known them for years. Years and years. Kids five years old can say the days of the week.'

But his mother was not listening. She was bending over the drawing table in the corner of the room. She had worked late on something last night. On his sofa bed in the opposite corner of the room, Victor had not been able to sleep until two in the morning, when his mother had finally gone to bed on the studio couch.

'Come here, Victor. Did you see this?'

Victor came on dragging feet, hands still in his pockets. No, he hadn't even glanced at her drawing board this morning, hadn't wanted to.

'This is Pedro, the Little Donkey. I invented him last night. What do you think? And this is Miguel, the little Mexican boy who rides him. They ride and ride over all of Mexico, and Miguel thinks they are lost, but Pedro knows the way home all the time, and . . .'

Victor did not listen. He deliberately shut his ears in a way he had learned to do from many years of practice; but boredom, frustration – he knew the word frustration, had read all about it – clamped his shoulders, weighed like a stone in his body, pressed hatred and tears up to his eyes as if a volcano were seething in him.

He had hoped his mother might take a hint from his saying he was too cold in his silly shorts. He had hoped his mother might remember what he had told her – that the fellow he had

119

wanted to get acquainted with downstairs, a fellow who looked about his own age, eleven, had laughed at his short pants on Monday afternoon. *They make you wear your kid brother's pants or something?* Victor had drifted away, mortified. What if the fellow knew he didn't even own any longer pants, not even a pair of knickers, much less *long* pants or even blue jeans!

His mother, for some cockeyed reason, wanted him to look 'French', and made him wear shorts and stockings that came to just below his knees, and dopey shirts with round collars. His mother wanted him to stay about six years old, for ever, all his life.

She liked to test out her drawings on him. *Victor is my sounding board*, she sometimes said to her friends. *I show my drawings to Victor and I know if children will like them.* Often Victor said he liked stories that he did not like, or drawings that he was indifferent to, because he felt sorry for his mother and because it put her in a better mood if he said he liked them. He was quite tired now of children's book illustrations, if he had ever in his life liked them – he really couldn't remember; and now he had only two favourites – Howard Pyle's illustrations in some of Robert Louis Stevenson's books and Cruickshank's in Dickens.

It was too bad, Victor thought, that he was absolutely the last person his mother should have asked an opinion of, because he simply *hated* children's illustrations. And it was a wonder his mother didn't see this, because she hadn't sold any illustrations for books for years and years – not since *Wimple-Dimple*, a book whose jacket was all torn and turning yellow now from age, which sat in the centre of the bookshelf in a little cleared spot, propped up against the back of the bookcase so that everyone could see it.

Victor had been seven years old when that book was printed. His mother liked to tell people – and remind him, too – that he had watched her make every drawing, had shown his opinion by laughing or not, and that she had been absolutely guided by him. Victor doubted this very much, because first of all the story was somebody else's and had been written before his mother did the drawings, and her drawings had had to follow the story closely.

Since *Wimple-Dimple*, his mother had done only a few illustrations now and then for children's magazines – how to make paper pumpkins and black paper cats for Hallowe'en and things like that – though she took her portfolio around to publishers all the time.

Their income came from his father, who was a wealthy businessman in France, an exporter of perfumes. His mother said he was very wealthy and very handsome. But he had married again, and he never wrote, and Victor had no interest in him, didn't even care if he never saw a picture of him, and he never had. His father was French with some Polish, his mother said, and she was Hungarian with some French. The word Hungarian made Victor think of gypsies, but when he had asked his mother once, she had said emphatically that she hadn't any gypsy blood, and she had been annoyed that Victor had brought the question up.

And now she was sounding him out again, poking him in the ribs to make him wake up, as she repeated. 'Listen to me! Which do you like better, Victor? "In all Mexico there was no bur-r-ro as wise as Miguel's Pedro," or "Miguel's Pedro was the wisest bur-r-ro in all Mexico"?'

'I think – I like it the first way better.'

'Which way is that?' demanded his mother, thumping her palm down on the illustration.

Victor tried to remember the wording, but realized he was only staring at the pencil smudges, the thumbprints on the edges of his mother's illustration board. The coloured drawing in its centre did not interest him at all. He was not thinking. This was a frequent, familiar sensation to him now; there was something exciting and important about not-thinking, Victor felt, and he thought that one day he would find out something about it – perhaps under another name – in the Public Library or in the psychology books around the house that he browsed in when his mother was out.

'Veec-tor! What are you doing?'

'Nothing, Mama.'

'That is exactly it! Nothing! Can you not even *think*?'

A warm shame spread through him. It was as if his mother read his thoughts about not-thinking. 'I am thinking,' he protested. 'I'm thinking about *not*-thinking.' His tone was defiant.

What could she do about it, after all?

'About what?' Her black, curly head tilted, her mascaraed eyes narrowed at him.

'Not-thinking.'

His mother put her jewelled hands on her hips. 'Do you know, Victor, you are a leetle bit strange in the head?' She nodded. 'You are seeck. Psychologically seeck. And retarded, do you know that? You have the behaviour of a leetle boy five years old,' she said slowly and weightily. 'It is just as well you spend your Saturdays indoors. Who knows if you would not walk in front of a car, eh? But that is why I love you, little Victor.'

She put her arm around his shoulders, pulled him against her, and for an instant Victor's nose pressed into her large, soft bosom. She was wearing her flesh-coloured knitted dress, the one you could see through a little where her breast stretched it out.

Victor jerked his head away in a confusion of emotions. He did not know if he wanted to laugh or cry.

His mother was laughing gaily, her head back. 'Seeck you are! Look at you! My lee-tle boy still, lee-tle short pants – ha! ha!'

Now the tears showed in his eyes, and his mother acted as if she were enjoying it! Victor turned his head away so that she would not see his eyes. Then suddenly he faced her. 'Do you think I *like* these pants? *You* like them, not me, so why do you have to make fun of them?'

'A lee-tle boy who's crying!' she went on laughing.

Victor made a dash for the bathroom, then swerved away and dived on to the sofa, his face towards the pillows. He shut his eyes tight and opened his mouth, crying but not-crying in a way he had also learned through long practice. With his mouth open, his throat tight, not breathing for nearly a minute, he could somehow get the satisfaction of crying, screaming even, without anybody knowing it.

He pushed his nose, his open mouth, his teeth, against the tomato-red sofa pillow, and though his mother's voice went on in a lazily mocking tone, and her laughter went on, he imagined that it was getting fainter and more distant from him.

He imagined, rigid in every muscle, that he was suffering the absolute worst that any human being could suffer. He imagined that he was dying. But he did not think of death as an escape, only as a concentrated and painful instant. This was the climax of his not-crying.

Then he breathed again, and his mother's voice intruded: 'Did you hear me? *Did you hear me?* Mrs Badzerkian is coming over for tea. I want you to wash your face and put on a clean shirt. I want you to recite something for her. Now what are you going to recite?'

' "In winter when I go to bed," ' said Victor. She was making him memorize every poem in *A Child's Garden of Verses*. He had said the first one that came in his head, and now there was an argument, because he had recited that the last time Mrs Badzerkian came to tea. 'I said it because I couldn't think of any other one right off the bat!' Victor shouted.

'Don't yell at me!' his mother cried, storming across the room at him.

She slapped his face before he knew what was happening.

He was up on one elbow on the sofa, on his back, his long, knobbly-kneed legs splayed out in front of him. All right, he thought, if that's the way it is, that's the way it is. He looked at her with loathing.

He would not show her that the slap had hurt, that it still stung. No more tears for today, he swore, not even any more not-crying. He would finish the day, go through the tea, like a stone, like a soldier, not wincing.

His mother paced the room, turning one of her rings round and round, glancing at him from time to time, looking quickly away from him. But his eyes were steady on her. He was not afraid. She could even slap him again and he wouldn't move.

At last she announced that she was going to wash her hair, and she went into the bathroom.

Victor got up from the sofa and wandered across the room. He wished he had a room of his own to go to. In the apartment on Riverside Drive there had been two rooms, a living-room and his mother's bedroom. When she was in the living-room, he had been able to go into the bedroom, and vice versa, but here – They were going to tear down the old building they had lived in on Riverside Drive. It was not a pleasant thing for Victor to think about.

Suddenly remembering the book that had fallen, he pulled out the sofa and reached for it. It was Menninger's *The Human Mind*, full of fascinating case histories of people. Victor put it back in its place on the bookshelf between a book on astrology and *How to Draw*.

His mother did not like him to read psychology books, but Victor loved them, especially ones with case histories in them. The people in the case histories did what they wanted to do. They were natural. Nobody bossed them. At the local branch library he spent hours browsing through the psychology shelves. They were in the adults' section, but the librarian did not mind him sitting at the tables there, because he was always so quiet.

Victor went into the kitchen and got a glass of water. As he was standing there drinking it, he heard a scratching noise coming from the paper bags on the counter. A mouse, he thought, but when he moved a couple of the bags he didn't see any mouse. The scratching was coming from inside one of the bags.

Gingerly, he opened the bag's end with his fingers and waited for something to jump out. Looking in, he saw a white paper carton. He pulled it out slowly. It's bottom was damp. It opened like a pastry box. Victor jumped in surprise. In the box was a turtle – a live turtle!

It was wriggling its legs in the air, trying to turn over. Victor moistened his lips, and frowning with concentration, took the turtle by its sides with both hands, turned him over, and let him down gently into the box again. The turtle drew its feet in then and its head stretched up a little and it looked right at him.

Victor smiled. Why hadn't his mother told him she'd brought him a present? A live turtle! Victor's eyes glazed with anticipation as he thought of taking the turtle down, maybe with a leash around its neck, to show the fellow who'd laughed at his short pants. The boy might change his mind about being friends with him, if he learned that Victor owned a live turtle.

'Hey, Mama! Mama!' Victor yelled at the bathroom door.

"You brought me a turtle?'

'A what?' The water shut off.

'A turtle! In the kitchen!' Victor had been jumping up and down in the hall. He stopped.

His mother had hesitated, too. The water came on again, and she said in a shrill tone, *'C'est une terrapène! Pour un ragout!'*

Victor understood, and a small chill went over him because his mother had spoken in French. His mother addressed him in French only when she was giving an order that had to be obeyed, or when she anticipated resistance from him.

So the terrapin was for a stew. Victor nodded to himself with a stunned resignation, and went back to the kitchen. For a stew. Well, the terrapin was not long for this world, as they say. What did a terrapin like to eat? Lettuce? Raw bacon? Boiled potato? Victor peered in the refrigerator.

He held a piece of lettuce near the terrapin's horny mouth. The terrapin did not open its mouth, but it looked at him. Victor held it near the two little dots of its nostrils, but if the terrapin smelled the lettuce, it showed no interest. Victor looked under the sink and pulled out a round wash pan. He put two inches of water into it. Then he gently dumped the terrapin into the pan. The terrapin paddled for a few seconds, as if it had to swim; then finding that its stomach sat on the bottom of the pan, it stopped, and drew its feet in.

Victor got down on his knees and studied the terrapin's face. Its upper lip overhung the lower, giving it a rather stubborn and unfriendly expression; but its eyes – they were bright and shining. Victor smiled when he looked hard at them.

'Okay, *Monsieur terrapène*,' he said, 'just tell me what you'd like to eat and we'll get it for you. Maybe some tuna?'

They had had tuna fish salad yesterday for dinner, and there was a small bowl of it left over. Victor got a little chunk of it in his fingers and offered it to the terrapin. The terrapin was not interested.

Victor looked around the kitchen, wondering; then seeing the sunlight on the floor of the living-room, he picked up the pan and carried it to the living-room and set it down so that the sunlight would fall on the terrapin's back. All turtles liked sunlight, Victor thought. He lay down on the floor on his side,

125

propped up on an elbow.

The terrapin stared at him for a moment, then very slowly and with an air of forethought and caution, put out its legs and advanced, found the circular boundary of the pan, and moved to the right, half its body out of the shallow water.

Obviously it wanted to get out, so Victor took it in one hand, by the sides, and said, 'You can come out and have a little walk.'

He smiled as the terrapin started to disappear under the sofa. He caught it easily, because it moved so slowly. When he put it down on the carpet, it was quite still, as if it had withdrawn a little to think what it should do next, where it should go.

The terrapin was brownish green. Looking at it, Victor thought of river bottoms, of river water flowing. Or maybe oceans. Where did terrapins come from? He jumped up and went to the dictionary on the bookshelf. The dictionary had a picture of a terrapin, but it was dull, black and white drawing, not so pretty as the live one. He learned nothing except that the name was of Algonquin origin, that the terrapin lived in fresh or brackish water, and that it was edible.

Edible. Well, that was bad luck, Victor thought. But he was not going to eat any *terrapène* tonight. It would be all for his mother, that ragout, and even if she slapped him, scolded him, and made him learn an extra two or three poems, he would not eat any terrapin tonight.

His mother came out of the bathroom. 'What are you doing there? – Victor?'

Victor put the dictionary back on the shelf. His mother had seen the pan. 'I'm looking at the terrapin,' he said, then realized the terrapin had disappeared. He got down on hands and knees and looked under the sofa.

'Don't put it on the furniture. It makes spots,' said his mother. She was standing in the foyer, rubbing her hair vigorously with a towel.

Victor found the terrapin between the wastebasket and the wall. He put it back in the pan.

'Have you changed your shirt?' asked his mother.

Victor changed his shirt, and then at his mother's order sat down on the sofa with *A Child's Garden of Verses* and tackled

another poem, a brand-new one for Mrs Badzerkian. He
learned two lines at a time, reading it aloud in a soft voice to
himself, then repeating it, then putting two, four, and six lines
together, until he had memorized the whole poem. He recited
it to the terrapin. Then Victor asked his mother if he could
play with the terrapin in the bathtub.

'No! And get your shirt all splashed?'

'I can put on my other shirt.'

'No! It's four o'clock now. Get that pan out of the living-
room!'

Victor carried the pan back to the kitchen. His mother took
the terrapin quite fearlessly out of the pan, put it back into the
white paper box, closed its lid, and stuck the box in the refrigerator.

Victor jumped a little as the refrigerator door slammed. It
would be awfully cold in there for the terrapin. But then, he
supposed, fresh or brackish water was cold too.

'Victor, cut the lemon,' said his mother. She was fixing the
big round tray with cups and saucers. The water was boiling in
the kettle.

Mrs Badzerkian was prompt as usual, and his mother
poured the tea as soon as her guest had deposited her coat and
pocket-book on the foyer chair and sat down. Mrs Badzerkian
smelled of cloves. She had a small, straight mouth and a thin
moustache on her upper lip which fascinated Victor, as he had
never seen one on a woman before – not at such short range,
anyway. He never had mentioned Mrs Badzerkian's moustache
to his mother, knowing it was considered ugly; but in a strange
way, her moustache was the thing he liked best about Mrs
Badzerkian.

The rest of her was dull, uninteresting, and vaguely unfriendly. She always pretended to listen carefully to his poetry
recitations, but he felt that she fidgeted, thought of other
things while he recited, and was glad when it was over.
Today, Victor recited very well and without any hesitation,
standing in the middle of the living-room floor and facing the
two women, who were then having their second cup of tea.

'Très bien,' said his mother. 'Now you may have a cookie.'

Victor chose from the plate a small round cookie with a
drop of orange goo in its centre. He kept his knees close to-

gether when he sat down. He always felt that Mrs Badzerkian looked at his knees, and with distaste. He often wished she would make some remark to his mother about his being old enough for long pants, but she never had – at least, not within his hearing.

Victor learned from his mother's conversation with Mrs Badzerkian that the Lorentzes were coming for dinner to-morrow evening. It was probably for them that the terrapin stew was going to be made. Victor was glad that he would have one more day to play with the terrapin. Tomorrow morning, he thought, he would ask his mother if he could take the ter-rapin down on the sidewalk for a while, either on a leash or, if his mother insisted, in the paper box.

'– like a chi-ild!' his mother was saying, laughing, with a glance at him, and Mrs. Badzerkian smiled shrewdly at him with her small, tight mouth.

Victor had been excused, and was sitting across the room with a book on the studio couch. His mother was telling Mrs. Badzerkian how he had played with the terrapin. Victor frowned down at his book, pretending not to hear. His mother did not like him to speak to her or her guests once he had been excused. But now she was calling him her 'lee-tle ba-aby Veec-tor . . .'

He stood up with his finger in the place in his book. 'I don't see why it's childish to look at a terrapin!' he said, flushing with sudden anger. 'They are very interesting animals. They –'

His mother interrupted him with a laugh, but at once the laugh disappeared and she said sternly, 'Victor, I thought I had excused you. Isn't that correct?'

He hesitated, seeing in a flash the scene that was going to take place when Mrs Badzerkian had left. 'Yes, Mama. I'm sorry,' he said. Then he sat down and bent over his book again.

Twenty minutes later Mrs Badzerkian left. His mother scolded him for being rude, but it was not a five or ten minute scolding of the kind he had expected. It lasted barely two minutes. She had forgotten to buy heavy cream, and she wanted Victor to go downstairs and get some.

Victor put on his grey woollen jacket and went out. He always felt embarrassed and conspicuous in the jacket, because it came just a little bit below his short pants, and it looked as if he had nothing on underneath the coat.

Victor looked around for Frank on the sidewalk, but he didn't see him. He crossed Third Avenue and went to a delicatessen in the big building that he could see from the living-room window. On his way back, he saw Frank walking along the sidewalk, bouncing a ball. Victor went right up to him.

'Hey,' Victor said. 'I've got a terrapin upstairs.'

'A what?' Frank caught the ball and stopped.

'A terrapin. You know, like a turtle. I'll bring it down tomorrow morning and show you, if you're around. It's pretty big.'

'Yeah? Why don't you bring it down now?'

'Because we're gonna eat now,' said Victor. 'See you.'

He went into his building. He felt he had achieved something. Frank had looked really interested. Victor wished he could bring the terrapin down now, but his mother never liked him to go out after dark, and it was practically dark now.

When Victor got upstairs, his mother was still in the kitchen. Eggs were boiling and she had put a big pot of water on a back burner. 'You took it out again!' Victor said, seeing the terrapin's box on the counter.

'Yes. I prepare the stew tonight,' said his mother. 'That is why I need the cream.'

Victor looked at her. 'You're going to – you have to kill it tonight?'

'Yes, my little one. Tonight.' She jiggled the pot of eggs.

'Mama, can I take it downstairs to show Frank?' Victor asked quickly. 'Just for five minutes, Mama. Frank's down there now.'

'Who is Frank?'

'He's that fellow you asked me about today. The blond fellow we always see. *Please*, Mama.'

His mother's black eyebrows frowned. 'Take the *terrapène* downstairs? Certainly not. Don't be absurd, my baby! The *terrapène* is not a toy!'

Victor tried to think of some other lever of persuasion. He had not removed his coat. 'You wanted me to get acquainted with Frank –'

'Yes. What has that got to do with the *terrapène*?'

The water on the back burner began to boil.

129

'You see, I promised him I'd –' Victor watched his mother lift the terrapin from the box, and as she dropped it into the boiling water his mouth fell open. '*Mama!*'

'What is this? What is this noise?'

Victor, open-mouthed, stared at the terrapin whose legs were now racing against the steep sides of the pot. The terrapin's mouth opened, its eyes looked right at Victor for an instant, its head arched back in torture, then the open mouth sank beneath the seething water – and that was the end.

Victor blinked. The terrapin was dead. He came closer, saw the four legs and the tail stretched out in the water. He looked at his mother.

She was drying her hands on a towel. She glanced at him, then said, 'Ugh!' She smelled her hands, then hung the towel back.

'Did you have to kill it like that?'

'How else? The same way you kill a lobster. Don't you know that? It doesn't hurt them.'

He stared at her. When she started to touch him, he stepped back. He thought of the terrapin's wide open mouth, and his eyes suddenly flooded with tears. Maybe the terrapin had been screaming and it hadn't been heard over the bubbling of the water. The terrapin had looked at him, wanting him to pull it out, and he hadn't moved to help it. His mother had tricked him, acted so fast that he couldn't save it. He stepped back again. 'No, don't touch me!'

His mother slapped his face, hard and quickly.

Victor set his jaw. Then he about-faced and went to the closet and threw his jacket on to a hanger and hung it up. He went into the living-room and fell down on the sofa. He was not crying now, but his mouth opened against the sofa pillow. Then he remembered the terrapin's mouth and he closed his lips. The terrapin had suffered, otherwise it would not have moved its legs so terribly fast to get out.

Then Victor wept, soundlessly as the terrapin, his mouth open. He put both hands over his face, so as not to wet the sofa. After a long while he got up.

In the kitchen his mother was humming, and every few seconds he heard her quick, firm steps as she went about her work. Victor had set his teeth again. He walked slowly to the kitchen doorway.

The terrapin was out on the wooden chopping board, and his mother, after a glance at him, still humming, took a knife and bore down on the blade, cutting off the terrapin's little nails. Victor half closed his eyes, but he watched steadily. His mother scooped the nails, with bits of skin attached to them, off the board into her palm and dumped them into the garbage bag.

Then she turned the terrapin on its back and with the same sharp, pointed knife she began to cut away the pale bottom shell. The terrapin's neck was bent sideways. Victor wanted to look away, but still he stared. Now the terrapin's insides were all exposed, red and white and greenish.

Victor did not listen to what his mother was saying – something about cooking terrapins in Europe before he was born. Her voice was gentle and soothing, not at all like what she was doing.

'All right, don't look at me like that!' she cried out suddenly, stomping her foot. 'What's the matter with you? Are you crazy? Yes, I think so! You are seeck, you know that?'

Victor could not touch any of his supper, and his mother could not force him to, even though she shook him by the shoulders and threatened to slap him. They had creamed chipped beef on toast. Victor did not say a word. He felt very remote from his mother, even when she screamed right into his face. He felt very odd, the way he did sometimes when he was sick to his stomach, but he was not sick to his stomach.

When they went to bed that night, he felt afraid of the dark. He saw the terrapin's face very large, its mouth open, its eyes wide and full of pain. Victor wished he could walk out the window and float, go anywhere he wanted to, disappear, yet be everywhere. He imagined his mother's hands on his shoulders, jerking him back, if he tried to step out the window. He hated his mother.

He got up and went quietly into the kitchen. The kitchen was absolutely dark, as there was no window, but he put his hand accurately on the knife rack and felt gently for the knife he wanted. He thought of the terrapin, in little pieces now, all mixed up in the sauce of cream and egg yolks and sherry in

131

the pot in the refrigerator.

His mother's cry was not silent – it seemed to tear his ears off. His second blow was in her body, and then he stabbed her throat again.

Only tiredness made him stop, and by then people were trying to bump the door in. Victor at last walked to the door, pulled the chain bolt back, and opened it for them.

He was taken to a large, old building full of nurses and doctors. Victor was very quiet and did everything he was asked to do, and answered the questions they put to him, but only those questions; and since they didn't ask him anything about a terrapin, he did not bring it up.

It seemed that Felton Spenser had committed suicide in a fit of depression. But the Czech detective, Dr Jan Czissar – 'Late Prague police. At your service (click, click)!' – was not convinced.

CASE OF THE GENTLEMAN POET

Eric Ambler

It was after the murderer of Felton Spenser had been tried and convicted that Assistant Commissioner Mercer finally became resigned to the occasional intrusions of Dr Jan Czissar into the affairs of New Scotland Yard.

For that reason alone, the case would be worth reporting. The conversion of an assistant commissioner of New Scotland Yard into an ordinary human being must be reckoned a major triumph of the power of reason over the force of habit. But the case has another claim to the interest of students of criminology in general and, in particular, of those who contemplate committing murders of their own. It demonstrated clearly that the first requisite for the committal of a perfect murder is the omniscience of a god.

The world first heard of the death of Felton Spenser late one January evening.

A B.B.C. announcer said: 'We regret to announce the death in London tonight of Mr Felton Spenser, the poet. He was 53. Although Mr Spenser was born in Manchester, the early years of his life were spent in the county of Flint, and it was in praise of the Flint countryside and scenery that much of his poetry was written. His first collection of poems, "The Merciful Light", was published in 1909. Mr Marshall Grieve, the critic and a friend of Spenser's, said of him tonight: "He was a man without enemies. His verse had a placid limpidity rarely met with nowadays and it flowed with the lyrical ease of his beloved Dee. Although of recent years his work has not received the attention which it has deserved, it remains an enduring monument to a man with many friends and an abiding love of nature." '

It was left to the newspapers to disclose the fact that Felton Spenser had been found shot in his Bloomsbury apartment. His friend, Mr Marshall Grieve, the author-critic, had reported finding him. There had been a revolver by his side, and it was said that Spenser had recently been suffering from fits of depression.

To Assistant Commissioner Mercer, Detective Inspector Denton ultimately brought further details.

Felton Spenser had lived in the top apartment of a converted house near Torrington Square. There were three other apartments below his. The ground floor was occupied by a dress-maker and her husband named Lobb. On the second floor lived Mr Marshall Grieve. The third floor was unoccupied. The dead man's apartment consisted of two large rooms, used as bedroom and sitting-room, a smaller room used as a study, a kitchen and a bathroom. It had been in the sitting-room that his body had been found.

At about 6.30 that evening the sound of a shot had come from the top of the house. The dressmaker's husband, Mr Lobb, who had just returned home, ran to the door of his apartment. At the same moment, Mr Grieve, who had also heard the shot, had appeared at his door at the head of the first flight of stairs. They had gone up together to investigate.

After breaking down the door of Felton Spenser's apartment, they had found Spenser half sitting, half lying on the sofa, his arms extended and his hands turned back as though he had in the throes of death gripped the edge of the sofa. The body had been rendered rigid by the cadaveric spasm. The appearance of the wound, which was such as to have caused instantaneous death, suggested that when the shot had been fired the revolver had been within an inch or two of the head.

Grieve stated that Spenser had been suffering for some time from fits of intense depression. He knew of several possible causes. Spenser had been profoundly disappointed by the reception accorded to a book of his poems published a year before and had spoken bitterly of being neglected. He had also been in financial difficulties. He had never earned a living from his work and had lived on a small income left to him by his wife, who had died five years previously.

He had, however, Grieve believed, been speculating with his capital. He had also been a very generous man and had lent large sums of money to his friends. Grieve had seen him earlier in the day of his death. Spenser had then told him that his affairs were in a bad way, that he was very worried, and that he was seeing his solicitor the following day in an effort to salvage some of his losses.

This statement was confirmed by the solicitor in question. Shortly before 5 o'clock in the afternoon of the day on which Spenser had died, he had received a telephone call from Spenser who asked for an appointment for the following day. Spenser had seemed agitated in his manner on the telephone, but that fact had not at the time impressed the solicitor, as his client had always seemed to him to be a trifle neurotic.

The revolver, reported Denton, was an old pin-fire weapon of French manufacture, and unregistered. Spenser could have obtained it in a variety of ways. The same applied to the ammunition. Only one shot had been fired from the revolver. The markings on the bullet extracted from the dead man's head showed that it had come from that particular revolver. The only distinguishing feature about the weapon was a series of marks near the muzzle which suggested that at some time a silencer had been fitted to it. No silencer had been found in the apartment. According to the medical report, the wound showed every sign of having been self-inflicted.

There was, in Denton's opinion, only one curious thing about the case. That thing was the draft of an unfinished letter lying on the desk in the study. It was written in pencil and much corrected, as if the writer had been choosing his words very carefully. It began:

'As I told you yesterday, I was serious when I said that unless the money was repaid to me by today I would place the matter in the hands of my legal advisers. You have seen fit to ignore my offer. Accordingly I have consulted my solicitor. Need I say that I regret the necessity which forces me to take this step? I think not. Need I say that, if I could afford to overlook the whole unpleasant matter, I would do so eagerly? Again, I do not think so. In asking for the return of the money, I...'

There the letter stopped.

135

Mercer considered it. 'Looks pretty straightforward to me,' he said at last. 'According to Grieve, he'd been in the habit of lending people money. It looks as though having found himself hard pressed he was trying to get a little of it back. What does his bank account show?'

'Well, sir, he'd certainly got rid of some money. He'd bought some doubtful stock and lost a bit that way. Six months ago he drew out £500. Maybe that was this loan he was trying to get back. Funny idea, though, handing it out in cash. I couldn't find any note of who had it, either. By the look of his place, I should say he was the sort who lights his pipe with important papers. I suppose it's being a poet that does that for you. My wife's got a book called "Pearls From the Lips of Poets" with one of his pieces in it. It's about a sunset and it's the kind that doesn't rhyme. I can't say I cared for it myself. A bit weird.' He caught Mercer's eye. 'But I thought that letter was a bit curious, sir. Why should he get up in the middle of writing a letter and shoot himself?'

Mercer pursed his lips. 'Ever heard of impulse, Denton? That's how half the suicides happen. One minute a man's looking cheerful. The next minute he's killed himself. "Suicide while the balance of his mind was disturbed" is the formula. Any life insurance?'

'Not that we can trace, sir. There's a cousin in Flint who inherits. Executors are Grieve and the solicitor.'

'Grieve's important. What sort of witness will he make?'

'Good, sir. He looks impressive.'

'All right, Denton. I'll leave it to you.'

And to Denton it was left – for the moment. It was not until the day before the inquest was due to be held that Dr Czissar sent his card in to Mercer's office.

For once, Mercer's excuse that he was too busy to see Dr Czissar was genuine. He was due at a conference with the commissioner and it was to Denton that he handed over the job of dealing with the refugee Czech detective.

Again and again during the subsequent conference Mercer wished that he had asked the doctor to wait and interviewed him himself. Since the first occasion on which Dr Czissar had entered New Scotland Yard armed with a letter of introduction from an influential home office official, he had visited

136

Mercer several times. And on every occasion he brought disaster with him – disaster in the shape of irrefutable proof that he, Dr Czissar, could be right about a case when Mercer was wrong.

He tried to put Dr Czissar out of his mind and concentrate on the business in hand; but he found his mind wandering from the larger questions of police administration to the smaller but more consuming questions raised by Dr Czissar's visit. What did Dr Czissar want to see him about this time? Could it be the Birmingham trouble? Surely not. The Soho stabbing? Scarcely. The Ferring business? Impossible. The questions continued. There was only one such question that Mercer did not ask himself: 'Is it the Spenser suicide?' The idea did not enter into his head.

When at last he returned to his office, Denton was waiting for him, and the expression of exasperated resignation on Denton's face told him all he wanted to know about Dr Czissar's visit. The worst had happened again. The only thing he could do now was to put as stony a face as possible on the impending humiliation. He set his teeth.

'Ah, Denton!' He bustled over to his desk. 'Have you got rid of Dr Czissar?'

Denton squared his shoulders. 'No, sir,' he said woodenly; 'he's waiting downstairs to see you.'

'But I told you to see him.'

'I have seen him, sir. But when I heard what he had to say, I thought I'd better keep him here until you were free. It's about this Spenser business, sir. I'm afraid I've tripped up badly. It's murder.

'No question of opinion, I'm afraid. A clear case. He got hold of some of the evidence from that newspaper friend of his who lends him his pass. I've given him the rest. He saw through the whole thing at once. If I'd have had my gumption I'd have seen through it too. He's darn clever, that Czech.'

Mercer choked down the words that rose to his lips. 'All right,' he said as calmly as he could, 'you'd better bring Dr Czissar up.'

Dr Czissar entered the room exactly as he had entered it so many times before – thousands of times, it seemed to Mercer. Inside the door, he clicked his heels, clapped his umbrella to his side as if it were a rifle, bowed, and announced loudly: 'Dr Jan Czissar. Late Prague police. At your service!'

Mercer said formally: 'How do you do, doctor. Sit down. I hear that you have something to tell us about the Spenser case.'

Dr Czissar's pale face relaxed. His tall, plump body drooped into its accustomed position beneath the long drab raincoat. The brown, cowlike eyes beamed through the thick spectacles.

'You are busy. I do not wish to interrupt. It is a small matter.'

'I understand that you think Felton Spenser was murdered.'

The mild eyes enlarged. 'Oh, yes. That is what I think, Assistant Commissioner Mercer.'

'And may I ask why, doctor?'

Dr Czissar cleared his throat and swallowed hard. 'Cadaveric spasm,' he declaimed as if he were addressing a group of students, 'is a sudden tightening of the muscles of the body at the moment of death, which produces a rigidity which remains until it is succeeded by the lesser rigidity of rigor mortis. The limbs of the dead person will thus remain in the positions in which they were immediately before death for some time. Cadaveric spasm occurs most frequently when the cause of death is accompanied by some violent disturbance of the nervous system such as would be produced by apoplexy or a shot through the head. In many cases of suicide by shooting through the head, the weapon is held so tightly by the cadaveric spasm in the dead hand that great force is required to remove it.'

Mercer gave a twisted smile. 'And although there was a cadaveric spasm, the revolver was found on the floor. Is that your point? I'm afraid, doctor, that we can't accept that as proof of murder. A cadaveric spasm may relax after quite a short time. The fact that the hand had not actually retained the weapon is not proof that it did not fire it. So...'

'Precisely,' interrupted Dr Czissar. 'But that was not my point, assistant commissioner. According to the medical report, which the inspector has been good enough to tell me, the body was in a state of unrelaxed cadaveric spasm when it was examined an hour after it was discovered. The fingers of both hands were slightly crooked, and both hands were drawn backwards almost at right angles to the forearms. But let us think.'

He drove one lank finger into his right temple. 'Let us think about the effect of a cadaveric spasm. It locks the muscles in the position assumed immediately before death. Very well, then. Mr Spenser's right hand immediately before his death was drawn backwards almost at right angles to the forearms. Also, the fingers of that hand were slightly crooked. It is not possible, Assistant Commissioner Mercer, to hold a revolver to the head and pull the trigger with the hand in that position. I contend, therefore, that Mr Spenser did not inflict the wound himself.'

Mercer looked sharply at Denton. 'You saw the body before it was moved. Do you agree with this?'

'I am afraid I do, sir,' said Denton.

Mercer contained himself with an effort. 'And what did happen, doctor?'

'In the first place,' said Dr Czissar, 'we have to consider the fact that on the evidence of the dressmaker no one left the house after Mr Spenser was killed. Therefore, when the police arrived, the murderer was still there. Inspector Denton tells me also that the entire house, including the empty apartment on the second floor, was searched by the police. Therefore, the murderer was one of the three persons in the house at the time – the dressmaker, Mrs Lobb, her husband, who returned home shortly before the shot was heard, and Mr Grieve. But which?

'Mr Lobb states that on hearing the shot, he ran to the door of his apartment and looked up the stairs where he saw Mr Grieve appear at the door of his flat. They then went up together to the scene of the crime. If both these men are innocent and telling the truth, then there is an absurdity – for if neither of them shot Mr Spenser, then Mrs Lobb shot him, although she was downstairs at the time of the shot. It is not possible. Nor is it possible for either of the men to have shot him unless they are both lying. Another absurdity. We are faced with the conclusion that someone has been ingenious.

'How was the murder committed?' Dr Czissar's eyes sought piteously for understanding. 'How? There is only one clue in our possession. It is that a microscope examination of the revolver barrel showed Inspector Denton that at some time a

139

silencer had been fitted to it. Yet no silencer is found in Mr Spenser's apartment. We should not expect to find it, for the revolver probably belongs to the murderer. Perhaps the murderer has the silencer? I think so. For only then can we explain the fact that when a shot is heard, *none of the three possible suspects is in Mr Spenser's room.*'

'But,' snapped Mercer, 'if a silencer had been fitted, the shot would not have been heard. It was heard.'

Dr Czissar smiled sadly. 'Precisely. Therefore, we must conclude that two shots were fired – one to kill Mr Spenser, the other to be heard by the dressmaker's husband, Mr Lobb.'

'But only one shot had been fired from the revolver that killed Spenser.'

'Oh, yes, assistant commissioner, that is true. But the murder was, I believe, committed with two revolvers. I believe that Mr Grieve went to Mr Spenser's apartment, armed with the revolver you found, at about six o'clock or perhaps earlier. There was a silencer fitted to the revolver, and when the opportunity came he shot Mr Spenser through the head. He then removed the silencer, smudged the fingerprints on the revolver and left it by Mr Spenser on the floor. He then returned to his own flat and hid the silencer. The next thing he did was to wait until Mr Lobb returned home, take a second revolver, which may, I think, have been of the useless kind which is sold for frightening burglars, go up into the empty flat, and fire a second but blank shot.

'Mr Lobb – he will be the most valuable witness for the prosecution – says in his evidence that, on hearing the shot, he ran to his door and saw Mr Grieve coming out of his apartment. It sounds very quick of him, but I think it must have taken Mr Lobb longer than he thinks. He would perhaps look at his wife, ask her what the noise was, and then go to his door. Yet even a few seconds would be plenty of time for Mr Grieve to fire the shot in the empty flat, descend one short flight of stairs, and pretend to be coming out of his door to see what had caused the noise.'

'I gathered that you had Grieve in mind,' said Mercer grimly; 'but may I remind you, doctor, that this is all the purest supposition. Where is the proof? What was Grieve's motive?'

140

'The proof,' said Dr Czissar comfortably, 'you will find in Mr Grieve's flat – the silencer, the second revolver, the perhaps pin-fire ammunition. He will not have got rid of these things for fear of being seen doing so. Also I suggest that Mr Lobb, the dressmaker's husband, be asked to sit in his room and listen to two shots – one fired in Mr Spenser's room from the revolver that killed Mr Spenser, the other, a blank shot, fired in the empty flat. You will find, I think, that he will swear that it was the second shot he heard. The two noises will be quite different.

'For the motive, I suggest that you consider Mr Grieve's financial arrangements. Some months ago Mr Spenser drew £500 in cash from his bank. There is no doubt, I think, that Mr Grieve had it. While we were waiting for you, assistant commissioner, I suggested to the inspector that some information about Mr Grieve's income would be helpful. Mr Grieve, we find, earns a little money writing. He is also an undischarged bankrupt. He would, therefore, prefer to receive so large a sum in notes instead of by cheque. Also, we have only his word that Mr Spenser lent money freely. I have no doubt that Mr Grieve obtained the money to invest on Mr Spenser's behalf, and that he took it for himself. Perhaps you will find some of it in his flat. Mr Spenser had discovered the theft and threatened to expose him. The letter he was writing was to Mr Grieve. But Mr Grieve did not wait to receive it. He decided to kill Mr Spenser. The fact that he had this old revolver and silencer no doubt suggested the method.'

Dr Czissar sighed and stood up. 'So kind of you to receive me, Assistant Commissioner Mercer. So kind, inspector.' He gave them a pale smile. 'Good afternoon.'

'One moment, doctor.'

Mercer had risen to his feet. There was nothing left for him to say that would change the fact of his defeat and he knew it. The hope that Dr Czissar would one day prove that he was no more infallible than other men had been deferred too often for him to derive any comfort from it. He did the only thing he could do under the circumstances.

'We're very much obliged to you, doctor,' he said. 'We'll always be glad of any help you can give us.'

Dr Czissar's pale face reddened. 'You are too kind,' he

141

stammered. And then for once, his English deserted him. 'It is to me a great . . .' he began, and then stopped. 'It is for me . . .' he said again. He could get no further, and abandoned the attempt to do so. Crimson in the face, he clicked his heels at each of them in turn. 'An honour,' he said in a strangled voice.

Then he was gone. They heard the long, drab raincoat flapping hastily down the corridor.

It certainly was a wonderful creation and a lot of fun for everyone. But occasionally, George felt, its clinical accuracy could be frightening ...

THE VELD

Ray Bradbury

'George, I wish you'd look at the nursery.'

'What's wrong with it?'

'I don't know.'

'Well, then.'

'I just want you to look at it, is all, or call a psychologist in to look at it.'

'What would a psychologist want with a nursery?'

'You know very well what he'd want.' His wife paused in the middle of the kitchen and watched the stove busy humming to itself, making supper for four.

'It's just that the nursery is different now than it was.'

'All right, let's have a look.'

They walked down the hall of their sound-proofed, Happy-life Home, which had cost them thirty thousand dollars installed, this house which clothed and fed and rocked them to sleep and played and sang and was good to them. Their approach sensitized a switch somewhere and the nursery light flicked on when they came within ten feet of it. Similarly, behind them, in the halls, lights went on and off as they left them behind, with a soft automaticity.

'Well,' said George Hadley.

They stood on the thatched floor of the nursery. It was forty feet across by forty feet long and thirty feet high, it had cost half again as much as the rest of the house. 'But nothing's too good for our children,' George had said.

The nursery was silent. It was empty as a jungle glade at hot high noon. The walls were blank and two-dimensional. Now, as George and Lydia Hadley stood in the centre of the room, the walls began to purr and recede into crystalline dis-

143

tance, it seemed, and presently an African veld appeared, in three dimensions, on all sides, in colour, reproduced to the final pebble and bit of straw. The ceiling above them became a deep sky with a hot yellow sun.

George Hadley felt the perspiration start on his brow.

'Let's get out of this sun,' he said. 'This is a little too real. But I don't see anything wrong.'

'Wait a moment, you'll see,' said his wife.

Now the hidden odorophonics were beginning to blow a wind of odour at the two people in the middle of the baked veldland. The hot straw smell of lion grass, the cool green smell of the hidden water hole, the great rusty smell of animals, the smell of dust like a red paprika in the hot air. And now the sounds: the thump of distant antelope feet on grassy sod, the papery rustling of vultures. A shadow passed through the sky. The shadow flickered on George Hadley's upturned, sweating face.

'Filthy creatures,' he heard his wife say.

'The vultures.'

'You see, there are the lions, far over, that way. Now they're on their way to the water hole. They've just been eating,' said Lydia. 'I don't know what.'

'Some animal.' George Hadley put his hand up to shield off the burning light from his squinted eyes. 'A zebra or a baby giraffe, maybe.'

'Are you *sure*?' His wife sounded peculiarly tense.

'No, it's a little late to be *sure*,' he said, amused. 'Nothing over there I can see but cleaned bone, and the vultures dropping for what's left.'

'Did you hear that scream?' she asked.

'No.'

'About a minute ago?'

'Sorry, no.'

The lions were coming. And again George Hadley was filled with admiration for the mechanical genius who had conceived this room. A miracle of efficiency selling for an absurdly low price. Every home should have one. Oh, occasionally they frightened you with their clinical accuracy, they startled you, gave you a twinge, but most of the time what fun for everyone, not only your own son and daughter, but for yourself when you

144

felt like a quick jaunt to a foreign land, a quick change of scenery. Well, here it was!

And here were the lions now, fifteen feet away, so real, so feverishly and startlingly real that you could feel the prickling fur on your hand, and your mouth was stuffed with the dusty upholstery smell of their heated pelts, and the yellow of them was in your eyes like the yellow of an exquisite French tapestry, the yellows of lions and summer grass, and the sound of the matted lion lungs exhaling on the silent noon-tide, and the smell of meat from the panting, dripping mouths.

The lions stood looking at George and Lydia Hadley with terrible green-yellow eyes.

'Watch out!' screamed Lydia.

The lions came running at them.

Lydia bolted and ran. Instinctively, George sprang after her. Outside, in the hall, with the door slammed, he was laughing and she was crying, and they both stood appalled at the other's reaction.

'George!'

'Lydia! Oh, my dear poor sweet Lydia!'

'They almost got us!'

'Walls, Lydia, remember; crystal walls, that's all they are. Oh, they look real, I must admit – Africa in your parlour – but it's all dimensional super-reactionary, super-sensitive colour film and mental tape film behind glass screens. It's all odorophonics and sonics, Lydia. Here's my handkerchief.'

'I'm afraid.' She came to him and put her body against him and cried steadily. 'Did you see? Did you feel? It's too real.'

'Now, Lydia . . .'

'You've got to tell Wendy and Peter not to read any more on Africa.'

'Of course – of course.' He patted her.

'Promise?'

'Sure.'

'And lock the nursery for a few days until I get my nerves settled.'

'You know how difficult Peter is about that. When I punished him a month ago by locking the nursery for even a few hours – the tantrum he threw! And Wendy too. They live for the nursery.'

'It's got to be locked, that's all there is to it.'

'All right.' Reluctantly he locked the huge door. 'You've been working too hard. You need a rest.'

'I don't know – I don't know,' she said, blowing her nose, sitting down in a chair that immediately began to rock and comfort her. 'Maybe I don't have enough to do. Maybe I have time to think too much. Why don't we shut the whole house off for a few days and take a vacation?'

'You mean you want to fry my eggs for me?'

'Yes.' She nodded.

'And darn my socks?'

'Yes.' A frantic, watery-eyed nodding.

'And sweep the house?'

'Yes, yes – oh, yes!'

'But I thought that's why we bought this house, so we wouldn't have to do anything?'

'That's just it. I feel like I don't belong here. The house is wife and mother now and nursemaid. Can I compete with an African veld? Can I give a bath and scrub the children as efficiently or quickly as the automatic scrub bath can? I cannot. And it isn't just me. It's you. You've been awfully nervous lately.'

'I suppose I have been smoking too much.'

'You look as if you didn't know what to do with yourself in this house, either. You smoke a little more every morning and drink a little more every afternoon and need a little more sedative every night. You're beginning to feel unnecessary too.'

'Am I?' He paused and tried to feel into himself to see what was really there.

'Oh, George!' She looked beyond him, at the nursery door. 'Those lions can't get out of there, can they?'

He looked at the door and saw it tremble as if something had jumped against it from the other side.

'Of course not,' he said.

At dinner they ate alone, for Wendy and Peter were at a special plastic carnival across town and had televised home to say they'd be late, to go ahead eating. So George Hadley, bemused, sat watching the dining-room table produce warm dishes of food from its mechanical interior.

'We forgot the ketchup,' he said.

'Sorry,' said a small voice within the table, and ketchup appeared.

As for the nursery, thought George Hadley, it won't hurt for the children to be locked out of it awhile. Too much of anything isn't good for anyone. And it was clearly indicated that the children had been spending a little too much time on Africa. That *sun*. He could feel it on his neck, still, like a hot paw. And the *lions*. And the smell of blood. Remarkable how the nursery caught the telepathic emanations of the children's minds and created life to fill their every desire. The children thought lions, and there were lions. The children thought zebras, and there were zebras. Sun – sun. Giraffes – giraffes. Death and death.

That *last*. He chewed tastelessly on the meat that the table had cut for him. Death thoughts. They were awfully young, Wendy and Peter, for death thoughts. Or, no, you were never too young, really. Long before you knew what death was you were wishing it on someone else. When you were two years old you were shooting people with cap pistols.

But this – the long, hot African veld – the awful death in the jaws of a lion. And repeated again and again.

'Where are you going?'

He didn't answer Lydia. Preoccupied, he let the lights glow softly on ahead of him, extinguish behind him as he padded to the nursery door. He listened against it. Far away, a lion roared.

He unlocked the door and opened it. Just before he stepped inside, he heard a far-away scream. And then another roar from the lions, which subsided quickly.

He stepped into Africa. How many times in the last year had he opened this door and found Wonderland, Alice, the Mock Turtle, or Aladdin and his Magical Lamp, or Jack Pumpkinhead of Oz, or Dr Doolittle, or the cow jumping over a very real-appearing moon – all the delightful contraptions of a make-believe world. How often had he seen Pegasus flying in the sky ceiling, or seen fountains of red fireworks, or heard angel voices singing. But now, this yellow hot Africa, this bake oven with murder in the heat. Perhaps Lydia was right. Perhaps they needed a little vacation from the fantasy which was growing a bit too real for ten-year-old children. It was all right to exercise one's mind with gymnastic fantasies, but when the lively child mind settled on one pattern...? It seemed that, at a distance, for the past month, he had heard lions roaring, and smelled their strong odour seeping as far away as his study door. But, being busy, he had paid it no attention.

George Hadley stood on the African grassland alone. The lions looked up from their feeding, watching him. The only flaw to the illusion was the open door through which he could see his wife, far down the dark hall, like a framed picture, eating her dinner abstractedly.

'Go away,' he said to the lions.

They did not go.

He knew the principle of the room exactly. You sent out your thoughts. Whatever you thought would appear.

'Let's have Aladdin and his lamp,' he snapped.

The veldland remained, the lions remained.

'Come on, room! I demand Aladdin!' he said.

Nothing happened. The lions mumbled in their baked pelts.

'Aladdin!'

He went back to dinner. 'The fool room's out of order,' he said. 'It won't respond.'

'Or –'

'Or what?'

'Or it *can't* respond,' said Lydia, 'because the children have thought about Africa and lions and killing so many days that the room's in a rut.'

'Could be.'

'Or Peter's set it to remain that way.'

'*Set* it?'

'He may have got into the machinery and fixed something.'

'Peter doesn't know machinery.'

'He's a wise one for ten. That I.Q. of his –'

'Nevertheless –'

'Hello, Mom. Hello, Dad.'

The Hadleys turned. Wendy and Peter were coming in the front door, cheeks like peppermint candy, eyes like bright blue agate marbles, a smell of ozone on their jumpers from their trip in the helicopter.

'You're just in time for supper,' said both parents.

'We're full of strawberry ice cream and hot dogs,' said the children, holding hands. 'But we'll sit and watch.'

'Yes, come tell us about the nursery,' said George Hadley.

The brother and sister blinked at him and then at each other. 'Nursery?'

'All about Africa and everything,' said the father with false joviality.

'I don't understand,' said Peter.

'Your mother and I were just travelling through Africa with rod and reel; Tom Swift and his Electric Lion,' said George Hadley.

'There's no Africa in the nursery,' said Peter simply.

'Oh, come now, Peter. We know better.'

'I don't remember any Africa,' said Peter to Wendy. 'Do you?'

'No.'

'Run see and come tell.'

She obeyed.

'Wendy, come back here!' said George Hadley, but she was gone. The house lights followed her like a flock of fireflies. Too late, he realized he had forgotten to lock the nursery door after his last inspection.

'Wendy'll look and come tell us,' said Peter.

'She doesn't have to tell *me*. I've seen it.'

'I'm sure you're mistaken, Father.'

'I'm not, Peter. Come along now.'

But Wendy was back. 'It's not Africa,' she said breathlessly.

'We'll see about this,' said George Hadley, and they all walked down the hall together and opened the nursery door.

There was a green, lovely forest, a lovely river, a purple mountain, high voices singing, and Rima, lovely and mysterious, lurking in the trees with colourful flights of butterflies, like animated bouquets, lingering in her long hair. The African veldland was gone. The lions were gone. Only Rima was here now, singing a song so beautiful that it brought tears to your eyes.

George Hadley looked in at the changed scene. 'Go to bed,' he said to the children.

They opened their mouths.

'You heard me,' he said.

They went off to the air closet, where a wind sucked them like brown leaves up the flue to their slumber rooms.

George Hadley walked through the singing glade and picked up something that lay in the corner near where the lions had been. He walked slowly back to his wife.

'What is that?' she asked.

'An old wallet of mine,' he said.

He showed it to her. The smell of hot grass was on it and the smell of a lion. There were drops of saliva on it, it had been chewed, and there were blood smears on both sides.

He closed the nursery door and locked it, tight.

In the middle of the night he was still awake and he knew his wife was awake. 'Do you think Wendy changed it?' she said at last, in the dark room.

'Of course.'

'Made it from a veld into a forest and put Rima there instead of lions?'

'Yes.'

'Why?'

'I don't know. But it's staying locked until I find out.'

'How did your wallet get there?'

'I don't know anything,' he said, 'except that I'm beginning to be sorry we bought that room for the children. If children are neurotic at all, a room like that –'

'It's supposed to help them work off their neuroses in a healthful way.'

'I'm starting to wonder.' He stared at the ceiling.

'We've given the children everything they ever wanted. Is this our reward – secrecy, disobedience?'

'Who was it said, "Children are carpets, they should be stepped on occasionally"? We've never lifted a hand. They're insufferable – let's admit it. They come and go when they like; they treat us as if *we* were offspring. They're spoiled and we're spoiled.'

'They've been acting funny ever since you forbade them to take the rocket to New York a few months ago.'

'They're not old enough to do that alone, I explained.'

'Nevertheless, I've noticed they've been decidedly cool towards us since.'

'I think I'll have David McClean come tomorrow morning to have a look at Africa.'

'But it's not Africa now, it's Green Mansions country and Rima.'

'I have a feeling it'll be Africa again before then.'

A moment later they heard the screams.

Two screams. Two people screaming from downstairs. And then a roar of lions.

'Wendy and Peter aren't in their rooms,' said his wife.

He lay in his bed with his beating heart. "No,' he said. 'They've broken into the nursery.'

'Those screams – they sound familiar.'

'Do they?'

'Yes, awfully.'

And although their beds tried very hard, the two adults couldn't be rocked to sleep for another hour. A smell of cats was in the night air.

'Father?' said Peter.

'Yes.'

Peter looked at his shoes. He never looked at his father any more, nor at his mother. 'You aren't going to lock up the nursery for good, are you?'

'That all depends.'

'On what?' snapped Peter.

'On you and your sister. If you intersperse this Africa with a little variety – oh, Sweden perhaps, or Denmark or China –'

'I thought we were free to play as we wished.'

'You are, within reasonable bounds.'

'What's wrong with Africa, Father?'

'Oh, so now you admit you have been conjuring up Africa, do you?'

'I wouldn't want the nursery locked up,' said Peter coldly. 'Ever.'

'Matter of fact, we're thinking of turning the whole house off for about a month. Live sort of carefree one-for-all existence.'

151

'That sounds dreadful! Would I have to tie my own shoes instead of letting the shoe tier do it? And brush my own teeth and comb my hair and give myself a bath?'

'It would be fun for a change, don't you think?'

'No, it would be horrid. I didn't like it when you took out the picture painter last month.'

'That's because I wanted you to learn to paint all by yourself, son.'

'I don't want to do anything but look and listen and smell; what else is there to do?'

'All right, go play in Africa.'

'Will you shut off the house sometime soon?'

'We're considering it.'

'I don't think you'd better consider it any more, Father.'

'I won't have any threats from my son!'

'Very well.' And Peter strolled off to the nursery.

'Am I on time?' said David McClean.

'Breakfast?' asked George Hadley.

'Thanks, had some. What's the trouble?'

'David, you're a psychologist.'

'I should hope so.'

'Well, then, have a look at our nursery. You saw it a year ago when you dropped by; did you notice anything peculiar about it then?'

'Can't say I did; the usual violences, a tendency towards a slight paranoia here or there, usual in children because they feel persecuted by parents constantly, but, oh, really nothing.'

They walked down the hall. 'I locked the nursery up,' explained the father, 'and the children broke back into it during the night. I let them stay so they could form the patterns for you to see.'

There was a terrible screaming from the nursery.

'There it is,' said George Hadley. 'See what you make of it.'

They walked in on the children without rapping.

The screams had faded. The lions were feeding.

'Run outside a moment, children,' said George Hadley. 'No, don't change the mental combination. Leave the walls as they

152

arc. Get!'

With the children gone, the two men stood studying the lions clustered at a distance, eating with great relish whatever it was they had caught.

'I wish I knew what it was,' said George Hadley. 'Sometimes I can almost see. Do you think if I brought high-powered binoculars here and —'

David McClean laughed dryly. 'Hardly.' He turned to study all four walls. 'How long has this been going on?'

'A little over a month.'

'It certainly doesn't feel good.'

'I want facts, not feelings.'

'My dear George, a psychologist never saw a fact in his life. He only heard about feelings; vague things. This doesn't feel good, I tell you. Trust my hunches and my instincts, I have a nose for something bad. This is very bad. My advice to you is to have the whole damn room torn down and your children brought to me every day during the next year for treatment.'

'Is it that bad?'

'I'm afraid so. One of the original uses of these nurseries was so that we could study the patterns left on the walls by the child's mind, study at our leisure, and help the child. In this case, however, the room has become a channel towards — destructive thoughts, instead of a release away from them.'

'Didn't you sense this before?'

'I sensed only that you had spoiled your children more than most. And now you're letting them down in some way. What way?'

'I wouldn't let them go to New York.'

'What else?'

'I've taken a few machines from the house and threatened them, a month ago, with closing up the nursery unless they did their homework. I did close it for a few days to show I meant business.'

'Ah, ha!'

'Does that mean anything?'

'Everything. Where before they had a Santa Claus now they have a Scrooge. Children prefer Santas. You've let this room and this house replace you and your wife in your children's affections. This room is their mother and father, far more

153

important in their lives than their real parents. And now you come along and want to shut it off. No wonder there's hatred here. You can feel it coming out of the sky. Feel that sun. George, you'll have to change your life. Like too many others, you've built it around creature comforts. Why, you'd starve tomorrow if something went wrong in your kitchen. You wouldn't know how to tap an egg. Nevertheless, turn everything off. Start new. It'll take time. But we'll make good children out of bad in a year, wait and see.'

'But won't the shock be too much for the children, shutting the room up abruptly, for good?'

'I don't want them going any deeper into this, that's all.'

The lions were finished with their red feast.

The lions were standing on the edge of the clearing watching the two men.

'Now *I'm* feeling persecuted,' said McClean. 'Let's get out of here. I never have cared for these damned rooms. Make me nervous.'

'The lions look real, don't they?' said George Hadley. 'I don't suppose there's any way –'

'What?'

'– that they could *become* real?'

'Not that I know.'

'Some flaw in the machinery, a tampering or something?'

'No.'

They went to the door.

'I don't imagine the room will like being turned off,' said the father.

'Nothing ever likes to die – even a room.'

'I wonder if it hates me for wanting to switch it off?'

'Paranoia is thick around here today,' said David McClean. 'You can follow it like a spoor. Hello.' He bent and picked up a bloody scarf. 'This yours?'

'No.' George Hadley's face was rigid. 'It belongs to Lydia.'

They went to the fuse box together and threw the switch that killed the nursery.

The two children were in hysterics. They screamed and pranced and threw things. They yelled and sobbed and swore and jumped at the furniture.

'You can't do that to the nursery, you can't!'

'Now, children.'

The children flung themselves on to a couch, weeping.

'George,' said Lydia Hadley, 'turn on the nursery, just for a few moments. You can't be so abrupt.'

'No.'

'You can't be so cruel.'

'Lydia, it's off, and it stays off. And the whole damn house dies as of here and now. The more I see of the mess we've put ourselves in, the more it sickens me. We've been contemplating our mechanical, electronic navels for too long. My God, how we need a breath of honest air!'

And he marched about the house turning off the voice clocks, the stoves, the heaters, the shoe shiners, the shoe lacers, the body scrubbers and swabbers and massagers, and every other machine he could put his hand to.

The house was full of dead bodies, it seemed. It felt like a mechanical cemetery. So silent. None of the humming hidden energy of machines waiting to function at the tap of a button.

'Don't let them do it!' wailed Peter at the ceiling, as if he was talking to the house, the nursery. 'Don't let Father kill everything.' He turned to his father. 'Oh, I hate you!'

'Insults won't get you anywhere.'

'I wish you were dead!'

'We were, for a long while. Now we're going to really start living. Instead of being handled and massaged, we're going to live.'

Wendy was still crying and Peter joined her again. 'Just a moment, just one moment, just another moment of nursery,' they wailed.

'Oh George,' said the wife, 'it can't hurt.'

'All right — all right, if they'll only just shut up. One minute, mind you, and then off for ever.'

'Daddy, Daddy, Daddy!' sang the children, smiling with wet faces.

'And then we're going on a vacation. David McClean is coming back in half an hour to help us move out and get to the airport. I'm going to dress. You turn the nursery on for a minute, Lydia, just a minute, mind you.'

And the three of them went babbling off while he let himself be vacuumed upstairs through the air flue and set about dressing himself. A minute later Lydia appeared.

'I'll be glad when we get away,' she sighed.

'Did you leave them in the nursery?'

'I wanted to dress too. Oh, that horrid Africa. What can they see in it?'

'Well, in five minutes we'll be on our way to Iowa. Lord, how did we ever get in this house? What prompted us to buy a nightmare?'

'Pride, money, foolishness.'

'I think we'd better get downstairs before those kids get engrossed with those damned beasts again.'

Just then they heard the children calling, 'Daddy, Mommy, come quick – quick!'

They went downstairs in the air flue and ran down the hall. The children were nowhere in sight. 'Wendy? Peter!'

They ran into the nursery. The veldland was empty save for the lions waiting, looking at them. 'Peter, Wendy?'

The door slammed.

'Wendy, Peter!'

George Hadley and his wife whirled and ran back to the door.

'Open the door!' cried George Hadley, trying the knob. 'Why, they've locked it from the outside! Peter!' He beat at the door. 'Open up!'

He heard Peter's voice outside, against the door.

'Don't let them switch off the nursery and the house,' he was saying.

Mr and Mrs George Hadley beat at the door. 'Now, don't be ridiculous, children. It's time to go. Mr McClean'll be here in a minute and ...'

And then they heard the sounds.

The lions on three sides of them, in the yellow veld grass, padding through the dry straw, rumbling and roaring in their throats.

The lions.

Mr Hadley looked at his wife and they turned and looked back at the beasts edging slowly forward, crouching, tails stiff.

Mr and Mrs Hadley screamed.

And suddenly they realized why those other screams had sounded familiar.

'Well, here I am,' said David McClean in the nursery doorway. 'Oh, hello.' He stared at the two children seated in the centre of the open glade eating a little picnic lunch. Beyond them was the water hole and the yellow veldland; above was the hot sun. He began to perspire. 'Where are your father and mother?'

The children looked up and smiled. 'Oh, they'll be here directly.'

'Good, we must get going.' At a distance Mr McClean saw the lions fighting and clawing and then quieting down to feed in silence under the shady trees.

He squinted at the lions with his hand up to his eyes.

Now the lions were done feeding. They moved to the water hole to drink.

A shadow flickered over Mr McClean's hot face. Many shadows flickered. The vultures were dropping down the blazing sky.

'A cup of tea?' asked Wendy in the silence.

Jaime was not a man to disappoint the tourists ... and he always made sure they got what they deserved.

POT LUCK

Stephen D. Frances

Jaime was building another boat. He sang happily as he worked, the muscles of his brown arms rippled in the sun, and crisply curling wood-shavings made a carpet between his bare feet and the sand.

Already the boat's keel and its skeleton ribs showed promise of the sweet and graceful lines the craft would have.

Presently Antonio strolled along the beach to Jaime's white-washed cottage and watched the fisherman working. After a time Antonio said softly: 'You work too hard, amigo. Let us smoke.'

Jaime willingly put aside his tools and sat relaxed on the hot sand. Antonio took out a bag of black tobacco, and there was a sympathetic silence between the two men as they rolled cigarettes.

Antonio exhaled a blue cloud of smoke and said conversationally: 'A foreign tourist has arrived at the hotel.'

Jaime's blue eyes stared at him wonderingly.

'It is late in the season,' he said. 'This foreigner will find the sea cold for swimming and the nights will be chilly.'

Antonio said: 'He is not a sunbathing tourist. He is an Englishman. He is very intelligent and also speaks Spanish.'

'Ah!' said Jaime softly. He rose to his feet, went into his cottage and returned bearing a wine-skin.

He offered it to Antonio, who threw back his head, squirted rich dark wine down his throat and wiped the back of his hand across his lips.

'This tourist has studied history,' continued Antonio.

'He knows that the Romans once landed on this part of the

158

Spanish coast and built towns. He also knows that Roman trading galleys, filled with rich merchandise, were often wrecked in the middle of the bay by storms.'

'So!' said Jaime, his eyes dreamy.

There was a pause while both men smoked contentedly.

'I suggested to this tourist that he should hire a fisherman to show him how squids are caught,' concluded Antonio.

Now Jaime was staring out across the smooth blue sea. 'Pedro the potter comes today,' he said meaningfully.

He paused to drink from the wine skin. 'Bring your tourist tomorrow and I will take him fishing.'

That afternoon, Pedro came down from the mountains driving a heavily-laden *burro* before him. Outside Jaime's cottage he unloaded six earthenware jars. Jaime examined the large, newly-baked vessels critically. 'You have made them well . . .' he approved.

When he had paid the potter for the jars, Jaime loaded them into his little fishing boat. Then he braced his sturdy shoulders against its hull and slid it down into the sea.

He brought the engine to life with one powerful tug on the starter cord and, two hours later, anchored his boat in a cove 12 miles along the rocky coast.

One by one Jaime dropped the new earthenware jars overboard and watched them sink. Then he lowered a sling made from a fishing net into the water, stripped off his clothes and put on a skin-diver's mask.

He was a powerful swimmer, and he reached the sea-bed 20 feet below with a few strokes. Jaime ignored the new jars, nestling in the soft mud, and swam to the last of six earthenware vessels he had deposited there the previous autumn.

After surfacing twice for air, he managed to get this jar in his fish-net sling.

Aboard his little boat again, Jaime hauled up the jar. After a year in the sea, it was thickly encrusted with barnacles.

The next morning, Antonio brought the tourist to Jaime's cottage. 'Senor Thomas Tilmane wishes to go fishing,' he told Jaime.

Tilmane was a tall, lean man with a high forehead, clear eyes and an open smile.

Gaily Jaime said: 'First, we must drink your health, amigo.' He led the other two men into his tiny, whitewashed living-room where he set three glasses upon the table and poured brandy generously.

But Tilmane was fascinated by the barnacle-encrusted earthenware jar in the corner.

'May I?' he asked breathlessly, and crossed to the jar. He examined it intently. When Tilmane looked round at Jaime his eyes were serious. 'Would you consider selling this?' he asked.

Jaime shrugged. 'It is an old jar I brought up in a fish-net,' he explained.

'Will you sell it?' persisted Tilmane.

'If it interests you to buy,' Jaime replied.

'How much do you ask?'

Now greed glinted in Jaime's eyes. 'Two thousand pesetas?' he asked. But he clearly expected to be scoffed at for naming such a sum – worth £14 in English money.

'I will buy it,' Tilmane said quickly. He counted the notes on to the table. But, before he pushed them across to Jaime, he hesitated.

Then the Englishman sighed and said quickly: 'I am sure this is a Roman *amphora*, probably from a wrecked galley.'

Tilmane added: 'After I have told you this, are you still willing to sell?'

Jaime's eyes had widened in gentle surprise. Now he shrugged his shoulders. 'If you wish to buy such an old jar, I will sell.'

Tilmane pushed the money across the table. But, before Jaime accepted it, the fisherman stipulated: 'The jar must remain here until you leave.'

'Agreed,' said Tilmane.

Antonio broke in: 'And now Jaime will show you how he catches squids.' Jaime's friend had the contented air of a man who has had a successful day.

When Tilmane was ready to leave for England, Antonio accompanied him to Jaime's cottage.

Jaime asked: 'Help me to carry the *amphora* to the car.' Antonio was surprised by the weight of the jar. He glanced down into its long wide neck – and choked when he saw a thick cork rammed tightly into it.

Between them, the two men wrestled the jar into the car. Then they stood in the roadway, waving farewell as Tilmane drove off.

Back in Jaime's living-room, Antonio pulled out his inevitable bag of black tobacco and they rolled cigarettes.

Antonio puffed a cloud of smoke towards the ceiling and asked bluntly: 'What did you put in the Englishman's jar to make it so heavy?'

Jaime raised the wine skin and squirted a refreshing jet into his mouth.

'Antonio,' he confessed, wiping his lips with the back of his hand, 'that tourist shamed me.'

'*Shamed* you?'

'He is not like the others,' sighed Jaime. 'He did not wish to take unfair advantage of an ignorant peasant and a stupid fisherman who knew nothing of history.

'This man was honest and told us what he believed. He shamed us, Antonio.'

Antonio was quietly persistent. 'What *did* you put in the jar, Jaime?'

Jaime mused: 'It is not seemly to be unfair to an honest man.' He again reached for the wine-skin. 'Tilmane will soon learn his jar has little money value.

'But our pride will be saved, Antonio, and Tilmane will not think too badly of us.

'Because he will have to comfort him, the dark wine of sunny Spain, which not even the Romans could make as richly as we make it in our village.'

He had a beak-like nose, grey hair and was wearing a Roman toga. Bizarre, yes – but one could not help sympathizing with his predicament

A CURIOUS STORY

James Pattinson

No doubt it was rude of me to stare, but I had some excuse for doing so. After all, it isn't every day of the week that you see a man dressed in a toga and Roman boots sitting on a bench in St James's Park.

It was a warm morning, and the garment, hanging in loose folds from his shoulders, was well enough suited to the weather, even though so out of place in its present surroundings. In Rome, some two thousand years ago, it would have aroused no comment whatsoever.

He was a man somewhat past middle age, with sparse, greying hair and a prominent, beak-like nose. He smiled when he saw me staring at him, but seemed neither surprised nor offended.

'I wonder,' he said, 'whether you could oblige me with a cigarette.'

I fumbled in my pocket and dragged out a packet. His voice and his whole manner were so majestic that I felt ashamed for not having a more expensive brand to offer him – Turkish perhaps or Egyptian – something exotic to match his appearance. He took one and I lit it for him. He sucked in a deep breath of smoke and let it float slowly out again from his mouth and nose.

'I am extremely obliged to you, my dear sir. I was in great need of that.'

I couldn't help laughing. Somehow, the sight of the patrician of ancient Rome sitting on a park bench and puffing at a cigarette was altogether too bizarre. He joined in my laughter, booming a little, not in the least put out.

'Won't you sit down? I am sure you wish to know why I am

dressed like this. You do, don't you?'

I sat down beside him. 'It is a little unusual, you know.'

'Unusual! It's unprecedented.' He took another long pull at the cigarette, obviously enjoying it. "It is rather a curious story. Indeed you may scarcely credit it. And what is more, it leaves me in a decidedly sticky situation.'

He adjusted the toga over his knees and turned to face me squarely. 'By all the rules I should at this moment be in the North Riding of Yorkshire. Had I not been overcome by weariness at an inauspicious time I should not now have been enjoying the pleasure of your company. Forgive me if I say that I should have been in a less unfortunate position.

'I am, my dear sir, a member of a company of travelling players. I have trodden the boards in more towns – ah, and villages too, heaven help me – than I care to remember. The years press upon one sadly.'

He shook his head, as though regretting the youthful vigour stamped out upon the stages of all those towns and villages. I almost suspected a tear in his beady eye. But he recovered his voice and went on.

'We were playing Shakespeare at a large country house not many miles from Thirsk – one of those local festivals, you know – art and culture and all that – thin sandwiches and fat contraltos – a stage in the great hall and tea on the lawn. To think that it was only yesterday.

'The play was "Julius Caesar" and I was Caesar. You see me still arrayed in all my glory – save for the laurel crown, and that has been lost.'

He coughed. A little colour flushed his hollow cheeks, then faded, as though it really had no business there.

'I was tired. I had had no sleep the previous night. Therefore I was glad when my part came to its ghostly close and I was able to creep away in search of solitude and rest.

'Alas, the house, though large and rambling, was full of people. Not a room unoccupied, not a corner in which I could take a gentle nap undisturbed by seekers of culture. At last I opened a door and found myself in a courtyard at the rear of the building, and there, standing completely unattended, was a furniture van. The back was open, and within its shadowy interior I could see just what I desired – a sofa.

163

'Without hesitation I climbed in and lay down. Oh, the joy of relaxation! In a moment my eyes had closed and I was in the arms of Morpheus.

'The next thing to impinge upon my senses was what I took to be a clap of thunder. I started up, imagining for a moment that I was on the stage and taking part in "The Tempest". All was dark. I heard the sound of a motor engine. My surroundings vibrated and, becoming fully awake, I realized what had happened: what I had supposed to be a clap of thunder had in fact been the slamming shut of the rear doors of the van. Now the vehicle was on its way, bound for I knew not where.

'I cried out. No one answered. I tried to scramble to the front of the van so that I could beat upon the partition separating me from the driver and his mate. It was useless; heavy furniture blocked the way and I could not move it.

'Fortunately I am not a man who gives way easily to despondency. Seeing that it was hopeless to try and get out of my prison, I did the next best thing: I lay down on the sofa and went to sleep.

'When I awoke all was still. From outside I could hear the intermittent sound of traffic, and I could see, high up in the rear doors of the van a chink of light. Groping about, I found a chair and, standing on this, I was just able to reach the chink and peer out.

'My view was restricted to a narrow compass, but I was able to discern some portion of a garish wooden building, blazing with electric light and bearing a sign which proclaimed: "Walter's Transport Café. All Night Service".

'I guessed then that the driver must have pulled up for refreshment and possibly a nap, and that my mobile prison was now at rest in the lorry park of Walter's café. I banged on the door, I shouted. Again to no purpose. All I got for my trouble was a sore throat and bruised knuckles.

'Again I resigned myself to my fate. I returned to the sofa and slept.

'I will not weary you, my dear sir, with further particulars of my Odyssey. Suffice it to say that at six o'clock this morning I was released from captivity to find myself no longer in Yorkshire but in the Great Metropolis.

'The reaction of my unwitting gaolers was amazement turning to hilarity. No doubt it was highly diverting for them to open their van and find therein a man dressed as I am now. When I explained to them my plight they laughed heartily, but they had little to offer in the way of assistance. The driver even had the effrontery to remark that it was the first time he'd had Julius flipping Caesar as a passenger. He wanted to know whether I thought the flipping van was a flipping chariot. "Cor stone the crows!" he said. "All the way from flipping Yorkshire an' we never knew you was there." '

Julius Caesar threw away the butt of his cigarette and trod on it with his Roman boot.

'It's an awkward situation,' I said.

He nodded. 'It is indeed awkward. Here am I with nothing but the clothes I stand up in – such as they are – and two or three hundred miles separating me from my luggage and my company. Moreover, I'm supposed to be playing Macbeth this evening. The question is – how am I to get back?'

'You have no money?'

He smiled ruefully. 'One of the drawbacks to a toga is its singular lack of pockets. I have not so much as a handkerchief.'

He was silent for a moment, gazing fixedly at the ground. I felt in a way responsible for him. By telling me his story he had, as it were, dragged me into the problem. I couldn't simply go away and leave him to his fate.

'How much do you suppose the rail fare is to Thirsk?' I asked.

He did not look up. 'Goodness knows. Five pounds; possibly eight. It might be more.'

I spoke rather diffidently. He was such a superior kind of person and it sounded almost like offering charity.

'I could lend you the money.'

He turned to face me, and again there was a suggestion of moisture in his eye, as though he were deeply moved.

'That is noble of you, my dear sir, truly noble. But I could not accept pecuniary assistance from a perfect stranger.'

'Nonsense,' I said. "You could pay me back.'

He nodded again. 'That is true. But there is another point.'

'Another?'

He indicated the toga. 'To travel on British Rail in such attire might arouse undesirable comment. If I could perhaps purchase a coat and trousers I should feel less conspicuous.'

'How much?' I asked.

'Eight pounds might do it – at a pinch. Ten would be better. Should we say ten pounds – a nice round sum?'

I took out my wallet and gave him the nice round sum. I wrote my name and address on a slip of paper and handed it to him. He wrung my hand.

'A Samaritan! Indeed, indeed, a Samaritan!' He was almost weeping.

After a week I gave up expecting the ten pounds. An actor in a touring company, I told myself, was bound to be hard up. Perhaps he had lost the address. It didn't worry me greatly. I felt a glow of satisfaction from having been able to help a fellow creature in distress. I hoped someone would have done as much for me.

About six months later, on a rather chilly day in November, I happened to be walking in Hyde Park when I overtook two men. One of them was dressed in the usual City style – dark overcoat, bowler hat, rolled umbrella – but the other was in a uniform which might have been that of a Cossack horseman from Czarist Russia. He wore tall leather boots, a long white coat, belted at the waist, and on his head was an Astrakhan cap set at a jaunty angle.

His voice sounded vaguely familiar – deep and sonorous. I caught a snatch of what he was saying.

'It is rather a curious story. We were playing "Anna Karenina" in Leeds . . .'

The Siren Goddess, found on Mars in 2012, was the Solar System's No. 1 mystery ... so it was not surprising someone should try to steal it.

CRIME ON MARS

Arthur C. Clarke

'We don't have much crime on Mars,' said Detective-Inspector Rawlings, a little sadly. 'In fact, that's the chief reason I'm going back to the Yard. If I stayed here much longer, I'd get completely out of practice.'

We were sitting in the main observation lounge of the Phobos Spaceport, looking out across the jagged sun-drenched crags of the tiny moon. The ferry rocket that had brought us up from Mars had left ten minutes ago and was now beginning the long fall back to the ochre-tinted globe hanging there against the stars. In half an hour we would be boarding the liner for Earth – a world on which most of the passengers had never set foot, but which they still called 'home'.

'At the same time,' continued the Inspector, 'now and then there's a case that makes life interesting. You're an art dealer, Mr Maccar; I'm sure you heard about that spot of bother at Meridian City a couple of months ago.'

'I don't think so,' replied the plump, olive-skinned little man I'd taken for just another returning tourist. Presumably the Inspector had already checked through the passenger list; I wondered how much he knew about me, and tried to reassure myself that my conscience was – well, reasonably clear. After all, everybody took *something* out through Martian Customs –

'It's been rather well hushed up,' said the Inspector, 'but you can't keep these things quiet for long. Anyway, a jewel thief from Earth tried to steal Meridian Museum's greatest treasure – the Siren Goddess.'

'But that's absurd!' I objected. "It's priceless, of course – but it's only a lump of sandstone. You couldn't sell it to anyone – you might just as well steal the Mona Lisa.'

The Inspector grinned, rather mirthlessly. '*That's* happened too,' he said. "Maybe the motive was the same. There are collectors who would give a fortune for such an object, even if they could only look at it themselves. Don't you agree, Mr Maccar?'

'That's perfectly true,' said the art dealer. 'In my business you meet all sorts of crazy people.'

'Well, this chappie – name's Danny Weaver – had been well paid by one of them. And if it hadn't been for a piece of fantastically bad luck, he might have brought it off.'

The Spaceport P.A. system apologized for a further slight delay owing to final fuel checks, and asked a number of passengers to report to Information. While we were waiting for the announcement to finish, I recalled what little I knew about the Siren Goddess. Although I'd never seen the original, like most other departing tourists I had a replica in my baggage. It bore the certificate of the Mars Bureau of Antiquities, guaranteeing that 'this full-scale reproduction is an exact copy of the so-called Siren Goddess, discovered in the Mare Sirenium by the Third Expedition, A.D. 2012 (A.M. 23).'

It's quite a tiny thing to have caused so much controversy, only eight or nine inches high – you wouldn't look at it twice if you saw it in a museum on Earth. The head of a young woman, with slightly oriental features, elongated ear-lobes, hair curled in tight ringlets close to the scalp, lips half parted in an expression of pleasure or surprise – and that's all.

But it's an enigma so baffling that it has inspired a hundred religious sects, and driven quite a few archaeologists out of their minds. For a perfectly human head had no right whatsoever to be found on Mars, whose only intelligent inhabitants were crustaceans – 'educated lobsters', as the newspapers are fond of calling them. The aboriginal Martians never came near to achieving space-flight, and in any event their civilization died before men existed on Earth.

No wonder the Goddess is the Solar System's Number One mystery. I don't suppose we'll find the answer in my lifetime – if we ever do.

'Danny's plan was beautifully simple,' continued the Inspector. 'You know how absolutely dead a Martian city gets on Sunday, when everything closes down and the colonists stay home to watch the TV from Earth. Danny was counting on this when he checked into the hotel in Meridian West, late Friday afternoon. He'd have Saturday for reconnoitring the Museum, and undisturbed Sunday for the job itself, and on Monday morning he'd be just another tourist leaving town . . .

'Early Saturday he strolled through the little park and crossed over into Meridian East, where the Museum stands. In case you don't know, the city gets its name because it's exactly on longitude 180 degrees; there's a big stone slab in the park with the Prime Meridian engraved on it, so that visitors can get themselves photographed standing in two hemispheres at once. Amazing what simple things amuse some people.

'Danny spent the day going over the Museum, exactly like any other tourist determined to get his money's worth. But at closing time he didn't leave; he'd holed up in one of the galleries not open to the public, where the Museum had been arranging a Late Canal Period reconstruction but had run out of money before the job could be finished. He stayed there until about midnight, just in case there were any enthusiastic researchers still in the building. Then he emerged and got to work.'

'Just a minute,' I interrupted. 'What about the night watchman?'

'My dear chap! They don't have such luxuries on Mars. There weren't even any burglar alarms, for who would bother to steal lumps of stone? True, the Goddess was sealed up neatly in a strong glass and metal cabinet, just in case some souvenir hunter took a fancy to her. But even if she were stolen, there was nowhere the thief could hide, and of course all outgoing traffic would be searched as soon as the statue was missed.'

That was true enough. I'd been thinking in terms of Earth, forgetting that every city on Mars is a closed little world of its own beneath the force-field that protects it from the freezing near-vacuum. Beyond those electronic shields is the utterly hostile emptiness of the Martian Outback, where a man will die in seconds without protection. That makes law enforcement very easy; no wonder there's so little crime on Mars . . .

'Danny had a beautiful set of tools, as specialized as a watchmaker's. The main item was a microsaw no bigger than a

169

soldering iron; it had a wafer-thin blade, driven at a million cycles a second by an ultrasonic power-pack. It would go through glass or metal like butter – and leave a cut only about as thick as a hair. Which was very important for Danny, as he could not leave any traces of his handiwork.

'I suppose you've guessed how he intended to operate. He was going to cut through the base of the cabinet and substitute one of those souvenir replicas for the genuine Goddess. It might be a couple of years before some inquisitive expert discovered the awful truth, and long before then the original would have been taken to Earth, perfectly disguised as a copy of itself, with a genuine certificate of authenticity. Pretty neat, eh?

'It must have been a weird business, working in that darkened gallery with all those million-year-old carvings and unexplainable artefacts around him. A museum on Earth is bad enough at night, but at least it's – well, *human*. And Gallery Three, which houses the Goddess, is particularly unsettling. It's full of bas-reliefs showing quite incredible animals fighting each other; they look rather like giant beetles, and most paleontologists flatly deny that they could ever have existed. But imaginary or not, they belonged to this world, and they didn't disturb Danny as much as the Goddess, staring at him across the ages and defying him to explain her presence here. She gave him the creeps. How do I know? He told me.

'Danny set to work on that cabinet as carefully as any diamond-cutter preparing to cleave a gem. It took most of the night to slice out the trap door, and it was nearly dawn when he relaxed and put down the saw. There was still a lot of work to do, but the hardest part was over. Putting the replica into the case, checking its appearance against the photos he'd thoughtfully brought with him, and covering up his traces might take a good part of Sunday, but that didn't worry him in the least. He had another twenty-four hours, and would positively welcome Monday's first visitors so that he could mingle with them and make his inconspicuous exit.

'It was a perfectly horrible shock to his nervous system, therefore, when the main doors were noisily unbarred at eight-thirty and the Museum staff – all six of them – started to open up for the day. Danny bolted for the emergency exit, leaving everything behind – tools, Goddesses, the lot.

'He had another big surprise when he found himself in the street: it should have been completely deserted at this time of day, with everyone at home reading the Sunday papers. But here were the citizens of Meridian East, as large as life, heading for plant or office on what was obviously a normal working day.

'By the time poor Danny got back to his hotel we were waiting for him. We couldn't claim much credit for deducing that only a visitor from Earth – and a very recent one at that – could have overlooked Meridian City's chief claim to fame. And I presume you know what *that* is.'

'Frankly, I don't,' I answered. 'You can't see much of Mars in six weeks, and I never went east of the Syrtis Major.'

'Well, it's absurdly simple, but we shouldn't be too hard on Danny – even the locals occasionally fall into the same trap. It's something that doesn't bother us on Earth, where we've been able to dump the problem in the Pacific Ocean. But Mars, of course, is all dry land; and that means that *somebody* is forced to live with the International Date Line . . .

'Danny, you see, had planned the job from Meridian West. It was Sunday over there all right – and it was still Sunday there when we picked him up at the hotel. But over in Meridian East, half a mile away, it was only Saturday. That little trip across the park had made all the difference! I told you it was rotten luck.'

There was a long moment of silent sympathy, then I asked, 'What did he get?'

'Three years,' said Inspector Rawlings.

'That doesn't seem very much.'

'Mars years – that makes it almost six of ours. And a whopping fine, which, by an odd coincidence, came to exactly the refund value of his return ticket to Earth. He isn't in jail, of course – Mars can't afford that kind of nonproductive luxury. Danny has to work for a living, under discreet surveillance. I told you that the Meridian Museum couldn't afford a night watchman. Well, it has one now. Guess who?'

'All passengers prepare to board in ten minutes! Please collect your hand-baggage!' ordered the loudspeakers.

As we started to move towards the airlock, I couldn't help

171

asking one more question.

'What about the people who put Danny up to it? There must have been a lot of money behind him. Did you get them?'

'Not yet; they'd covered their tracks pretty thoroughly, and I believe Danny was telling the truth when he said he couldn't give us a lead. Still, it's not my case. As I told you, I'm going back to my old job at the Yard. But a policeman always keeps his eyes open – like an art dealer, eh, Mr Maccar? Why, you look a bit green about the gills. Have one of my space-sickness tablets.'

'No, thank you,' answered Mr Maccar, 'I'm quite all right.'

His tone was distinctly unfriendly; the social temperature seemed to have dropped below zero in the last few minutes. I looked at Mr Maccar, and I looked at the Inspector. And suddenly I realized that we were going to have a very interesting trip.

When Mrs Bradley was called in on the lighthouse murder she
applied a little feminine psychology ...

A LIGHT ON MURDER

Gladys Mitchell

The body had been there for five days, and the men in the
lighthouse could not get to it. Their relief was overdue, but
before any of them looked southward for the welcome sight of
their boat, he would first look to the west, to the black rocks
against whose smooth-washed crevices the pale face and hands
of the dead man showed up like pieces of paper.

They had no doubt of the identity of the corpse. They who
had been four were now three. At night the great light, revolving its god-like eye, would pick out the form of their com-
rade, and then, as though to hide the sight from everything
save the stars, it would sweep on until the next revolution
again revealed the unthinkable thought – that Dick was dead.

'He must have jumped,' said Tom, the oldest and most experienced of the men. 'It's a bad thing for Maggie. Who's to
tell her?'

'Funny how the sea picked him up and chucked him on the
rocks and then never swept him off again,' said Dugald, the
youngest man.

'It seems as if he'd been there a year,' said Walt, who was
almost new to the lighthouse. 'I wonder what his trouble was?
He never said anything, did he?'

'You don't need to have trouble to do a thing like that,' said
old Tom. 'It takes fellows that way sometimes. You get
browned-off on a light. Then you get to looking down at the
sea from the gallery round the lamp, and then you do it. I
knew a fellow once on the Dymballs – but Dick never seemed
that sort.'

The relief boat arrived two days later, and, in spite of a still-
heavy swell, it took the dead man from the rocks. But when
the captain looked at the body he refused to take anybody off

the lighthouse. He returned to shore with poor Dick as fast as his boat could churn the seas. There was a knife between the dead man's shoulder-blades.

The police went out to the lighthouse and questioned the three keepers. It was soon proved that the knife had been the property of the dead man himself, but as it was impossible that he could have thrust it into his own back, there remained the question: which of his three companions had murdered him?

The fingerprints of all three men were taken but proved useless. There were no prints on the haft of the knife, and in the lamp-room and on the gallery (the only two places in which the murder was at all likely to have been committed unless more than one of the men had been concerned in it) there were the prints of all the keepers, the dead man himself included, on the railings and on the gear.

Kitbags, lockers and clothes were minutely inspected for traces of blood, but the wound had not bled very much, and when no such traces were found nobody was particularly surprised.

Medical evidence at the inquest established that the man had been dead for eight or nine days. This coincided with the story of the keepers that about thirty-six hours after Dick had disappeared his body had been seen on the rocks and was there seven days. There was no other evidence worth considering, so the police decided to take the line that all three men were equally guilty of murder. No arrest was made, but the men were closely tailed and were not sent back to their duty.

'But, of course, they're not all guilty,' said the Inspector in charge of the case, 'and what we have got to do is to sort out the wheat from the chaff. The sooner the better, too. Trinity House don't like it that we've practically pinched three of their men. But we can't have them back on the light to destroy or to fake the evidence. But how to get at the truth –'

'We want a psychologist, sir,' said his bright young sergeant from Hendon. 'Why don't we brief Mrs Lestrange Bradley?'

'Mrs How-Much?'

'Lestrange Bradley, sir. The psychologist. Her speciality is solving murder cases.'

'Oh – her. Yes, well, it might be an idea. I don't like the

thought of jugging an honest chap like a blinking prize turkey at a show.'

Mrs Bradley was interested in her new task. The men, at her instigation, were taken, one at a time, to revisit the lighthouse in her company. The fact that two police officers in plain clothes accompanied each man was neither here nor there. Nothing was said on either side.

Mrs Bradley took the men in reverse order of age. She was anxious to present old Tom (whom, privately and off the record, she did not suspect of the murder) with the evidence of the other two as a guarantee of and a check upon their truthfulness. His long experience of lighthouse work would be invaluable, she decided.

Young Dugald was her first victim. He was a red-haired, raw-looking, chunky man of twenty-eight, married, with two children. The dead man had been thirty-two, not very happily married, and without children. As the keepers were relieved on a rota, there might possibly have been trouble, Mrs Bradley thought, if Dick had known Dugald's wife.

'We wass neffer relieved at the same time, Dick and myself,' said Dugald, gazing out to sea with his warm, green-hazel eyes, and speaking in the sing-song voice of West Scotland. 'But we wass friendly, for all tha-at. I would not serve Dick a dirty turn, Cruachan, no! Not for gold!'

'Well, if you didn't, who did?' Mrs Bradley inquired briskly, for she dreaded a Highland lament for the dead man. Dugald turned his head and looked thoughtfully at her. He saw a black-eyed, yellow-skinned, elderly woman, not at all prepossessing to look at. Her appearance did not seem to affect him. He had not a very high standard of physical beauty.

'I will wish to be knowing that, myself,' he replied. 'You see, it wass this way.' He paused, collecting his thoughts. 'The pollissmen haff put it all out of my head,' he said sadly. 'It wass so clear before all the argument.'

Mrs Bradley could believe this. She waited patiently.

'You see, it wass this way,' Dugald repeated in his soft, sad tones. 'Dick wass on duty in the lamp-room, and the three of us, we wass in the bunk-room. Dick wass on duty from da-ark until midnight, then I wass to be on until two, Walt from two until four, and Tom from four until daylight.' Mrs Bradley

175

made a note of these times.

'But when I went up to relieve him, the poor man was gone,' concluded Dugald. 'He wass not there. There wass no one.' So Dick had been killed before midnight. That was fact, unless contradicted later, Mrs Bradley noted.

'Yes, I see,' she said encouragingly. 'Did anything else happen that was out of the ordinary?'

'Well, you see, it wass a queer thing, so it wass, and I do not remember it happening effer before, but while Dick wass on duty that efening all of us, myself too, wass not feeling ferra well, and we went out from the bunk-room – but it is not manners I should be telling this to a lady.'

'But I understand perfectly,' Mrs Bradley assured him. 'You all had upset stomachs, and a need to leave the bunk-room. No explanation is necessary. You are telling me that, in your opinion, any one of you could have killed Dick. Were you all absent long enough for that?'

'You wouldn't watch the clock on such an occasion,' explained Dugald. 'You would be trying to sleep until you would need to go outside to be sick.'

Mrs Bradley nodded.

'And you were on duty immediately after Dick,' she remarked in an innocent tone. Dugald gave her a quick glance.

'That is so,' he replied. 'But, my sorrow! You must not be thinking I killed the poor man! Ochen, och, no! I would neffer haff been doing that! By Cruachan, no!'

Mrs Bradley accepted this denial with tolerant indifference, and Dugald was taken off. She spent the intervening time in drinking tea with the relief men – three instead of the usual four – and in being taken on an exhaustive tour of the lighthouse. She was shown the great lamp and received an explanation of its workings. She inspected the fog-signals apparatus, and did an immense amount of climbing up and down the spiral iron staircase and in gazing at the sea through unexpected windows which lit the upper floors of the tower.

She was particularly interested in the domestic side of the keepers' lonely lives. She saw the galley and received details of food, cooking, washing up, and laundering.

'You must all be a great comfort to your wives and mothers,' she remarked as she sat down on one of the bunks.

The men grinned.

'Funny thing,' one of them remarked, 'but it's the single ones that are handiest at cooking the grub. It's the married chaps as does the chores.'

'I suppose it is understandable that the single men should be cooks,' Mrs Bradley observed. 'They are the ones who often have to fend for themselves on shore.'

One of the men agreed and the other one debated the point. The third man was on duty, for a watch had to be kept, and the log written up, by day as well as by night.

Soon the boat which had taken off Dugald returned with Walt. Mrs Bradley took him and his police escort up to the lamp-room again, as that seemed to her, as well as to the police, the most likely place for the murder. There was no doubt that the dead man had been on duty when he was killed; that is, if Dugald's evidence could be trusted; and it could easily be refuted by the others if he were lying. In any case, the gallery outside the lamp-room was easily the simplest place from which the body could have been tumbled into the sea. She looked forward to her interview with Walt.

Walt was a tough-looking six-foot man with fair hair and grey-blue eyes. He measured up the little old woman with a quick, sardonic stare, and shrugged his broad shoulders as he answered her first question offhandedly.

'Why, Duggie told us,' he said. 'He had to go on duty at twelve, but I reckon he took his time getting up there, because we all – well, p'raps he told you.'

'Yes, I've had that point put to me,' Mrs Bradley replied. 'You are about to tell me, I think, that although Dugald went to take over his watch before you were compelled to leave the bunk-room for the second or third time, you had returned to the bunk-room before he came down with the news that Dick was not to be found, and you thought him a long time gone.'

'No, it was the first time with me, but I reckon he wasn't gone as long as I thought. Besides, I don't blame him. It's no odds to anybody if a chap goes into the galley to see whether there's another cup of cocoa left in the jug, and hots it up before he goes on duty, and takes it up there with him.'

'So the mug was up there in the lamp-room when you and Tom went up?'

177

'I can't remember whether it was or not. What odds, anyway?'

'None, probably. How did the two men get on?'

'What, Duggie and Dick? All right, so far as I know. You *have* to get on with the other blokes on a light.'

'I should imagine so. Yet someone didn't hit it off with Dick.'

'I can't make it out,' said Walt.

The relief crew looked at the small elderly woman and the tall young man with some curiosity as they came back into the bunk-room with their escort. The plain-clothes officers then went off with Walt, took him ashore to the waiting police car and brought off old Tom to the light.

'Are you any forwarder, mam?' old Tom inquired when he had been disembarked at the lighthouse steps and had climbed to the galley for a mug of tea before Mrs Bradley questioned him.

'I shall be, by the time you go back,' she answered. 'No, none for me, Tom, thank you. I've already had some with the relief men.'

'I'll be glad to be back on here,' said old Tom wistfully. 'Rough on my missus, this is. She bears up well, but it's the disgrace. It'll get her down if things don't go right and I'm arrested. And one of us'll have to be, won't we?'

'It would interest me very much to know your opinion as to which one, Tom,' said Mrs Bradley. 'Who did it? Who committed the murder? You must have a pretty shrewd idea.'

But Tom was staunch. All three men had already been asked by the police (indirectly, of course, but sufficiently plainly) this very same question. None would give another away.

'Thinking ain't knowing,' said Tom. 'All I know is the one that *didn't* do it, and that there one is me. But all that's got to be proved.'

'Do you all carry knives around with you? Does a man have his knife with him all the time?'

'Yes, I reckon we always have a knife on us. It comes in handy, and a man don't always want to be climbing up and down them stairs, especially at my age.'

'I suppose not. What do you do with yourselves when you're off duty?'

'I dunno as we ever are off duty much in the daytime. On *and* off, as you might say. We don't reckon much on an eight-hour day, or anything of that kind, off here. We cooks and mends and washes and swabs up and plays cards and does knitting. I be the champion knitter and mender, and Dick, he were chief handyman. Dugald and him done the swabbing up, too, and Walt were main handy in the galley.'

'So Dugald and Dick were more often together on the job than either of you others?'

'Well,' said Tom, choosing his words, 'that might be so, but it weren't nothing to signify, and they always seemed to rub along all right.'

'Yes, I see. Now, Tom, there's one more thing. Dugald had to take over the duty from Dick at midnight.'

'Ay, that's right.'

'He went up to the lamp-room, found that Dick had disappeared – or so he says –'

'I reckon he meant it,' said Tom, in a tone of obstinacy. Mrs Bradley, having made the point, abandoned it.

'How long was he gone before he came down and told you two that Dick had disappeared?'

Tom searched her quick black eyes, but they told him nothing.

'I couldn't rightly say,' he replied. 'But I reckon he didn't go straight up. We'd often hot up a drink for ourselves and take the jug and two mugs up with us – one for the bloke on watch and the other for ourself, and drink it together before the watch came down to turn in.'

'Did you see a jug and two mugs up there in the lamp-room, Tom, when Dugald called you that night to say Dick had gone?'

'There was the jug, half full, and one mug, not used, mam.'

'Looks bad for Dugald, doesn't it?' said Mrs Bradley pleasantly. 'It looks as though he didn't *expect* to find anybody else up there. How much do the mugs hold?'

'Best part of three-quarters of a pint,' said Tom hoarsely, 'but young Dugald –'

'And the jug?'

179

'It's a two-pint size.'

'Were you surprised to see the body thrown up on the rocks, Tom?'

Tom stared, astonished at the sudden change of ground.

'No,' he said. "Of course not. The way these currents run it was bound to be like that. The chap as chucked Dick overboard was a fool.'

'No. Ignorant. Murderers often are. How many times did you have to leave your bunk that night, Tom?'

'Three times, and Dugald twice and Walt twice. They got stronger stomachs than me. Sick as toads we was, all three of us.'

'You can arrest Walt for the murder,' said Mrs Bradley, later, astonishing the Inspector by her satisfied, confident tone.

'But how do you know?' he inquired.

'Tom knew the body would be washed up on to the rocks. Therefore I suggest that Tom is innocent.'

'We've thought that all along. It was rough on the old fellow we had to mix the sheep and the goats. But what about Dugald? Your point about the jug and the mug struck my men as pointing to his guilt. They thought you'd got him properly there.'

'I think not. Had there been more cocoa in the jug I might agree. What Dugald did was to take up one mug only – with the idea of dividing the rather inconsiderable amount of cocoa between himself and Dick, one having the mug and the other what remained in the jug. Did you ever know a man wash up an extra utensil when he need not? *I* never did.'

'I believe you. But how do you pin it on Walt? I agree you've eliminated the others, but will all this convince a jury?'

'Yes, when you've found the woman in the case – Dick's wife, I should rather imagine. Meanwhile, here is your evidence. Something had upset the men's stomachs that night – and lighthouse keepers don't have queasy insides. Each man had to leave the bunk-room from time to time during the early part of the night. You'll be able to find out what they had to eat. The point is that Walt was the cook. He could, and you'll find that he did, doctor the suppers of Dugald and Tom. He would

180

not have doctored his own, but he made the same excuse as they did, to leave the bunk-room. What's more, I'm sure he's lying when he says he only went out once. The first time he went out he killed Dick, and the second time he tumbled the body over the gallery rail. He did not dare to risk staying away long enough to do both deeds at one time. His mistake was that he had not studied the tides. He was almost new to that lighthouse.'

The boy's mistake was in coming back to his parents' home. You could see his father resented his presence, almost as if they were rivals.

THE OLD MAN

Daphne du Maurier

Did I hear you asking about the Old Man? I thought so. You're a newcomer to the district, here on holiday. We get plenty these days, during the summer months. Somehow they always find their way eventually over the cliffs down to this beach, and then they pause and look from the sea back to the lake. Just as you did.

It's a lovely spot, isn't it? Quiet and remote. You can't wonder at the old man choosing to live here.

I don't remember when he first came. Nobody can. Many years ago, it must have been. He was here when I arrived, long before the war. Perhaps he came to escape from civilization, much as I did myself. Or maybe, where he lived before, the folks around made things too hot for him. It's hard to say. I had the feeling, from the very first, that he had done something, or something had been done to him, that gave him a grudge against the world. I remember the first time I set eyes on him I said to myself, 'I bet that old fellow is one hell of a character.'

Yes, he was living here beside the lake, along of his missus. Funny sort of lash-up they had, exposed to all the weather, but they didn't seem to mind.

I had been warned about him by one of the fellows from the farm, who advised me, with a grin, to give the old man who lived down by the lake a wide berth – he didn't care for strangers. So I went warily, and I didn't stay to pass the time of day. Nor would it have been any use if I had, not knowing a word of his lingo. The first time I saw him he was standing by the edge of the lake, looking out to sea, and from tact I avoided the piece of planking over the stream, which meant passing close to him, and crossed to the other side of the lake by the beach instead. Then, with an awkward feeling that I was trespassing and had no business to be there, I bobbed down behind a clump of gorse, took out my spy-glass, and had a peep at him.

He was a big fellow, broad and strong – he's aged, of course, lately; I'm speaking of several years back – but even now you can see what he must have been once. Such power and drive behind him, and that fine head, which he carried like a king. There's an idea in that, too. No, I'm not joking. Who knows what royal blood he carries inside him, harking back to some remote ancestor? And now and again, surging in him – not through his own fault – it gets the better of him and drives him fighting mad. I didn't think about that at the time. I just looked at him, and ducked behind the gorse when I saw him turn, and I wondered to myself what went on in his mind, whether he knew I was there, watching him.

If he should decide to come up the lake after me I should look pretty foolish. He must have thought better of it, though, or perhaps he did not care. He went on staring out to sea, watching the gulls and the incoming tide, and presently he ambled off his side of the lake, heading for the missus and home and maybe supper.

I didn't catch a glimpse of her that first day. She just wasn't around. Living as they so, close in by the left bank of the lake, with no proper track to the place, I hardly had the nerve to venture close and come upon her face to face. When I did see her, though, I was disappointed. She wasn't much to look at after all. What I mean is, she hadn't got anything like his character. A placid, mild-tempered creature, I judged her.

They had both come back from fishing when I saw them, and were making their way up from the beach to the lake. He was in front, of course. She tagged along behind. Neither of them took the slightest notice of me, and I was glad, because the old man might have paused, and waited, and told her to get on back home, and then come down towards the rocks where I was sitting. You ask what I would have said, had he done so? I'm damned if I know. Maybe I would have got up, whistling and seeming unconcerned, and then, with a nod and a smile – useless, really, but instinctive, if you know what I mean – said good day and pottered off. I don't think he would have done anything. He'd just have stared after me, with those strange narrow eyes of his, and let me go.

After that, winter and summer, I was always down on the beach or the rocks, and they went on living their curious, remote existence, sometimes fishing in the lake, sometimes at sea. Occasionally I'd come across them in the harbour on the estuary, taking a look at the yachts anchored there, and the shipping. I used to wonder which of them made the suggestion. Perhaps suddenly he would be lured by the thought of the bustle and life of the harbour, and all the things he had either wantonly given up or never known, and he would say to her, 'Today we are going into town.' And she, happy to do whatever pleased him best, followed along.

You see, one thing that stood out – and you couldn't help noticing it – was that the pair of them were devoted to one another. I've seen her greet him when he came back from a day's fishing and had left her back home, and towards evening she'd come down the lake and on to the beach and down to the sea to wait for him. She'd see him coming from a long way off, and I would see him too, rounding the corner of the bay. He'd come straight in to the beach, and she would go to meet him, and they would embrace each other, not caring a damn who saw them. It was touching, if you know what I mean. You felt there was something lovable about the old man, if that's how things were between them. He might be a devil to outsiders, but he was all the world to her. It gave me a warm feeling for him, when I saw them together like that.

You asked if they had any family? I was coming to that. It's about the family I really wanted to tell you. Because there was a tragedy, you see. And nobody knows anything about it except me. I suppose I could have told someone, but if I had, I don't know ... They might have taken the old man away, and she'd have broken her heart without him, and anyway, when all's said and done, it wasn't my business. I know the evidence against the old man was strong, but I hadn't positive proof, it might have been some sort of accident, and anyway, nobody made any inquiries at the time the boy disappeared, so who was I to turn busybody and informer?

I'll try and explain what happened. But you must understand that all this took place over quite a time, and sometimes I was away from home or busy, and didn't go near the lake. Nobody seemed to take any interest in the couple living there but myself, so that it was only what I observed with my own eyes that makes this story, nothing that I heard from anybody else, no scraps of gossip, or tales told about them behind their backs.

Yes, they weren't always alone, as they are now. They had four kids. Three girls and a boy. They brought up the four of them in that ramshackle old place by the lake, and it was always a wonder to me how they did it. God, I've known days when the rain lashed the lake into little waves that burst and broke on the muddy shore near by their place, and turned the marsh into a swamp, and the wind driving straight in. You'd have thought anyone with a grain of sense would have taken his missus and his kids out of it and gone off somewhere where they could get some creature comforts at least. Not the old man. If he could stick it, I guess he decided she could too, and the kids as well. Maybe he wanted to bring them up the hard way.

Mark you, they were attractive youngsters. Especially the youngest girl. I never knew her name, but I called her Tiny, she had so much go to her. Chip off the old block, in spite of her size. I can see her now, as a little thing, the first to venture paddling in the lake, on a fine morning, way ahead of her sisters and the brother.

The brother I nicknamed Boy. He was the eldest, and between you and me a bit of a fool. He hadn't the looks of his sisters and was a clumsy sort of fellow. The girls would play around on their own, and go fishing, and he'd hang about in the background, not knowing what to do with himself. If he possibly could he'd stay around home, near his mother. Proper mother's boy. That's why I gave him the name. Not that she seemed to fuss over him any more than she did the others. She treated the four alike, as far as I could tell. Her thoughts were always for the old man rather than for them. But Boy was just a great baby, and I have an idea he was simple.

Like the parents, the youngsters kept themselves to themselves. Been dinned into them, I dare say, by the old man. They never came down to the beach on their own and played;

185

and it must have been a temptation, I thought, in full summer, when people came walking over the cliffs down to the beach to bathe and picnic. I suppose, for those strange reasons best known to himself, the old man had warned them to have no truck with strangers.

They were used to me pottering, day in, day out, fetching driftwood and that. And often I would pause and watch the kids playing by the lake. I didn't talk to them, though. They might have gone back and told the old man. They used to look up when I passed by, then glance away again, sort of shy. All but Tiny. Tiny would toss her head and do a somersault, just to show off.

I sometimes watched them go off, the six of them – the old man, the missus, Boy, and the three girls, for a day's fishing out to sea. The old man, of course, in charge; Tiny eager to help, close to her dad; the missus looking about her to see if the weather was going to keep fine; the two other girls along-side; and Boy, poor simple Boy, always the last to leave home. I never knew what sport they had. They used to stay out late, and I'd have left the beach by the time they came back again. But I guess they did well. They must have lived almost entirely on what they caught. Well, fish is said to be full of vitamins, isn't it? Perhaps the old man was a food faddist in his way.

Time passed, and the youngsters began to grow up. Tiny lost something of her individuality then, it seemed to me. She grew more like her sisters. They were a nice-looking trio, all the same. Quiet, you know, well-behaved.

As for Boy, he was enormous. Almost as big as the old man, but with what a difference! He had none of his father's looks, or strength, or personality; he was nothing but a great clumsy lout. And the trouble was, I believe the old man was ashamed of him. He didn't pull his weight in the home, I'm certain of that. And out fishing he was perfectly useless. The girls would work away like beetles, with Boy, always in the background, making a mess of things. If his mother was there he just stayed by her side.

I could see it rattled the old man to have such an oaf of a son. Irritated him, too, because Boy was so big. It probably didn't make sense to his intolerant mind. Strength and stupidity didn't go together. In any normal family, of course, Boy would have left home by now and gone out to work. I used to wonder if they argued about it back in the evenings, the missus and the old man, or if it was something never admitted between them but tacitly understood – Boy was no good.

Well, they did leave home at last. At least, the girls did.

I'll tell you how it happened.

It was a day in late autumn, and I happened to be over doing some shopping in the little town overlooking the harbour, three miles from this place, and suddenly I saw the old man, the missus, the three girls and Boy all making their way up to Pont – that's at the head of a creek going eastward from the harbour. There are a few cottages at Pont, and a farm and a church up behind. The family looked washed and spruced up, and so did the old man and the missus, and I wondered if they were going visiting. If they were, it was an unusual thing for them to do. But it's possible they had friends or acquaintances up there, of whom I knew nothing. Anyway, that was the last I saw of them, on the fine Saturday afternoon, making for Pont.

It blew hard over the week-end, a proper easterly gale. I kept indoors and didn't go out at all. I knew the seas would be breaking good and hard on the beach. I wondered if the old man and the family had been able to get back. They would have been wise to stay with their friends up Pont, if they had friends there.

It was Tuesday before the wind dropped and I went down to the beach again. Seaweed, driftwood, tar and oil all over the place. It's always the same after an easterly blow. I looked up the lake, towards the old man's shack, and I saw him there, with the missus, just by the edge of the lake. But there was no sign of the youngsters.

I thought it a bit funny, and waited around in case they should appear. They never did. I walked right round the lake, and from the opposite bank I had a good view of their place, and even took out my old spy-glass to have a closer look. They just weren't there. The old man was pottering about as he often did when he wasn't fishing, and the missus had settled herself down to bask in the sun. There was only one explanation. They had left the family with friends in Pont. They had sent the family for a holiday.

I can't help admitting I was relieved, because for one fright-ful moment I thought maybe they had started off back home on the Saturday night and got struck by the gale; and, well – that the old man and his missus had got back safely, but not the kids. It couldn't be that, though. I should have heard. Someone would have said something. The old man wouldn't be pottering there in his usual unconcerned fashion and the missus basking in the sun. No, that must have been it. They had left the family with friends. Or maybe the girls and Boy had gone up country, gone to find themselves jobs at last.

Somehow it left a gap, I felt sad. So long now I had been used to seeing them all around, Tiny and the others. I had a strange sort of feeling that they had gone for good. Silly, wasn't it? To mind, I mean. There was the old man, and his missus, and the four youngsters, and I'd more or less watched them grow up, and now for no reason they had gone.

I wished then I knew even a word or two of his language, so that I could have called out to him, neighbour-like, and said, 'I see you and the missus are on your own. Nothing wrong, I hope?'

But there, it wasn't any use. He'd have looked at me with his strange eyes and told me to go to hell.

I never saw the girls again. No, never. They just didn't come back. Once I thought I saw Tiny, somewhere up the estuary, with a group of friends, but I couldn't be sure. If it was, she'd grown, she looked different. I tell you what I think. I think the old man and the missus took them with a definite end in view, that last week-end, and either settled them with friends they knew or told them to shift for themselves.

I know it sounds hard, not what you'd do for your own son and daughters, but you have to remember the old man was a tough customer, a law unto himself. No doubt he thought it would be for the best, and so it probably was, and if only I could know for certain what happened to the girls, especially Tiny, I wouldn't worry.

But I do worry sometimes, because of what happened to Boy.

You see, Boy was fool enough to come back. He came back about three weeks after that final week-end. I had walked

188

down through the woods – not my usual way, but down to the lake by the stream that feeds it from a higher level. I rounded the lake by the marshes to the north, some distance from the old man's place, and the first thing I saw was Boy.

He wasn't doing anything. He was just standing by the marsh. He looked dazed. He was too far off for me to hail him; besides, I didn't have the nerve. But I watched him, as he stood there in his clumsy loutish way, and I saw him staring at the far end of the lake. He was staring in the direction of the old man.

The old man, and the missus with him, took not the slightest notice of Boy. They were close to the beach, by the plank bridge, and were either just going out to fish or coming back. And here was Boy, with his dazed stupid face, but not only stupid – frightened.

I wanted to say, 'Is anything the matter?' but I didn't know how to say it. I stood there, like Boy, staring at the old man.

Then what we both must have feared would happen, happened.

The old man lifted his head, and saw Boy.

He must have said a word to his missus, because she didn't move, she stayed where she was, by the bridge, but the old man turned like a flash of lightning and came down the other side of the lake towards the marshes, towards Boy. He looked terrible. I shall never forget his appearance. The magnificent head I had always admired now angry, evil; and he was cursing Boy as he came. I tell you, I heard him.

Boy, bewildered, scared, looked hopelsssly about him for cover. There was none. Only the thin reeds that grew beside the marsh. But the poor fellow was so dumb he went in there, and crouched, and believed himself safe – it was a horrible sight.

I was just getting my own courage up to interfere when the old man stopped suddenly in his tracks, pulled up short as it were, and then, still cursing, muttering, turned back again and returned to the bridge. Boy watched him, from his cover of reeds, then, poor clot that he was, came out on to the marsh again, with some idea, I suppose, of striking for home.

I looked about me. There was no one to call. No one to give any help. And if I went and tried to get someone from the farm they would tell me not to interfere, that the old man was best left alone when he got in one of his rages, and anyway that Boy was old enough to take care of himself. He was as big as the old man. He could give as good as he got. I knew different. Boy was no fighter. He didn't know how.

I waited quite a time beside the lake but nothing happened. It began to grow dark. It was no use my waiting there. The old man and the missus left the bridge and went on home. Boy was still standing there on the marsh, by the lake's edge.

I called to him, softly. 'It's no use. He won't let you in. Go back to Pont, or wherever it is you've been. Go to some place, anywhere, but get out of here.'

He looked up, that same queer dazed expression on his face, and I could tell he hadn't understood a word I said.

I felt powerless to do any more. I went home myself. But I thought about Boy all evening, and in the morning I went down to the lake again, and I took a great stick with me to give me courage. Not that it would have been much good. Not against the old man.

Well ... I suppose they had come to some sort of agreement, during the night. There was Boy, by his mother's side, and the old man was pottering on his own.

I must say, it was a great relief. Because, after all, what could I have said or done? If the old man didn't want Boy home, it was really his affair. And if Boy was too stupid to go, that was Boy's affair.

But I blamed the mother a good deal. After all, it was up to her to tell Boy he was in the way, and the old man was in one of his moods, and Boy had best get out while the going was good. But I never did think she had great intelligence. She did not seem to show much spirit at any time.

However, what arrangement they had come to worked for a time. Boy stuck close to his mother – I suppose he helped her at home, I don't know – and the old man left them alone and was more and more by himself.

He took to sitting down by the bridge, humped, staring out to sea, with a queer brooding look on him. He seemed strange, and lonely. I didn't like it. I don't know what his thoughts were, but I'm sure they were evil. It suddenly seemed a very long time since he and the missus and the whole family had gone fishing, a happy, contented party. Now everything had changed for him. He was thrust out in the cold, and the missus and Boy stayed together.

I felt sorry for him, but I felt frightened too. Because I felt it could not go on like this indefinitely; something would happen.

One day I went down to the beach for driftwood – it had been blowing in the night – and when I glanced towards the lake I saw that Boy wasn't with his mother. He was back where I had seen him that first day, on the edge of the marsh. He was as big as his father. If he'd known how to use his strength he'd have been a match for him any day, but he hadn't the brains. There he was, back on the marsh, a great big frightened foolish fellow, and there was the old man, outside his home, staring down towards his son with murder in his eyes.

I said to myself, 'He's going to kill him.' But I didn't know how or when or where, whether by night, when they were sleeping, or by day, when they were fishing. The mother was useless, she would not prevent it. It was no use appealing to the mother. If only Boy would use one little grain of sense, and go...

I watched and waited until nightfall. Nothing happened.

It rained in the night. It was grey, and cold, and dim. December was everywhere, trees all bare and bleak. I couldn't get down to the lake until late afternoon, and then the skies had cleared and the sun was shining in that watery way it does in winter, a burst of it, just before setting below the sea.

I saw the old man, and the missus too. They were close together, by the old shack, and they saw me coming for they looked towards me. Boy wasn't there. He wasn't on the marsh, either. Nor by the side of the lake.

I crossed the bridge and went along the right bank of the lake, and I had my spy-glass with me, but I couldn't see Boy. Yet all the time I was aware of the old man watching me.

Then I saw him. I scrambled down the bank, and crossed the marsh, and went to the thing I saw lying there, behind the reeds.

He was dead. There was a great gash on his body. Dried blood on his back. But he had lain there all night. His body was sodden with the rain.

Maybe you'll think I'm a fool, but I began to cry, like an idiot, and I shouted across to the old man, 'You murderer, you bloody God-damned murderer.' He did not answer. He did not move. He stood there, outside his shack with the missus, watching me.

You'll want to know what I did. I went back and got a spade, and I dug a grave for Boy, in the reeds behind the marsh, and I said one of my own prayers for him, being uncertain of his religion. When I had finished I looked across the lake to the old man.

And do you know what I saw?

I saw him lower his great head, and bend towards her and embrace her. And she lifted her head to him and embraced him too. It was both a requiem and a benediction. An atonement, and a giving of praise. In their strange way they knew they had done evil, but now it was over, because I had buried Boy and he was gone. They were free to be together again, and there was no longer a third to divide them.

They came out into the middle of the lake, and suddenly I saw the old man stretch his neck and beat his wings, and he took off from the water, full of power, and she followed him. I watched the two swans fly out to sea right into the face of the setting sun, and I tell you it was one of the most beautiful sights I ever saw in my life: the two swans flying there, alone, in winter.

Dangerous things, storms ... they can bring down power-lines, endanger life, and reveal a flaw in a murderer's alibi.

GALE WARNING

Josephine Bell

'You're very late,' Jill called from the kitchen, where she was dishing up an over-cooked dinner.

David shouted back from the hall, 'I dropped in to see Steve Mitchell. Interesting case on hand.'

Jill asked no more questions until he had eaten, then she demanded the full story.

'An old gentleman called Ballantyre has been murdered in his house on the Sussex coast. Only two people had any motive for killing him. We have barred the casual stranger, which I think we may do, as, in spite of the fact that the doors were not locked, nothing was stolen from the house. The two suspects, who each swear the other must have done it, are the old man's nephew, who has recently had serious money losses in his business, and the manservant at the house, Rogers, who has been betting too heavily at the racetrack. Both these stand to gain by Mr Ballantyre's death, and I understand the old man had told them both that they were mentioned in his will. Mrs Rogers, who does the cooking, also stood to gain, but she is a stout, middle-aged woman of little brain and lethargic habits, who would, I think, be physically incapable of doing it the way it was done.'

'How was that?' Jill asked, and added, 'Half a minute I'll get the coffee. We'll leave clearing this up till you have finished telling me the story.'

When she came back with the coffee tray David answered her question.

'He was stabbed – in the chest – three times, with some sharp, short weapon, such as a clasp-knife. He must have died at midnight, or a little after: one of the wounds involved the heart, so death must have been rapid. He was found lying on a flight of stairs that leads to a beacon tower, a sort of lighthouse, that he had built on the roof of his house. He was lying near the top of the stairs, sprawled across them, with his head up the flight, and his legs down. The door of his tower room was open, and the beacon light was on.'

'Oh,' said Jill. 'I was going to say he must have been going up to the room, but it looks as if he had been there, gone down without shutting the door, and left the light on. And then never got back.'

'Quite right. He had been up there all the evening. He was expecting his nephew to visit him – from the sea.'

'From the sea?' Jill echoed.

'Yes.' David pulled out an envelope and began to draw for her. 'Ballantyre's house is near a creek or small natural harbour – like this. Rather like Chichester, on a very much smaller scale. Not so very far from Chichester either, as it happens. The house is on rising ground, with a garden all round, a couple of fields, a marsh with a causeway through it, and then the creek. At high tide all but a couple of yards of muddy shingle are covered. There is about seven feet of water at the centre of the little harbour at low tide, but the rest dries out. Except for very small craft no boat can get in or out at low tide. The object of the beacon tower is to guide boats in at night. There is a powerful set of bulbs against a big reflector. The tower, in line with a permanent coastguard light a few miles up the coast, gives the entrance. Ballantyre had a good many yachting friends who used to sail into his harbour. He was accustomed to light up for them.'

'Then I suppose the nephew had a boat,' said Jill.

'He had. He had also written to say he was sailing at the week-end, and would put into the harbour. So on Saturday last Mr Ballantyre put on his light at nine, when dusk fell, and sat in his tower, reading. An open book was found on the table. His nephew's boat draws five foot six inches. He could only get in, and out again, over the bar of the harbour, one hour before, or one hour after, high tide. On that day this meant at the end of the morning, or between eleven at night and one on Sunday morning. High tide was at midnight.'

'When Mr Ballantyre was murdered,' said Jill with a little shiver.

'Precisely. The time would be right for the nephew to do the deed.'

'Would he have to enter the harbour? Couldn't he anchor outside in the channel leading to it?'

'Not in any safety. The bar is half a mile out, at least. There are strong cross-currents and a shingle bottom. An anchor might easily drag, especially as he was sailing alone, and would have to leave his ship unattended. It would not be an easy job to row in, either, in the usual small yacht's dinghy. No, very unlikely he would risk dropping an anchor outside.'

'Oh, besides,' said Jill, 'there was a storm last Saturday, wasn't there? I listened to gale warnings at six, I know, because we'd been having Children's Hour for Peter.'

'Yes, and the storm arrived at that part of the coast about eleven, or just after. It did not blow out until three next morning.'

'Still, the nephew *could* have got into the harbour at eleven?'

'He could.'

'And got out again in spite of the weather?'

'With difficulty – but a desperate man will take chances, and the storm is his alibi, as I'll tell you in a minute.'

Jill wrinkled up her nose.

'If he anchored in the harbour, and went ashore in his dinghy, wouldn't there be footprints on the mud above the tide mark?'

'I thought of that. So had Mitchell. Unfortunately it was a spring tide that night and, with the storm, a particularly high one. It had run right up on to the marsh. Any footprints there may have been washed away.'

'Difficult,' Jill said. "You spoke of alibis. I suppose this nephew and the man Rogers both have them?'

'Apparently watertight in each case. I'll give you the nephew's first, because Steve thinks he is our most likely bet. He wanted cash more urgently than Rogers, he had arranged to see the old man that night, and he was much more upset than the servant after the murder, though on other counts you would expect him to have greater powers of control. He agrees that he wrote to his uncle and says he was going to borrow money from him, so as to avoid having to sell his yacht, to

195

which he is very much attached.'

'Go on.'

'He says he got the gale warning on his wireless as he came up the coast, and decided not to try for the harbour at all, as it had to be after eleven. A yacht is much safer in deep water in a storm, and he was on a lee shore anyway. So he stood off five or six miles, and when the storm came took down his sails, put out a sea-anchor, and went below. He waited until it blew out at three next morning, then hoisted his sails again, and went on towards the Isle of Wight. He reached Cowes at one in the afternoon on Sunday, and dropped anchor there. Then he went ashore to telephone his uncle as to why he had failed to turn up. He was answered by a constable, who told him the old boy had been murdered. He went back to the ship in a stunned state of mind, only to find the police had boarded her. But they found no evidence of his having been into the harbour the night before. Her anchor was by that time stuck into Solent mud, his clasp-knife was clean, there was no blood anywhere. But the sea is a good cleanser, and several of his clothes were wet, whether from the storm or not is anybody's guess.'

'What about the other man – Rogers?'

'He is equally frank. He had asked his master for a rise in wages, and been refused. It was on this occasion that Mr Ballantyre told him he was provided for in his will; he offered this bit of information without being asked. On Saturday night he went out about ten o'clock into the neighbouring woods to do a spot of poaching. He saw the beacon light shining, but he knew already that the nephew was expected, because Mr Ballantyre had told him, and Mrs Rogers had been ordered to leave some soup prepared in the larder. Rogers says he reached home (he lives in a cottage on the edge of the grounds) about twelve-thirty, and found his wife asleep. He did not wake her. This is confirmed by the wife, for what her word is worth. She went to bed at ten, and as she sleeps very soundly she has no idea when he came back. Two pheasants and three rabbits in the cottage larder confirm Rogers' night's work, and will get him into another kind of trouble in due course. The local police found a neighbour who went down the coast road at ten-thirty that night. The beacon tower-light was shining and the Rogers' cottage was in darkness.'

'It won't be easy to shake either of those alibis,' said Jill. 'They are negative and unconfirmed, but quite plausible.'

'Too true.'

'Who found the body?'

'Rogers. Yes, I know. He may have rigged things to suit himself. But that usually shows, and here it hasn't — so far. Mrs Rogers generally gets over to the house first in the morning, to start things in the kitchen. Her husband is supposed to sweep up outside at this time, but he often does not arrive until it is time to take up Mr Ballantyre's early morning tea. On Sunday morning he was extra late, being tired by the poaching, I expect. When he hurried upstairs with the tea he found Mr Ballantyre's bedroom empty and the bed not slept in. He went down and called his wife. He says he thought the old boy might have had a stroke in the bathroom. They tried that, and the other rooms, and then went up the tower stairs, and found him. They both say they thought it was a stroke or a heart atack until they saw the blood on the front of his shirt. When Rogers touched him he found to his horror that the body was all sprinkled with paraffin.'

'What?' Jill cried.

'Yes. Paraffin.'

'Why?'

'Steve thinks the murderer was aiming at a funeral pyre. There was no one else in the house, remember. And then perhaps he lost his nerve, or did not have time.'

'The nephew? Time to leave the harbour, you mean?'

'Yes.'

'I wonder,' said Jill in a puzzled voice, 'why Rogers was *horrified* by the paraffin?'

'The whole affair was upsetting for him, wasn't it? Whether he is guilty or innocent. And then the suggestion of burning the body!'

'Yes, but no one had set it alight, and he isn't a man to take fright easily, you'd think, if he is a practised poacher. So why was he horrified? Or did Steve just report him like that?'

'No, it was in the statement Rogers made. I saw that this afternoon.'

'Either it's out of character,' persisted Jill, 'or it had some extra meaning for Rogers. Are you quite sure the nephew is

197

the guilty one? If only you could prove it!'

'By no means. Steve thinks so. I think he's the more likely, but no more than that.'

They both thought for a time, then Jill said, 'There must be some more clues you haven't got yet. Has Steve been down to the place?'

'No. The Yard were only asked to join in today, and I happened to be round there, so Steve told me about it. He goes down tomorrow.'

'Something local,' said Jill. 'I bet all the inhabitants are seething with it and dodging reporters and mobbing poor Mrs Rogers. Sukie!' she cried, and darted to the telephone.

'Sukie who?' David asked, 'and why?'

'Gardiner,' said Jill, dialling O and giving a number. 'You must remember the Gardiners who had a flat in Well Walk just after the war.'

'What about them?'

'They live somewhere on that coast now; beyond the Witterings and Bognor. They may have picked up something. Just possibly.'

She turned to the receiver as a voice came through.

'Sukie? Jill here. Jill Wintringham. Don't sound so surprised. No, it can't be as long as that, can it? ... Listen. You must have heard about this murder of old Mr Ballantyre ... I knew you would ... Well, David wants to solve it tonight, before Steve Mitchell ... Who is that? He's a detective superintendent at Scotland Yard ... Yes, before Steve goes down to the place and finds the vital clues ... I know, but he can't help doing it, and he does it so well, and not in any morbid spirit. Shut up, David! ... Yes, he always has these competitions with Steve ... No, I don't think they are being slow. It was only three days ago, wasn't it? ... I know. So have you heard anything locally, that might be helpful? Not a thing? Oh, Sukie, do *think*! ... Well, *try*!'

'Ask her what she was doing on the night of the crime,' said David idly.

'Look, David says what were you doing on the night of the crime? Sleeping, I suppose? ... No?'

There was a long pause in the Wintringhams' sitting-room while Jill listened to her friend's story.

'Relay it,' said David, getting up to go nearer to the telephone.

'She says they were kept awake by the wind and then at one in the morning the hen-house blew over and they had to go out and rescue the hens. Ordinarily, she says, that wouldn't be too difficult because when the back door is open, and the kitchen and hall lights are on, you can see all down the back garden path right away to the hen-house. But the storm had upset the grid or something in their district and they had to do it in darkness.'

'The grid?' David snatched the receiver from Jill and asked tautly: 'Sukie? David here. What time did your lights go off? Eleven-thirty? And come on again? One-thirty? Was a large area affected? Well, about what radius? Would it include Ballantyre's house? It would. Bless you, my child. I'll give you and Bob a theatre in town for this.'

He clapped down the receiver and dialled Scotland Yard, demanding to be put through to Superintendent Mitchell.

'Steve? Still at it, old mole? I've news for you – I think. But first, have you got a Reed's Almanack handy? No, don't blaspheme! Never mind, if you haven't. Can you remember was there a moon last Saturday? Not. Yes, I know the storm clouds would have covered it, but it makes quite a difference to the light or otherwise, in spite of cloud. Yes, I suppose I might have guessed.'

'What?' asked Jill at his side.

'Jill says, what. That a poacher usually chooses a dark night. Well then, Steve, Rogers is your man. Shall I tell you how I know the nephew didn't do it? All right, you'll soon pick it up down there. I know I'm not giving you proof of Rogers' guilt, but you'll find it if you concentrate on him. The nephew's story is true, and his isn't. Or at least, it's incomplete.'

'Now explain,' said Jill, as David turned away from the telephone.

'I'll tell you what I think happened. Rogers says in his statement that he saw the beacon light from where he was poaching. So he could also have seen it go out. He may have decided then and there to attack his master under cover of darkness, but I think most probably he wondered what was

199

wrong and went to find out, thinking a fuse had blown. When he found the whole house in darkness his plan may have come to him. I think he went up to the tower room and found the door open and no one there. And then I think he saw Mr Ballantyre coming up the stairs.'

'Saw?'

'With a hurricane lamp,' said David, 'filled with paraffin. To light the beacon. It would have showed fairly well against the big reflector; enough, probably. He must have thought the nephew might be trying to make the harbour. Rogers took what seemed a good opportunity and killed him. The lamp fell and the paraffin was spilt on the old man's clothes. Rogers took the lamp down, put it in its usual place and went home – at twelve-thirty as he stated. At one-thirty the light came on again. It was burning in the tower in the morning, because no one was there to turn it off.'

'That would explain why Rogers put "horrified" in his statement,' said Jill. 'The lamp bothered him a lot.'

'Or was he really horrified when he saw the old man had a lamp and recognized him? He may have banked on doing it in the dark, unknown to the victim.'

'He may have been out to steal, not kill, and attacked when he was discovered? Horror is the right word, either way,' said Jill in a low voice. She added thoughtfully, 'But that story is all pure invention. You have no proof for any of it. And I don't see why it all could not apply equally well to the nephew. He could have come into the harbour between eleven and half-past.'

'He could.'

'And done all you have described Rogers as doing.'

'Yes.'

'And you said he might, if desperate, brave the weather to go out again.'

'I did, as long as he was over the bar by one in the morning.'

'Well, what's the difficulty, then?'

'Only that you need your leading marks or lights to leave a harbour just as much as you need them to enter it. And at one o'clock the beacon light was out.'

'So if he had come in he would have had to stay?'

'With no moon and that storm even a desperate man would

be unlikely to try to get out against a head wind. You remember he said he was on a lee shore and so stood away to sea after the gale warning? At best he risked going aground in the entrance to the harbour, and very suspicious that would have been next morning. At worst he might have been wrecked outside it. But his yacht was not there next day: it was at Cowes.'

'Has he got an engine on the boat, or only sails?' Jill asked.

'He has an auxiliary. Yes, I asked Steve that. But he would not have risked the noise it would make coming in and going out, if murder was his intention. As well as the Rogers' cottage, there are the neighbours I mentioned, and one or two other houses, all near the creek.'

'I suppose he couldn't have put the paraffin lamp up to light himself out?' suggested Jill.

'Then it would have been in the tower next morning, and not in its usual place. Rogers' line is that he didn't touch anything when he found the body, and Mrs Rogers confirms it. A very correct line for him to take, and true, as it happens. But his accusation of the nephew falls down.'

Jill nodded. David switched on the wireless. Before it began to speak she said dreamily, 'I'm glad it wasn't the nephew. Rogers would always be the more *likely*, wouldn't he, because poachers are hunting animals; he would be used to killing creatures weaker than himself. And sailing people, all the ones I've met at any rate, are always so nice, aren't they?'

'Dear idiot,' said David.

The short-crust pastry, and a tinge of admiration for the killer, inspired Inspector Halliday to relive the old murder case.

PEOPLE KEEP DYING ROUND HERE

Rhona Petrie

'Ah,' said Inspector Halliday with appreciation, and slowly considering withdrawal from the dining table, 'you're a lucky young fellow. As bonny a lass as ever trotted up the High Street with a shopping basket on her arm. Knows what to do with the groceries too. My, that was good pie! I only knew one woman could make a short-crust pastry like that.'

'And you let her get away?' asked Constable Morris with a grin, presuming somewhat on the meal's success.

'Well, I won't say I never fancied her,' admitted the old inspector. 'I'd been widowed a couple of years by then. Only thing was, rumour had it the lady was someone else's intended. Our Superintendent's, no less. That put me clean out of the running.'

Lucy deftly whipped the table cloth from under the men's elbows, took it away, and returned with the coffee percolator. Ears alerted, she recognized the tone of voice as Halliday lowered himself into an armchair and stretched his bony, black-socked ankles towards the fire.

'Elinor Barnett her name was, and she wasn't a local product. Fuddy-duddy old Prof Barnett had brought her back from one of those Hellenic cruises. An instant wife, you might say. Shuddered the specs off the whole university, it did. A dried-up old beanpole like him and this – this soft little brown-eyed woman with a bent for domesticity.'

Done, Lucy's eyes signalled to her husband. (Just get him reminiscing on a full stomach and it's in the bag, Jim had said. If he starts telling stories after dinner, promotion is as good as mine. He may be a moralizing old bore, but his recommendation carries weight.)

'But if she was married to the old professor ...?' the young policeman prompted.

'Oh, he died. Had a whale of a time before he went, though. Kicked over the traces completely. Changed overnight, you might say. Even wrote himself new lectures. Bought a big Queen Anne house out by the common, furnished it, and filled it with parties. Good food and good conversation – you know the sort of thing the university crowd goes in for. And there was Elinor, mothering all the lads, making sure they all had a balanced diet and got their laundry back and kept in touch with their parents – a real home away from home it was. Many's the meal I had there myself as some student's guest when I took a short course at the university. Great days they were, but they didn't last all that long.

'The sudden speed-up in his whole way of living must have overtaxed the old chap because Professor Barnett got himself virus pneumonia from a faculty moor-hiking weekend two winters later and promptly died. Everyone thought he'd have left Elinor well off, with a good-sized insurance policy and all; but it turned out she could just about make things pay if she partitioned off some of the larger rooms and crammed in a lot of student boarders. She insisted on keeping the house – said it was the only real home she'd ever had. And she seemed content enough to go on working hard to pay for its upkeep. Of course, nobody imagined she'd be on her own long. It was a good setup: professor's widow, good house in a nice neighbourhood, all mod. cons. laid on, so to speak. Ideal background for a middle-aged chap of good professional standing, you might say.'

'Which is where your Superintendent came in,' supposed Jim, pressing the cream jug into Halliday's not unwilling hand.

'Ah,' confided the old Inspector, 'and so he might have, if it hadn't been for young Tommy Prescott's accident. Which is what brought me back on the scene, as it happened. And I ought to warn you, young Lucy, that the rest of the tale's not pretty at all.'

'What sort of accident was it?' she asked, absently receiving back the coffee crystals from her guest and prodding at his

203

story as though it were a reluctant log smouldering in the hearth.

'A toss off his motorbike. Nothing special, they thought at Casualty. Put a plaster over one cheek and bandaged his hands, sent him home to take life easy for a day or two. Home, of course, was his room at Mrs Barnett's. Tommy was a second-year classicist, an orphan raised by an uncle in London. He had various aunts and uncles in the Midlands but no one of his own generation. He'd been across to Northampton to visit an old aunt that very afternoon and had this spill on the way back. Elinor Barnett, of course, was mother, sister, and guardian angel to the injured lad.'

'Ooh,' said Lucy with delight, scenting at last a story to her own taste. 'Was there a scandal then?'

Halliday stopped in his narrative, mouth still open, and rolled on his hostess the blank, brown, dog-like eyes that he had reproachfully rolled on so many generations of suspects in the C.I.D. Interrogation Room. 'You misunderstand me,' he rebuked her soberly, 'this was a *murder* case.'

At once the atmosphere in the comfortable little living-room changed. Constable Jim Morris, on temporary loan to C.I.D., snapped mentally to attention. Can't be so, he told himself. A *local murder* within recent memory and I've never even heard of it? The old buzzard's making it up as he goes along. Setting a test case, that's it. Thinks he'll baffle my wits. Well, I'll show him!

Stirring stolidly away at his over-sweetened coffee, Halliday noted with satisfaction how the young couple edged forward in their chairs, eyes wide with impatient curiosity. He chuckled inside himself to see the constable's mind racing ahead into all the possible alleys and byways of the narrative, sniffing at the story, doubting that it was genuine, scenting in it an ulterior motive. Switched on, he looked: registering intelligence at full power, cocking his eager-examinee's head with jaunty confidence.

Halliday ponderously examined his spoon. (I've fooled better men than you, young 'un, and shall do it again.)

Reassured now that his listeners' suspicions were well engaged in the wrong direction, he launched on the sudden death of Tommy Prescott.

'She did all that anyone could,' he said sadly. 'Perhaps if she'd looked in on him during the night there would have been time to save him. But why should she? They hadn't said anything at the hospital about checking on him for twenty-four hours. When Elinor saw him next morning she realized at once. He'd been vomiting; only spoke a few words – about his Aunt Pat. He seemed very anxious about the old lady – then his breathing changed. The pupils of his eyes were fully dilated. He went rapidly into a coma.'

'Cerebral pressure,' Jim Morris pronounced, managing to sound both smug and slightly shocked. 'Unsuspected concussion. They ought to have been more careful at the hospital.'

'No,' insisted Lucy, bouncing in her chair, "*she* did it, didn't she?'

As Halliday slowly shook his head she sank back, disappointed. 'But you did say it was a murder case, Inspector.'

'Never jump to conclusions,' her husband warned severely. 'What did the post-mortem examination show, sir?'

'A vee of fine cracks in the skull – too fine apparently to show on the X-ray – damage to the soft tissue at the point and a corresponding bruise on the opposite side of the brain. Precisely what one would expect, according to an eyewitness's description of the accident. There was never any question about it: Tommy Prescott died as a result of injuries received when he was tossed off his motorbike. It was his own fault too – took a left turn too wide and met a lamppost on the wrong side of the road.'

Inspector Halliday serenely emptied his coffee cup and considered the fine grounds that remained. He waited for Lucy to offer a refill, provide it, and add the accessories to his taste. Seeing that things were going so well, Jim Morris tiptoed over to the sideboard for the bottle of brandy he'd hoarded since Christmas. Top him up, he told himself. Let the lonely old boy remember this evening as a gold and rosy glow. An investment, after all.

'Poor Elinor. She took it badly, blamed herself for negligence. As if it could have been foreseen from the little she knew of his condition.' Halliday sighed into the fire, then held up the small liqueur glass to centre the logs' red glow in the heart of the translucent amber spirit, sighed again, this time more happily, and bent a forbidding aspect on Lucy.

'Not,' he said severely, 'that you should misunderstand that either. Elinor Barnett was a respectable woman. Her grief was genuine concern, real sorrow at such a hopeful young life cut short. She told me – for I was at the lad's bedside at the end – she told me she was determined to go and see this old Aunt Pat the boy had had so much on his mind. Perhaps she was in need, or unwell. There was certainly something about the aunt that had upset young Tommy.

'I told Elinor not to be in too great a hurry. It so happened I had a trip to Northampton in the offing myself, to do with an inquiry into the theft of a collection of foreign postage stamps. If I worked it in right I'd have pleasant company on the way. And if rumour was right about Elinor and Superintendent Ellis, it could do me no harm to have her speak well of me.'

'*Ellis!*' almost shouted Jim Morris, sitting suddenly erect so that brandy slopped over the chair.

'Recognize the name, do you?' grunted Halliday. 'Retired a good ten years back, but not entirely gone from memory, it seems. Well, as I was saying' – and he turned a blank stare on the couple – 'an ambitious young policeman sometimes imagines he can get a long way on a broad smile and a smart salute, not that Ellis was any more easy to fool than we would be today.'

He lowered his gaze and allowed Jim's eyes to meet Lucy's briefly in a mixture of guilt and accusation.

'– so I jollied her along, hoping to get dividends out of it in one way or another.'

Halliday paused and gazed into the fire again. 'I was still a youngish man then, newly made sergeant, had a little car of my own, and could claim for mileage on a duty run. It was a perfect spring day and Elinor looked good enough to eat, in a little brown squirrel jacket and mustard-coloured dress. I'll never forget how she looked. Little did we dream she had only a matter of days to live. If she hadn't been feeling a little anxious about the dead boy's aunt I would have said she hadn't a care in the world.'

'Was it Elinor who got murdered?' cried Lucy.

Halliday didn't speak for a full half minute and Jim Morris, watching the leathery old face harden under the firelight into an implacable, Neanderthal mask, knew that the real story would be coming now. The crime was not a local one at all and that was why he'd never heard of it before.

'She'd written to the old aunt to warn her we were coming,' Halliday went on, 'and when we peeped through the mail slot, having had no reply to our knocking, her letter was the first thing we saw in the hall, lying where the postman had slipped it through. We went next door and inquired about Miss Prescott. They told us she was in the local hospital. Just after Tommy left her, it seems, she'd suffered a stroke and was partially paralysed.'

Lucy opened her mouth to demand 'Did she die?' – still eager for corpses; but her husband quickly hushed her.

'I was due at Northampton Central Police Station,' said Halliday in a heavy voice, 'but I dropped Elinor at the hospital on my way, promising to phone her when I'd pick her up.

'Northampton police had the postage stamp theft well in hand. It remained just to take a statement and get it properly signed. I gave the local sergeant a lift out to the witness's house and on the way back, because it was on our route, we dropped in at the hospital.'

In a single movement Halliday drained the brandy, as though the memory required some obliterating. 'I was appalled when I saw Elinor again. You wouldn't have thought it was the same woman.'

'What had happened?' asked Lucy hoarsely.

'That's what I asked her, of course. She told me. It was queer enough, but even Elinor admitted there could have been a reasonable explanation.

'She'd been shown to the old lady's bed, in a curtained-off corner of a small ward. The nurse warned her the old lady couldn't move or talk, but, being Elinor, she decided to wade in and cheer the old soul up. She mentioned that she was Tommy's landlady and the boy wanted her to visit his aunt. He was anxious about her, she said. She didn't mention Tommy's accident, of course, and certainly not that he was dead.

'Well, it didn't take long to exhaust the general topics and the old lady was certainly listening because she followed every movement of Elinor's lips with her eyes. Then, unthinkingly, Elinor asked if she was comfortable in this hospital.

'Quite deliberately old Miss Prescott moved her head to stare straight at Elinor. "It's all right," she said distinctly, "but people keep dying round here." The voice was thin and petulant, but in no way distorted.

'Elinor positively shot off for the nurse and they both hurried back to hear more. Guess what? – old Miss Prescott had gone dumb on them again.

'It had upset Elinor, feeling that the nurse might decide she'd imagined it or had some reason to lie to them; but the nurse laughed and said that old folks were funny sometimes. They liked to make their illnesses stretch out to insure extra attention. Let her go on pretending until tomorrow – if she could keep it up. In the morning they could test precisely how far the paralysis was letting up. As for "people keep dying round here", it was true the woman in the next bed had passed away the previous night. She hadn't realized that Miss Prescott was conscious of them moving out the body. There was another patient in that bed today, a middle-aged woman with a broken leg. The nurse nodded across to her. Mrs Barnett had been good enough to go over and pour a tumbler of water for her as she couldn't reach it herself.

'I thought that should have reassured Elinor, but it didn't entirely, and then Rogers, the police sergeant, had to stir things up again.

' "Had you met Miss Prescott before, ma'am?" ' he asked Elinor.

'She shook her head. "I only knew that she existed. I found her address among Tommy's things."

' "Good enough," he said cockily. "That proves she did speak to you. It's exactly what she would say – she used to say it all the time, before her stroke. She was really quite gaga, you know, and thought she had special powers. Anyone who crossed her, or who didn't particularly please her, came to a sticky end. Peculiarly enough, there *had* been one or two sudden deaths in her neighbourhood. That's probably the reason she got such a fantastic notion. We first heard about it from her neighbours, and then she started turning up at Central Police Station, wanting to sign confessions. Completely dotty, poor old soul. If this stroke hadn't happened, I guess she'd have been admitted to a Home in any case. That's why young Tommy was so worried about her, you may be sure."

'It horrified Elinor, and the rest of the evening was hardly a success. She wouldn't go out for a meal with me, just wanted to get back and rest. She sat in a sort of glazed black despair all the way home in the car and nothing I could say would relieve it. Of course, old age is a very sad thing, but what, after all, can you do to cure it?

'Next morning, when I'd heard the shocking news, I persuaded myself she had felt some presentiment of evil.'

'What news?'

'About the murder. At the Northampton hospital. Someone had put a pillow on a patient's face as she slept and leaned on it until the woman was dead.'

'Tommy's Aunt Pat?'

'No. The woman next to her – the one with the broken leg. And nothing at all to show who had done it. The night nurse was heating up milk in the kitchen and when she got back in the ward, it was done.'

'And Miss Prescott?' demanded Jim Morris. 'Didn't they make those tests to prove the paralysis had receded?'

'Pointless,' answered the old inspector heavily. 'You see, that night she'd had her second stroke, a more serious one this time. They discovered her like that, straight after the murder. Her bed was in confusion, blankets on the floor. A real mess.'

'You mean...?' faltered Lucy. 'She'd killed the woman next to her, tried to get back in her own bed, and then – How horrible!'

'I had a phone call later that morning from Elinor. She wanted me to come and see something she'd found.

'I went, of course, and it rocked me back on my heels. It was Tommy's motorbike, which had been dumped in her garage since his accident. She said she'd begun to wonder about this strange old Aunt Pat and her fatal effect on those who displeased her. So she'd taken a closer look at the connection of the brake pedal which had come off in the smashup. Under magnification she found file marks. Someone had almost severed the connection. Small wonder Tommy went off the track at a sharp turn. His second or two of unconsciousness

209

would be enough to cut off any precise memory of the sequence of events. Like everyone else, Tommy could have assumed the pedal came off at the moment of impact.'

Constable Morris shook his head in wonder. 'Killing her own nephew too. Unfit to plead, of course. I guess that's why I never heard of the case. They must have simply locked her away somewhere until she died.'

'What a shocking old woman,' breathed Lucy, hunched in her chair.

'She died two days later,' said Halliday briefly. 'Predeceased Elinor by some nine or ten hours.'

'Oh, no! Not Elinor too? How did the aunt do it?'

'Mrs Barnet was poisoned, Lucy.'

'Slipped it to her at the hospital,' suggested Jim Morris. 'It looked like aspirin, so the next time Mrs B. had a headache –'

'Ingenious,' the old inspector agreed, 'but incorrect. The poison was a barbiturate. And Elinor took an overdose when she knew she'd been found out.'

'*Elinor?* Elinor *found out?* Doing what?'

'Committing murder. First her husband, then the woman with the broken leg. Not Tommy, though. His death, like his aunt's, just happened. Though the aunt's was really Elinor's fault. Miss Prescott must have watched Elinor kill the woman in the next bed.'

'And Tommy's sawed-off brake pedal? What about those file marks?' demanded Morris, jabbing a stiff forefinger into the padding of Halliday's armchair.

'I told you it rocked me back on my heels when I saw it. That was because I'd already gone over the motorbike minutely myself. What's more, I'd retained the pedal – which showed a clean break. Now, with the file marks added, the joint didn't mate. No, Elinor did that herself – to make us sure that Miss Prescott was a real killer. And this was necessary to Elinor's plan because the woman in the next bed *had* to die at once.'

'Now who's jumping to conclusions?' snorted Lucy.

'Oh, I didn't jump,' the old inspector assured her. 'I shied off it as long as I could – until, in fact, I had a full story of that unknown woman's life. And then the connecting link could no longer be ignored. Miss Mavis Garner – registered nurse Garner – had once been in private attendance on Professor Barnett. It was during his last illness. She recognized Elinor at once when she came visiting the next patient. She couldn't have failed to, having lived for more than a fortnight under Elinor's roof, some seventeen months before.'

'But why *kill* her?' Lucy demanded, almost in tears now. 'How can you *know* what there was between them?'

'Blackmail,' said her husband, scowling and kneading his knuckles. 'She had something on Mrs Barnett, had proof maybe that she'd been the cause of her husband's death –'

'Pneumonia he died of,' Halliday reminded them. 'So what do you think?'

'She could hardly infect him.'

'But once infected – and in February too.'

'Exposure, of course! She waited until the nurse's back was turned, then stripped the bed and opened all the windows. When Nurse Garner came back he was very much worse, in a coma perhaps, and maybe she felt the room much too cold –'

'She had found it at barely thirty-eight, when she'd kept it for days at a steady seventy-four.'

Halliday had aged in the last ten minutes, reliving the crimes of the woman he had admired.

'She left us the details in her confession. She'd given five thousand pounds to Nurse Garner to insure her silence. Small wonder she wasn't left as well provided for as we'd expected. Anyway, Garner took the money and not being a professional blackmailer, but even, it seems, capable of a sense of guilt, she had never come back for more. But now, suddenly confronted by Elinor again, she was ashamed of her own part in the arrangement and ready to confess openly how she'd permitted murder to go unsuspected.'

'Accessory,' said Jim Morris, gnawing at his underlip, 'after the fact.'

'So Mrs Barnett took out her car after dark,' went on Halliday, not hearing the interruption, 'and drove back to Northampton. She hung about there until the coast was clear. Hospitals, after all, are wide-open all the time. When the nurse was not in the ward and all but the luckless Miss Prescott asleep, she murdered the one woman and mussed up the bed of the other. Then she drove home and put in some work with a file on Tommy's motorbike.

'You remember her name was being linked with that of our Superintendent? She couldn't afford any accusations then, however improbable or unprovable. Some mud would have stuck to her, even if Nurse Garner was laughed out of town. So you see, like many another cornered criminal' – Halliday's mouth set in an ugly grin – 'this one killed again to cover a murder already committed. A double murderess – that soft little brown-eyed woman with a bent for domesticity. She'd be here today if she hadn't felt sorry for a lad whose dotty old aunt kept complaining, "People keep dying round here!" So *more* had to.'

They were all silent a while. The coffee was finished, the charred logs fell in on an empty cave of embers. The evening was over.

'I warned you it wasn't a pretty tale,' the old inspector growled, heaving himself to his feet, and the young couple made no move to prevent his leaving.

'She was as bonny a lass,' he echoed, 'as ever trotted up the High Street with a shopping basket on her arm. And what a cook she was! But ambitious, and ambition's a dangerous thing in women. It made her too ready to plan others' lives for her own use. Or deaths, for that matter. But there's no easy road, you know – no honest short cuts to getting on in the world. Just work. Bloody hard work, if you'll excuse the word, m'dear.

'Well, thank you again, young Jim and Lucy. It was a wonderful meal you gave me. I'll not forget it; and don't you either. Like I said, I only knew one woman who could make short-crust pastry as good as yours!'

Claude lived well on his salary as a professor of English Literature and Poetry. Winston, on the other hand, was 'a genuinely starving poet who lived in a genuine garret'. Theirs was a curious friendship ...

THE BABY SPOON

Patricia Highsmith

Claude Lamm, Professor of English Literature and Poetry, had been on the faculty of Columbia University for ten years. Short and inclined to plumpness, with a bald spot in the middle of his close-cropped black hair, he did not look like a college professor, but rather like a small businessman hiding in clothes he thought a college professor should wear – good tweed jackets with leather patches on the elbows, unpressed grey flannels, and unshined shoes.

He lived in one of the great dreary apartment houses that clump east and south of Columbia University, a gloomy, ash-coloured building with a shaky elevator and an ugly miscellany of smells old and new inside it. Claude Lamm rendered his sunless, five-room apartment still more sombre by cramming it with sodden looking sofas, with books and periodicals and photographs of classic edifices and landscapes about which he professed to be sentimental but actually was not.

Seven years ago he had married Margaret Cullen, one of those humdrum, colourless individuals who look as if they might be from anywhere except New York and turn out, incredibly, to be native New Yorkers. She was 50, eight years older than Claude, with a plain, open countenance and an air of desperate inferiority. Claude had met her through another professor who had known Margaret's father, and had married her because of certain unconscious drives in himself towards the maternal.

But under Margaret's matronly exterior lay a nature that was half childish, too, and peculiarly irritating to Claude. Outside of her cooking and sewing – she did neither well – and the

213

uninspired routine that might be called the running of the house, she had no interests. Except for an occasional exchange of letters, which she bored Claude by reading aloud at the table, she had detached herself from her old friends.

Claude came home at 5 most afternoons, had some tea, and planned his work and reading for the evening. At 6.15 he drank a martini without ice and read the evening paper in the living-room, while Margaret prepared their early dinner. They dined on shoulder lamb chops or meat loaf, often on cheese and macaroni which Margaret was fond of, and Margaret stirred her coffee with the silver baby spoon she had used the first evening Claude had met her, holding the spoon by the tip end of the handle in order to reach the bottom of the cup.

After dinner Claude would retire to his study – a book-glutted cubicle with an old black-leather couch in it – to read and correct papers and to browse in his bookshelves for anything that piqued his aimless curiosity.

Every two weeks he asked Professor Millikin, a Shakespeare scholar, or Assistant Professor George and his wife to come to dinner. Three times a year the apartment was thrown open to twelve students from his special readings classes, who came and ate Dundee cake and drank tea. Margaret would sit on a cushion on the floor, because there were never enough chairs, and of course one young man after another would offer his chair to her.

'Oh, no, thank you!' Margaret would protest with a lisping coyness quite unlike her usual manner. 'I'm perfectly comfortable here. Sitting on the floor makes me feel like a little girl again.'

She would look up at the young men as if she expected them to tell her she did look like a little girl, which to Claude's disgust the young men sometimes did. The 'little girl' mood always came over Margaret in the company of men, and always made Claude sneer when he saw it.

Claude sneered easily and uncontrollably, hiding it in the act of putting his cigarette holder between his teeth or by rubbing the side of his nose with a forefinger. Claude had keen, suspicious brown eyes. No feature of his face was remarkable, but it was not a face one forgot easily. It was the restlessness, the furtiveness in his face that one noticed and

214

remembered. At the teas Margaret would use her baby spoon, which as likely as not would start a conversation. Then Claude would move out of hearing.

Claude did not like the way the young men looked at his wife – disappointedly, a little pityingly, always solemnly. Claude was ashamed of her before them. She should have been beautiful and vivacious, a nymph of the soul, with a fair face that would accord with the love poems of Donne and Sidney. Well, she wasn't.

Claude's marriage to Margaret might have been comparable to a marriage with his housekeeper, if not for emotional entanglements that made him passionately hate her as well as passionately need her. He hated her childishness with a vicious and personal resentment. He hated almost as much her competent, maternal ministerings to him – her taking his clothes to the cleaner's, for instance – which was all he tolerated her for, he knew, and why he had *her* now instead of his nymph.

When he had been down with flu one winter and Margaret had waited on him hand and foot, he had sneered often at her retreating back, hating her, really hating her obsequious devotion to him. Claude had despised his mother and she, too, between periods of neglect and erratic ill temper, had been capable of smothering him with affection and attention. But the nearest he came to expressing his hatred of Margaret was to announce casually once a week, 'Winston's coming over for a while tonight.'

'Oh,' Margaret would reply with a tremor in her voice. 'Well I suppose he'd like some of the raisin cake later. Or maybe a sandwich of the meat loaf.'

Winston loved to eat at Claude's house. Or rather, he was always hungry. Winston was a genuinely starving poet who lived in a genuine garret at the top of a brownstone house in the West Seventies. He had been a student of Claude's three years ago, a highly promising student whose brilliant, aggressive mind had so dominated his classmates that the classes had been hardly more than conversations between Claude and Winston. Claude was immensely fond of Winston and flattered by Winston's fondness for him. From the first it had excited Claude in a strange and pleasant way to catch Winston's smile, Winston's wink even, the glint of mad humour in his eyes, in

215

the midst of Winston's flurry of words in class.

While at Columbia, Winston had published several poems in poetry magazines and literary magazines. He had written a poem called 'The Booming Bittern', a mournful satire on an undergraduate's life and on directionless rebellion that Claude had thought might take the place in Winston's career that 'The Love Song of J. Alfred Prufrock' had taken in T. S. Eliot's. The poem had been published in some quarterly, but had attracted no important attention.

Claude had expected Winston to go far and do him credit. But Winston had published only one thin book of verse since leaving college. Something had happened to Winston's easy, original flow of thought. Something had happened to his self-confidence after leaving Columbia, as if the wells of inspiration were drying up along with the sap and vitality of his twenty-four-year-old body. Winston was thin as a rail now. He had always been thin, but now he slouched, hung his head like a wronged and resentful man, and his eyes under the hard straight brows looked anxious, hostile, and unhappy.

He clung to Claude with the persistence of a maltreated child clinging to the one human being who had ever given him kindness and encouragement. Winston was working now on a novel in the form of a long poem. He had submitted part of it to his publishers a year ago, and they had refused to give him an advance. But Claude liked it, and Winston's attitude was, the rest of the world be damned.

Claude was keenly aware of Winston's emotional dependence on him, and managed to hide his own dependence on Winston in the superior, patronizing manner he assumed with Winston. Claude's hostility to Margaret found some further release in the contempt that Winston openly showed for her intellect.

One evening, more than usually late in arriving, Winston slouched into the living-room without a reply to Claude's greeting. He was a head and a half taller than Claude, even when he stooped; his dark brown hair was untidy with wind and rain, his overcoat was clutched about his splinter of a body by the hands rammed into its pockets. Slowly and without a glance at Margaret, Winston walked across the living-room towards Claude's study.

Claude was a little annoyed. This was a mood he didn't know.

'Listen, old man, can you lend me some money?' Winston asked when they were alone in the study, then continued over Claude's surprised murmur, 'You've no idea what it took for me to come here and ask you, but now it's done, anyway.' He sighed heavily.

Claude had a sudden feeling it hadn't taken anything, and that the despondent mood was only play-acting. 'You know I've always let you have money if you needed it, Winston. Don't take it so seriously. Sit down.' Claude sat down.

Winston did not move. His eyes had their usual fierceness, yet there was an impatient pleading in them, too, like the eyes of a child demanding something rightfully his own. 'I mean a lot of money. Five hundred dollars. I need it to work on. Five hundred will see me through six weeks, and I can finish my book without any more interruptions.'

Claude winced a little. He'd never see the money again if he lent it to Winston, who already owed him about two hundred. It occurred to Claude that Winston had not been so intense about anything since his university days. And it also came to him, swiftly and tragically, that Winston would never finish his book. Winston would always be stuck at the anxious, furious pitch he was now, which was contingent on his not finishing the book.

'You've got to help me out this last time, Claude,' Winston said in a begging tone.

'Let me think it over. I'll write you a note about it tomorrow. How's that, fellow?'

Claude got up and went to his desk for a cigarette. Suddenly he hated Winston for standing there begging for money. Like anybody else, Claude thought bitterly. His lip lifted as he set the cigarette holder between his teeth, and Winston saw it, he knew Winston never missed anything. Why couldn't tonight have been like all the other evenings, Claude thought, Winston smoking Claude's cigarettes, propping his feet on the corner of Claude's desk, Winston laughing and making him laugh, Winston adoring him for all the jibes he threw at the teaching profession?

'You crumb,' Winston's voice said steadily. 'You fat smug

217

jerk of a college professor. You stultifier and castrator of the intellect.'

Claude stood where he was, half turned away from Winston. The words might have been a blunt ramrod that Winston had thrust through Claude's skull and down to his feet. Winston had never spoken to him like that, and Claude literally did not know how to take it. Claude was not used to reacting to Winston as he reacted to other people.

'I'll write you a note about it tomorrow. I'll just have to figure out how and when,' he said shortly, with the dignity of a professor whose position, though not handsomely paid, commanded a certain respect.

'I'm sorry,' Winston said, hanging his head.

'Winston, what's the matter with you?'

'I don't know.' Winston covered his face with his hands.

Claude felt a swift sense of regret, of disappointment at Winston's weakness. He mustn't let Margaret know, he thought. 'Sit down.'

Winston sat down. He sipped the little glass of whisky that Claude poured from the bottle in his desk as if it were a medicine he desperately needed. Then he sprawled his scarecrow legs out in front of him and said something about a book that Claude had lent him the last time he was here, a book of poetry criticism.

Claude was grateful for the change of subject. Winston talked with his eyes sleepily half shut, moving his big head suddenly now and then for emphasis; but Claude could see the glint of interest, of affection, of some indefinable speculation about himself through the half-closed lids, and could feel the focus of Winston's intense and personal interest like the life-bringing rays of a sun.

Later they had coffee and sandwiches and cake in the living-room with Margaret. Winston grew very animated and entertained them with a story of his quest for a hotel room in the town of Jalapa in Mexico, a story pulled like an unexpected toy from the hotchpotch of Winston's mind, and by Winston's words set in motion and given a life of its own. Claude felt proud of Winston. 'See what I amuse myself with behind the door of my study, while you creep about in the dull prison of your own mind,' Claude might have been saying aloud as he glanced at Margaret to see if she was appreciating Winston.

Claude did not write to Winston the next day. He felt that Winston was in no more need of money than usual, and that Winston's crisis would pass if the two of them didn't communicate for a while. Then on the second evening Margaret told Claude that she had lost her baby spoon. She had looked all over the house for it, she said.

'Maybe it fell behind the refrigerator,' Claude suggested.

'I was hoping you'd help me move it.'

A smile pulled at Claude's mouth as he jockeyed the refrigerator away from the wall. He hoped she had lost the spoon. It was a silly thing to treasure at the age of 50, sillier than her high-school scrapbooks and the bronzed baby shoe that had sat on her father's desk and that Margaret had claimed after his death. Claude hoped she had swept the spoon into the garbage by accident and that it was out of the house for ever.

'Nothing but dust,' Claude said, looking down at the mess of fine sticky grey dust on the floor and the refrigerator cord.

The refrigerator was only the beginning. Claude's cooperation inspired Margaret. That evening she turned the kitchen inside out, looked behind all the furniture in the living-room, even looked in the bathroom medicine cabinet and in the clothes hamper.

'It's just not in the house,' she kept saying to Claude in a lost way. After another day of searching she gave up.

Claude heard her telling the woman next door about it.

'You remember it, I suppose. I think I once showed it to you when we had coffee and cake here.'

'Yes, I do remember. That's too bad,' said the neighbour.

Margaret told the newsstore man, too. It embarrassed Claude painfully as he stood there staring at the rows of candy bars and Margaret said hesitantly to the man she'd hardly dared speak to before, 'I did mean to pay our bill yesterday, but I've been a little distracted. I lost a very old keepsake – an old piece of silver I was very fond of. A baby spoon.'

Then at the phrase 'an old piece of silver', Claude realized that Winston had taken it. Winston might have thought it had a quick cash value at the pawnbroker, or he might have taken it out of malice. He could have palmed it that last night he was at the house. Claude smiled to himself.

Claude had known for years that Winston stole little things – a glass paperweight, an old cigarette lighter that didn't work, a photograph of Claude. Until now Winston had chosen only Claude's possessions. For sentimental reasons, Claude thought.

Three more days passed and the spoon did not turn up. And there was no word from Winston. Margaret wrote some letters in the evenings, and Claude knew she was saying in each and every one of them that she had lost her baby spoon and that it was unforgivably careless of her. It was like a confession of some terrible sin that she had to make to everyone she knew. And more, she seemed to want to tell everyone, 'Here I stand, bereft.'

She wanted to hear their words of comfort, their reassuring phrases about such things happening to everybody. Claude had seen her devouring the sympathy that the delicatessen woman had offered her. And he saw her anxiety in the way she opened the letter from her sister in Staten Island. Margaret read the letter at the table, and though it didn't say anything about the baby spoon it seemed to put Margaret in better spirits, as if her sister's not mentioning it were a guarantee of her absolution.

Assistant Professor Leonard George and his wife Lydia came to dinner one evening, and Margaret told them about the spoon. Lydia, who was by no means stupid but very good at talking about nothing, went on and on about how disquieting the losses of keepsakes were at first, and how unimportant they seemed later. Margaret's face grew gradually less troubled until finally she was smiling. After dinner she said on her own initiative, 'Well, who wants to play some bridge?'

Margaret put on a little lipstick now when they sat down to dinner. It all happened in about ten days. The inevitable pardons she got from people after confessing the loss of her baby spoon seemed to break the barriers between herself and the adult world. Claude began to think he might never see that horrible coyness again when young men came to semester teas. He really ought to thank Winston for it, he supposed. It amused him to think of grasping Winston's hand and thanking him for relieving the household of the accursed baby spoon. He would have to be careful how he did it, because Winston

220

didn't know that Claude knew about his petty thieveries. But perhaps it was time Winston did. Claude still resented Winston's begging for money and those shocking moments of rudeness the last time he had visited.

Yes, Winston wanted bringing into line. Claude would let Winston know he knew about the spoon, and he would also let him have $300.

Winston hadn't yet called, so Claude wrote a note to him, inviting him to dinner Sunday night, and saying he was prepared to lend him $300. 'Come early so we can have a little talk first,' Claude wrote.

Winston was smiling when he arrived, and he was wearing a clean white shirt. But the white collar only accentuated the greyness of his face, the shadows in his cheeks.

'Working hard?' Claude asked as they went into his study.

'You bet,' Winston said. 'I want to read you a couple of pages about the subway ride Jake takes.' Jake was the main character in Winston's book.

Winston was about to begin reading when Margaret arrived with a shaker of whisky sours and a plate of canapés.

'By the way, Winston,' Claude began when Margaret had left. 'I want to thank you for a little service I think you rendered me the last time you were here.'

Winston looked at him. 'What was that?'

'Did you see anything of a silver spoon, a little silver baby spoon?' Claude asked him with a smile.

Winston's eyes were suddenly wary. 'No. No, I didn't.'

Claude saw that Winston was guilty, and embarrassed. Claude laughed easily. 'Didn't you take it, Winston? I'd be delighted if you did.'

'Take it? No, I certainly didn't.' Winston started towards the cocktail tray and stopped, frowning harder at Claude, his stooped figure rigid.

'Now look here —' Why had he begun it before Winston had had a couple of cocktails? Claude thought of Winston's hollow stomach and felt as if his words were dropping into it. 'Look here, Winston, you know I'm terribly fond of you.'

'What's this all about?' Winston demanded, and now his voice shook and he looked completely helpless to conceal his guilt. He half turned round, then turned back again, as if guilt pinned his big shoes to the floor.

Claude tipped his head back and drank the entire contents of his glass. He said with a smile. 'You know I know you've taken a few things from me. It couldn't matter to me less. I'm glad you wanted to take them, in fact.'

'What things? That's not true, Claude.' Winston laid his sprawling hand over the conch shell on the bookcase. He stood upright now and there was something even militant about his tall figure and the affronted stare he gave Claude.

'Winston, have a drink.' Claude wished now that he hadn't begun it. He should have known Winston wouldn't be able to take it. Maybe he had destroyed their friendship – for nothing. Claude wondered if he should try to take it all back, pretend he had been joking. 'Have a drink,' he repeated.

'But you can't accuse me of being a thief!' Winston said in a horrified tone. And suddenly his body began to tremble.

'No, no, you've got the whole thing wrong,' Claude said. He walked slowly across the room to get a cigarette from the box on his desk.

'That's what you said, isn't it?' Winston's voice cracked.

'No, I didn't. Now let's sit down and have a drink and forget it.' Claude spoke with elaborate casualness, but he knew it sounded patronizing just the same. Maybe Winston *hadn't* stolen the spoon – after all, it belonged to Margaret, not to Claude. Maybe Winston was reacting with guilt because he had taken the other things, and he now knew that Claude realized it.

Those were Claude's last two thoughts – that he had sounded false and patronizing, that Winston might not have taken the baby spoon – before there was a quick step behind him, a brief whir of something moving fast through the air, and a shattering impact at the back of his head that caused his arms to fling up in a last empty, convulsive gesture.

He wasn't much to look at — 'drooping grey moustache and pale-blue eyes' — but he had a special reason for being unafraid of killers

OLD WILLIE

William McGivern

This is a story I've heard told by old-timers around Chicago newspaper offices. They don't insist it's true, of course, since it hangs chiefly on the word of a reporter who was far more at home in speak-easies than he ever was at a typewriter. Still, parts of the tale can't be explained away as the splintered dreams of a drunk. Maybe that's why the old-timers go on telling the story ...

It begins in 1927, Prohibition-time, when Chicago was run by a band of Sicilian immigrants under the austere leadership of a man named Al Capone. And it also begins when an amiable little man, whom everyone knew only as Old Willie, became interested in a shy Danish girl named Inger Anderson.

Willie was the handy man and janitor around the West Side boarding house where Inger roomed. He was a straight-backed, light-stepping character, with drooping grey moustache and pale-blue eyes. He could have been in his middle sixties or seventies – it was hard to say. Everyone at the boarding-house liked him because of his obliging, courteous manner, and consistent good humour, but they didn't know very much about him; nor care a great deal.

Old Willie's interest in Inger was purely fatherly, of course. He knew she'd come from a Minnesota village and he felt she needed looking after in the big city. He fussed over her as if she were a baby. Inger was pretty capable despite her shyness, but she was touched by Old Willie's interest in her, and they became good friends.

Inger's ambition was to become a concert singer. She had a pleasant, untrained voice which wouldn't have excited a small-town choirmaster, but she loved to sing and was ready to do almost anything to fulfil her dreams. She signed up for voice lessons in the evenings and found herself a job as a hotel maid through an employment agency. She was thrilled at her luck in finding work so quickly. What she didn't know was that the employment agency director, spotting her as an earnest but unknowing Minnesota specimen, had assigned her to the hotel which was the headquarters of the Capone mob – the old Star at Wabash Avenue near Twelfth Street. Considering this, considering that the Star was filled with as choice a collection of gorillas as were ever assembled under one roof, Inger got along okay for the first few weeks. She cleaned rooms, made beds, and kept her eyes cast down when the sharply-dressed torpedoes stared insolently at her lovely, graceful figure and beautiful legs. One of the hoodlums, Blackie Cardina, a Sardinian with alert eyes and a strong, bold jaw, stared longer than any of the others and then grinned.

Old Willie was horrified when Inger told him where she was working. They were talking in the parlour at the time. Inger had just finished her lessons and had been telling Old Willie about the skating and sledding in Minnesota, and about a boy named Lars who wanted to marry her, and then she said something about the Star Hotel.

'Listen, you get out of that place,' Old Willie said, shaking his head sternly. 'Those are bad men, worse than rattlesnakes, and it's no place for a girl like you.'

Inger was amused by Willie's anxiety. She was young and very confident, and the thought that she couldn't look out for herself struck her as funny. After all, she reasoned, she had been at the Star a month and no one had bothered her yet.

About a week after this talk, Inger came home much later than usual and went straight to her room. She didn't come down to eat, and she didn't practise her scales that night. Old Willie, vaguely troubled, tried to find out what was wrong, but she wouldn't open her door, or even talk to him. The next day the landlady brought Inger up some food, and talked to her for an hour or so. When she come out her eyes were red, and that night she glared at all the men boarders as if they were particularly repellent species of vermin.

For a month things went on this way. Inger wasn't working at the Star any more. She stuck close to her room and wouldn't

224

see anyone, not even Old Willie. Then he learned from the landlady that Inger was leaving. She wasn't going home. She was just leaving.

That brought him to a decision. He went up and knocked firmly on the door. 'You might as well open up,' he said. 'I'm sticking here until you do.'

There was a wait, and then, in a tired voice, Inger told him to come in. She was in bed looking pale and ill. Old Willie sat beside her and patted her arm with a thin, long-fingered hand.

'You're in trouble, aren't you, Inger?' he said.

She looked away from him, staring out at the bare, black, winter trees.

'Who is it?' Old Willie said. Something had changed in his voice; it was curiously hard, insistent.

'I can't talk about it.'

'You've got to, Inger. You got no father or brothers here.'

She moaned softly. 'They mustn't ever know.'

'No need for that. Tell me about it.'

Finally she told him, crying openly, her hand clutching his with desperate strength. It was the one they called Blackie, Blackie Cardina. He had followed her into a room, grinning. She had pleaded with him, begged him, and at last she had fought and screamed. But nothing had made any difference to Blackie. He had taken what he wanted . . .

When she finished, Old Willie sighed. 'I'll have a talk with him,' he said.

'No, no,' Inger cried. 'They – he'd kill you. You don't know what they're like.'

'Now don't worry about me,' Old Willie said in a soothing voice. 'You try to sleep, and don't be fretting.'

And with that he left her. Old Willie went first to his own room and reappeared in a few minutes wearing a long, black frayed overcoat. The landlady met him at the foot of the stairs and asked him where he was going. Old Willie didn't answer. He walked past her, his eyes fixed straight ahead, a tense, angry frown on his old face.

Old Willie reached the Star Hotel a little after noon. He stopped inside the revolving doors, looking like some country bumpkin who'd got into the wrong pew by mistake. And now, right at this point, is where the drunken reporter, Jake Mac-

225

key, enters the story in the role of an eye-witness. Jake was at the Star that afternoon, sitting on a sofa and talking to one of Capone's men. Maybe Jake was on a story. Maybe he was just hanging round for a drink. Anyway, he was there, slightly drunker than usual, and he noticed Old Willie immediately, because Old Willie with his drooping moustaches and long black overcoat was a sight to catch and hold the eye.

Old Willie stopped a bellboy and asked him where he might find Blackie Cardina. The bellboy jerked his thumb towards a card game at the far end of the lobby. Blackie was there, sitting behind a high stack of chips, a cigar in his strong teeth, and grinning like a wolf because he was winning, and because, at that precise moment of his life, he thought the world was a place that had been kindly provided for him to loot, ravish, and otherwise do with as he pleased.

He glanced up a few seconds later and saw the old man with drooping moustaches studying him sombrely. Blackie paid no attention to him; he had looked up as he figured the odds against filling a belly straight.

'Okay, I take a card,' Blackie said, and snapped his fingers.

'Hold the deal,' Old Willie said quietly. 'Which of you is a rat called Blackie Cardina?'

Blackie looked up again, seeing Old Willie for sure this time, and his little dark eyes narrowed dangerously. 'You aren't funny, old man,' he said.

'I ain't trying to be,' Old Willie said. 'I'm a friend of a girl used to work here. You had your fun with her, you slimy snake-eating bastard, and now you're going to pay for it. I want a thousand dollars from you. That'll help her out some. And you can figure the price cheap.'

Blackie got to his feet and it was difficult to judge from his expression whether he would start laughing or cussing. 'Look, old man, get out,' he said, at last, pointing to the door. 'Get out. You hear? I don't want to kick an old man into the street. I'll let you walk, understand.' He got madder as he talked, and a flush of colour surged up his throat and stained his dark features. 'Get out!' he shouted. 'Get out, you dirty, rotten old bum. Get out of here!'

'One thousand dollars,' Old Willie said, casually unbuttoning his long black overcoat.

The kill-look in Blackie's eyes deepened. 'Who sent you here? Who are you?' he shouted, and reached for the gun in his shoulder holster. 'I'll teach you a lesson, goddamn it.'

Old Willie said something then, something which only Jake Mackey seems to have heard, and he said it in a voice that was proud and hard and confident. After that, although it was all part of one smoothly connected motion, Old Willie yelled, 'Draw, you bastard!' and threw himself swiftly to one side in a low, springy crouch.

There was a lot of discussion later as to what exactly happened in the next few seconds. Two facts were incontrovertible: one, Old Willie somehow got a gun into his hand, and, two, Blackie Cardina fell across the card table with a black hole burned neatly into his forehead. No one actually saw Old Willie draw a gun. The onlookers decided later it was probably fastened to a spring arrangement in his holster. Anyway, it got into his hand very fast, and the bullet from it got into Blackie's skull even faster.

Old Willie didn't let things get out of control. With a little wave of his big, old-fashioned revolver he backed Blackie's friends away from the table, and then coolly plucked a wallet from Blackie's hip pocket.

He inspected the contents and stuffed the wallet into a pocket of his overcoat. After that he backed towards the doors, moving easily and lightly, the gun in his hand as steady as something carved from rock.

Jack Mackey said there was something about Old Willie then, something in his eye and manner, that made you want to shrink down in your chair and stay very quiet.

At the doors Old Willie made a short speech. 'Sit tight for five minutes. First man don't think that's a good idea is going to get himself killed.'

And then he walked out into the street and for five minutes a half-dozen of Al Capone's hoodlums looked uneasily at Blackie's body, and occasionally glanced up at the clock above the lobby desk.

They weren't afraid to go outside, they said later. They weren't afraid of an old man in a tattered overcoat who'd been lucky enough to plug Blackie between the eyes. Still, they didn't go out and they didn't move.

Jake Mackey got on Old Willie's trail right after the five minutes were up, and by checking the cab companies he found a hackie who had picked up an old party answering Willie's description at the intersections of Twelfth Street and Wabash Avenue. This took time, of course; it was late in the afternoon when Jake cautiously approached the boarding-house where the cab driver had taken Old Willie and had dropped him.

And by then it was too late. Old Willie had been there, all right, but only long enough to give Inger a roll of money, and then pack up his few things and leave.

He didn't say good-bye to anyone, but simply strolled off down the darkening street, a slender old man with faded blue eyes and a curiously youthful stride. No one watched him leave.

Jake Mackey was fascinated by what he'd seen at the Star Hotel and he hung round Inger to get all the facts she could recall about Old Willie.

She told him how secretive Old Willie had always been, and how he liked to listen to her sing, and so forth, but she couldn't tell him very much more.

He and Inger became good friends in the next week or so, and for a while Jake even thought he was falling in love with her. But nothing came of that. Inger had a miscarriage a week later, and after that packed up and went back to Minnesota.

She married the boy named Lars, and Jake carried the wedding announcement in his wallet, but finally lost it in a bar, the way clippings get lost in bars.

He never did pin down his story. He did a lot of checking on it, and spent a good deal of time in the library, but he never could prove it, and so he never wrote it.

Still, he *knew* that he had missed a great story by a hair's breadth, and in the years that followed he told the story round Chicago bars to anyone who would listen to him.

The thing that convinced him his story was true was the way Old Willie had handled that gun, and what Old Willie had said when Blackie asked him who he was – Blackie had asked him who he was, remember, just before digging for the gun in his shoulder holster. Old Willie's answer had held no significance for the Sicilian immigrants at the card table, but it had raised the hairs on the back of Jake Mackey's neck.

Old Willie had said, in a proud, hard, confident voice, 'When I was a kid they called me Billy.'

And that's the way the old-timers tell Jake Mackey's story. They don't insist it's true, of course – but they go on telling it.

There are things most of us would say we'd never eat in any circumstances. But do any of us really know to what lengths we could be driven by hunger?

IN THE RUINS

Roald Dahl

Somewhere among the bricks and stones, I came across a man sitting on the ground in his underpants, sawing off his left leg. There was a black bag beside him, and the bag was open, and I could see a hypodermic needle lying there among all the rest of the stuff.

'Do you want some?' he asked, looking up. 'I am quite uncontaminated.'

'Yes, please,' I said. I was going crazy with hunger.

'I don't mind giving you a bit so long as you promise to produce the next meal.'

'All right,' I said. 'Yes.'

'Caudal injection,' he said. 'Base of the spine. You don't feel a thing.'

The leg was off now and the doctor was busy putting little clips on to the places that were bleeding badly.

I found a few bits of wood and I made a fire in the ruins and started roasting a piece of the meat. The doctor sat on the ground, still doing things to the stump of his leg.

A child came up, a girl about four years old. She had probably seen the smoke from the fire or smelled the smell of cooking. She was very unsteady on her feet.

'You want some, too?' the doctor asked.

She nodded.

'You'll have to pay it back later,' the doctor said.

The child stood there looking at the piece of meat I was holding over the fire on the end of a bent curtain-rod.

'You know something,' the doctor said, 'with all three of us here we ought to be able to survive for quite a long time.'

'I want my mummy,' the child said, starting to cry.

'Sit down,' the doctor told her. 'I'll take care of you.'

230

CONTRIBUTORS

CHRISTIANNA BRAND. Born in Malaya of English parentage and educated at a Franciscan convent at Taunton, Devon. She wrote her first crime novel *Death In High Heels* while working in London as an Aga cooker salesgirl. Married to a retired Harley Street surgeon, she is a past president of the Crime Writers' Association and her many books include *Green For Danger*, *London Particular*, and *Cat and Mouse*.

DICK FRANCIS. Born in 1920, he was educated at Maidenhead County Boys' School. He served as a pilot in the R.A.F. during the Second World War. He was champion National Hunt jockey in 1953 and turned to journalism at the end of his professional racing career. His books include *Dead Cert*, *Odds Against*, and *Smoke Screen*.

LESLIE CHARTERIS. Born in 1907, he has been a professional writer since his early thirties. He has written more than forty Saint novels but says *The Saint And The People Importers* (1971) was his last. His most recent publication was *Paleneo*, an international language based on signs and symbols. Current hobbies are 'eating, drinking, sailing, fishing, and lying in the sun'.

AGATHA CHRISTIE. Was created a Dame of the British Empire in 1971 and was without doubt the world's most famous exponent of the whodunit. Her first novel was *The Mysterious Affair At Styles*, published in 1920. Since then bestsellers have poured from her fluent pen – *Ten Little Niggers*, *Murder On The Nile*, *Murder On The Orient Express* and countless others. Her play *The Mousetrap* is in its 24th year in the West End and looks like running for ever! She died in January, 1976.

ROALD DAHL. Was born in Llandaff, South Wales, in 1916. He is married to the actress Patricia Neal. He has contributed to many leading periodicals including *The New Yorker*. His books include *Over To You*, *The Gremlins*, *Kiss, Kiss*, and *Someone Like You*.

STANLEY ELLIN. Was born in New York City in 1916. He has been a 'pusher' for a newspaper distributor, dairy farmer, teacher, steelworker and went into the Army during the Second World War. After the war he turned to writing. His books include *House of Cards*, *The Blessington Method*, and *The Eighth Circle*. He has won the 'Edgar' Award from the Mystery Writers of America three times.

MICHAEL GILBERT. He does most of his writing on the train commuting from his home at Cobham, Kent, to the London firm of solicitors in which he is a partner. A founder member of the Crime Writers' Association, he has written many crime novels, radio and TV scripts. His hobbies are archery, walking, and contract bridge.

HERBERT HARRIS. He is listed in the *Guinness Book Of Records* as Britain's most prolific short story writer – with more than 3,000 published. He is a founder member and past president of the Crime Writers' Association and lives on the Isle of Wight.

PATRICIA HIGHSMITH. She was educated at Columbia University, New York, and was a freelance journalist before publishing her first novel, *Strangers On A Train* (filmed by Alfred Hitchcock). She now lives in France and enjoys snail-watching, carpentry, and travelling by train.

EDGAR LUSTGARTEN. Born in 1907, he was educated at Manchester grammar school and St John's College, Oxford. He was a practising barrister from 1930–40. Since the war he has become widely known as an author, journalist and broadcaster. His books on crime include *Verdict In Dispute* and *The Business Of Murder*.

JULIAN SYMONS. Born in 1912, he has been writing crime novels and historical biographies since 1942. He is a past president of the Crime Writers' Association and won the Mystery Writers of America's Edgar Allan Poe Award in 1960. His novels include *The Man Who Killed Himself* and *The Gigantic Shadow*.

DENNIS WHEATLEY. Born in 1897 and educated at boarding school in Margate and HMS *Worcester*, he has written more than 75 novels. He worked in his family's Mayfair wine business before turning to writing in 1932. Many of his novels, like *The Devil Rides Out*, are perennial bestsellers. He is now writing five volumes of memoirs.

TONY WILMOT. A Fleet Street journalist, he has written more than 120 short stories (mostly crime); was a Crime Writers' Association best story prizewinner in 1972. His first novel *The Last Bohemian*, based on the life of Modigliani, was published last year.

JOSEPHINE BELL. Born in Manchester, the daughter of Joseph Collier, surgeon. Studied medicine at Newnham College, Cambridge, and at University College Hospital, London; practised in Greenwich from 1927–1935. Has written thirty-seven crime novels and twenty-one straight novels. She gave up practising medicine in 1954 to write full time.

RHONA PETRIE. Born in Hastings, Sussex, she is an Honours graduate of London University and 'has lived in several countries as translator, social secretary and sun addict'. Her main crime novels are *Running Deep*, *Thorne In The Flesh*, *MacLurg Goes West*, and *Death In Deakins Wood*.

JAMES PATTINSON. Born in Norfolk, he was educated at Thetford Grammar School and served in Maritime Royal Artillery in the Second World War. His first novel, *Soldier Sail North* was based on experience in Russian convoys. His thirty-five other novels include *The Rodriguez Affair*, *Search Warrant*, and *Away With Murder*.

RAY BRADBURY. He was born in Waukegan, Illinois, in 1920 and was educated at Los Angeles High School. First Sci-Fi stories published in 1941. His many books and collections of stories include *The Golden Apples Of The Sun*, *Fahrenheit 451*, *The Illustrated Man*, and *The Martian Chronicles*. Hobbies are oil painting, ceramics, and collecting native masks.

STEPHEN D. FRANCES. Was raised by his widowed mother in South London during the twenties. He created the highly successful Hank Janson novels of the forties and fifties. For the past twenty years he has lived in Spain. His many novels include *One Man In His Time*, *La Guerra: A Spanish Saga*, *Cry for My Lovely*, and *This Woman Is Death*.

DAPHNE DU MAURIER. The daughter of the late Sir Gerald du Maurier, she was educated mainly in Paris. Began writing stories in 1928 and published her first novel in 1931. Her many novels include *Jamaica Inn*, *My Cousin Rachel*, *Rebecca*, and *Frenchman's Creek*. For many years she has lived in Cornwall and enjoys walking and sailing.

ERIC AMBLER. Born in 1909, he was an apprentice engineer and advertising copywriter before turning to writing fiction. He has written many screenplays, including *The Cruel Sea* and *The Purple Plain*. His novels include *The Mask Of Dimitrios*, *The Light Of Day*, *A Kind Of Anger*, and *The Levanter*. He now lives in Switzerland.

ARTHUR C. CLARKE. Born in 1917, he was educated at Huish's Grammar School, Taunton, and King's College, London, where he obtained a B.Sc. Served in the R.A.F. during the Second World War and was chairman of the British Interplanetary Society, 1946–7. His many S.F. novels include *The Sands of Mars*, *Glide Path*, and *Rendezvous with Rama*. He lives in Sri Lanka.

GLADYS MITCHELL. Published her first detective story in 1929. Her fiftieth story *Late, Late In The Evening* was published in 1975. Educated at Goldsmiths and University College, University of London, she taught English and History from 1921 to 1961. Her novels include *The Murder Of Busy Lizzie* and *Convent On Styx*. Hobbies: reading, watching athletics, and telling ghost stories.

WILLIAM McGIVERN. Chicago-born, he served in the Artillery in the Second World War, and was a police reporter on the *Philadelphia Evening Bulletin* before turning to crime fiction. His novels include *Odds Against Tomorrow* and *Rogue Cop*. His latest, *Night Of The Juggler*, is soon to be filmed.

ACKNOWLEDGEMENTS

William Heinemann Ltd. and Doubleday & Co. Inc. and *Ellery Queen's Mystery Magazine* for *The Terrapin* © 1962 by Patricia Highsmith; *Ellery Queen's Mystery Magazine* for *Speciality of The House* by Stanley Ellin and *After All These Years* by Michael Gilbert; Hodder & Stoughton Ltd. for *The Unblemished Bootlegger* from *The Brighter Buccaneer* by Leslie Charteris; *Edgar Wallace Mystery Magazine* for *The Murder Of Stanford White* by Edgar Lustgarten; Murray Pollinger and A. Watkins Inc. for *In The Ruins* © 1964 by Roald Dahl; *Evening Standard* for *A Nice Cup Of Tea* by Herbert Harris, and *The Case Of The Unhappy Piano-Tuner* by Julian Symons; *Evening News* and Laurence Pollinger Ltd. for *The Last Of The Midnight Gardeners* by Tony Wilmot; Dennis Wheatley and Hutchinson Ltd. for *Death At Three-Thirty* from *Mediterranean Nights* by Dennis Wheatley; William Collins Sons & Co. Ltd. for *Four And Twenty Blackbirds* © Agatha Christie Ltd. 1960; John Johnson and *The Times* for *Nightmare* by Dick Francis. William McGivern for *Old Willie*. *Evening Standard* for *A Light On Murder* by Gladys Mitchell, *Gale Warning* by Josephine Bell. *John O' London's* for *A Curious Story* by James Pattinson. Gollancz Ltd. for *Crime on Mars* by Arthur C. Clarke, reprinted by permission of the author and the author's agents, Scott Meredith Literary Agency Inc., New York. *Weekend* for *Pot Luck* by Stephen D. Frances. Hart Davis MacGibbon Ltd. for *The Veld* by Ray Bradbury, reprinted by permission of A. D. Peters & Co. Ltd. Gollancz Ltd. and Penguin Books for *The Old Man* by Daphne du Maurier. *Ellery Queen's Mystery Magazine* for *People Keep Dying Round Here* by Rhona Petrie, *The Baby Spoon* © 1973 by Patricia Highsmith, and *Case of the Gentleman Poet*, © 1939 by Eric Ambler.

The BIG thriller of 1976

THE OLYMPIC MISSION

Pamela Ferguson   **60p**

Fact: Security for the Montreal Olympics is the toughest, most costly and most comprehensive ever.

Fiction: it is not sufficient.

Fact: There is an international chain of brothels posing as health and leisure centres.

Fiction: The Syndicate wants a piece of the action.

Fact: The Olympic Games provide a tailor-made opportunity for terrorism.

Fiction: A top Middle East politician is mingling with the crowds.

Fact: Priests act as couriers transferring Vatican jewels around the world.

Fiction: A theft is planned – in Montreal.

Fact: Hordes of people pour into the Olympic city for the Games.

Fiction: One of them is a killer . . .

Fact and fiction are ingeniously interwoven in this supercharged thriller, which reaches its explosive conclusion at the ceremonial climax of the Games.

Use the special order form at the end of this book

Armchair bookshop

All good bookshops stock Everest titles. If you have any difficulty getting our books – or if you prefer to shop from home – please fill in this form.

To: Armchair bookshop, Everest Books, 4 Valentine Place, London SE1.

Please send me the following titles. I enclose purchase price plus 15p (postage & packing) by cheque, postal or money order (no currency).

....

....

....

....

....

....

....

NAME (*block letters*) ....

ADDRESS ....

....

....

....
